ONLY PRETTY BETAS

REBEL WEREWOLVES BOOK TWO

ROSEMARY A. JOHNS

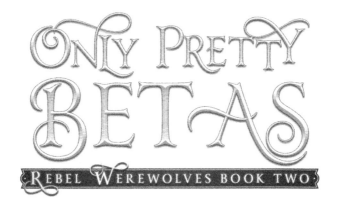

ONLY PRETTY BETAS

REBEL WEREWOLVES BOOK TWO

USA TODAY BESTSELLING AUTHOR

ROSEMARY A JOHNS

ONLY PRETTY BETAS

REBEL WEREWOLVES BOOK TWO

When the witches throw me to the wolves…

…they don't mean the cute-as-a-button kind.

The shifters are hot, deadly, and our enemies for centuries. Luckily, I'm Crimson, the last Wolf Charmer with the badass magical power to control the gorgeous werewolves.

Except, my powers have been bound, and I'm at their mercy.

It's make or break time in the savage kingdoms behind the wall. I have to trust my wolf princes:

Moon — my magical rebel Omega

Amadeus — my hot incubus Beta

Emperor — my dominant protective Alpha

I know that they hold dark secrets. Will the princes choose me, even when their loyalties are tested?

To survive amongst the wolves, I must:

Rule #1 Never be seduced by the wicked prettiness of a Beta

Am I wrong to give in to temptation…and pleasure? Either I'll find a way to turn around and lead the wolves with stronger powers than before…

…or like my parents, I'll be devoured by wolves.

BOOKS IN THE REBEL VERSE

REBEL ANGELS - COMPLETE SERIES

COMPLETE SERIES BOX SET: BOOKS 1-5
VAMPIRE HUNTRESS
VAMPIRE PRINCESS
VAMPIRE DEVIL
VAMPIRE MAGE
VAMPIRE GOD
VAMPIRE SECRET: REBELS AND RENEGADES

REBEL VAMPIRES - COMPLETE SERIES

COMPLETE SERIES BOX SET BOOKS 1-3
BLOOD DRAGONS

BLOOD SHACKLES
BLOOD RENEGADES
STANDALONE NOVELLA - BLOOD GODS

REBEL WEREWOLVES

ONLY PERFECT OMEGAS
ONLY PRETTY BETAS
ONLY PROTECTOR ALPHAS

CHAPTER 1

Behind the crescent-shaped screens that divided prisoners from servants, writhed beasts with beautiful faces.

Only Pretty Betas, promised the painted sign.

If I hadn't known better, I'd have thought that I was rubbing my wrists raw against rope that tied me to a tent pole in a sultan's harem, except for the fact that it was sinfully hot wolf shifters trapped in here with me.

Plus, boy did I know better.

I choked on the amber incense that hung over the Beta Apprentice's orgy in an intoxicating cloud. The outline of the wolf servants in the dark rose and fell behind the gossamer screens like they were in a wild dance. Yet their pleasured cries and moans made me blush.

Those Apprentices knew how to have mind-blowing sexy times... Even if I was at the mercy of their Alphas, at least the Betas were enjoying themselves.

I bit my lip. *Yep, I wasn't even slightly envious...*

Liar, liar, witchy pants on fire.

I sighed, banging my head against the pole that held me on my aching toes with my hands above my head like a sacrificial offering. Bite marks had been daubed all around the tent in scarlet paint and stood out as livid wounds.

Only a couple of weeks ago, I'd been running my art gallery in East Hampton, rather than being caught up trying to prevent a supernatural war. I knew more about mixing paints than mixing it up with wolves and witches.

My red hair curled in sweaty tangles. Beads of sweat dripped down my neck, dampening my mom's velvet cape, which I was still wearing. I'd been terrified that the wolves would steal it from me, just like they'd stolen her life. Despite that, I still struggled to believe that witches were the ancient enemies of both wolves and mages, since I'd Claimed three wolf princes as my Charms and was engaged to marry a mage.

Okay, so I *also* knew an angelic royal prick of a mage who happened to be a god...but even he'd become like family.

Or pack.

I'd only been back from America for less than a week, which is where I'd lived for the last decade after the murder of my parents by shifters. Yet instead of reclaiming my heritage as the last Wolf Charmer with the power to control werewolves here in Oxford, I'd already been thrown to the wolves by the House of Blood for becoming a rebel witch.

Honestly, my Welcome Home had sucked.

It'd doubly sucked because my crimson shadow magic had been temporarily bound. I hadn't been without my magic for over a decade and I shook with the loss.

Plus, the House of Blood had chosen to toss my Charms and me into the one kingdom out of the three Wolf Kingdoms — the Wilds — where I'd humiliated every Alpha on my wedding day to their prince, as if their wood of outlaws wasn't dangerous enough. So, I had a feeling that their welcome wouldn't be any warmer. Unless, you know, it came with a match and a bonfire…and for witches that was a joke in bad taste.

Come on, Crimson, breathe…

A warm hand slid along my back, calming my panic, before slipping to my neck and gently squeezing.

I looked into Emperor's large amber eyes.

Emperor was my third Charm, the Prince of the Alphas: tall, golden-haired, and as hot as a lord in any romance…*and the shameless asshole knew it.*

Emperor rested his forehead against mine. His lips ghost touched my mouth. He didn't kiss me, although *hocus pocus and unholy hexes*, how I wished that he would. His muscled chest pressed against mine, and his silky golden robes that hung open brushed my skin.

"By my hide, the infamous Wolf Charmer surely isn't afraid?" Emperor forced his thigh between mine, and I gasped, as his hard-on pushed against me. He lifted his brow. "If you're thrown to the wolves, then isn't the quaint saying that you find a way to turn around and lead the pack?"

I lifted my leg, rubbing against his dick, and it was his turn to gasp and hiss. He licked against the seam of my lips in retaliation, and I smiled, before capturing his mouth in a tender kiss that despite everything, caught him by surprise. "Trust me, I don't intend to be devoured tonight or let anyone else that I..." Why was it so hard to say *love...*? "No one else is being devoured either because of me. But we're in the middle of the Kingdom of the Wilds without my magic, and I'm tied up in the nonkinky way."

Emperor tested the ropes that bound me, masking the move by clasping my hands as if we were in the throes of passion.

Then he whispered into my ear, "The first time that we were alone together, it was *I* who was tied up. I'm rather enjoying the reversal."

I frowned at his cocky grin, even if it made warmth

unfurl inside me.

"Aw, is wolfie shivering with his need to Dom as an Alpha?" When I rubbed my cheek against his soft hair in reminder of his secret — *that he was in fact an Alpha who was masquerading as an Omega* — he growled.

"So, you *did* notice that I'm all Alpha right now." He bared his teeth, which elongated just enough to be fangs...and why was that hot enough to make *me* shiver? His fingers worked at the knots in the rope, even as he nibbled at my ear. "Interesting that you choose to tempt me."

His grin was wicked, as he ground his hips against mine.

Oh, two could play at that game.

"Because you're so dangerous that the Alphas didn't chain you but left you free with the pretty Betas," I teased.

Stop panting...kissing his throat...arching into him... Witching heavens, I was waving the white flag.

Emperor chuckled. "I'm playing the perfect *Omega,* remember? I'm meant to be too well behaved to do anything naughty with a dirty little witch..."

My jaw set, as my gaze sharpened. Even though my skin tingled everywhere that he touched me, I was back in the game. I raised my knee, rubbing it in circles across his groin, at the same time as I sucked on his neck, as if I meant to bite.

Although, I'd never do that without permission.

5

Emperor's eyes instantly closed, and he groaned, stiffening against me, whilst his hands clutched mine. At the same time, the ropes slithered free from my wrists.

He'd freed me.

Still, however, Emperor didn't pull away; he was lost in our bond, even if it'd begun as a trick.

"Dirty little witch, huh?" I couldn't help the secret smile. When I'd Claimed Emperor, we'd only pretended to my English witch aunt, Stella, that we'd screwed, and it'd become a joke between us. Just about now, it was feeling a lot more real. "The type who'd make you come in your pants?"

Emperor pulled back affronted. "These pants are my favorite suit." He wrinkled his nose. "And dry clean only."

I laughed. *Well, if I was going to Claim a haughty prince…*

A silky wolf head nosed out of my jeans' pocket. I eased my aching arms down, rubbing at my wrists, before stroking over Okami's head.

Okami was the magical wolf that I'd created after the death of my parents for comfort, but now he was as much part of my pack as the angels, mages, and wolves who'd become my family since I returned to England.

Suddenly, the predatory passion of Mikky Ekko's "We Must Be Killers" burst through the tent. I shuddered, as the music thrummed through me as powerfully as Emperor's touch had, mingling with the heady amber scent. The Betas howled, working themselves to a frenzy.

Emperor nodded towards the screens, and we crept towards them. Then I peered around.

The Betas sprawled over log benches in nothing but leather trousers, whilst their silvery gray hair glimmered in the low light of the lamps. In their own ethereal way, the Betas were every bit as pretty as the Omegas had been in the Omega Training Center. Like all wolves, they had collars around their necks, which the witches had forced the shifters to wear ever since they'd been defeated in the Wolf War.

The true beauty that made my breath hitch was the way that they flickered from male to female because Betas alone could shift in the collars. Yet by Royal Decree, they were only allowed to become female during *play*.

Emperor rested his hand on my shoulder. "Goddess Moon! Lucky that no one worked me all up and then left me hanging…" I smirked unapologetically. "This'll be the reason that our so-called bodyguards were so distracted."

I snorted. "Can you blame them?"

Emperor shook his head. "Not when our sexy incubus prince must've started the party. I assure you that I know both his scheming and how irresistible he can be."

My second Charm — the half incubus Prince of the Gods — Amadeus reclined on a bench, which was surrounded by Betas who danced to the music like he was the sultan and they were *his* harem.

Betas pet Amadeus' midnight black hair or simply knelt staring adoringly into his crimson eyes, which had been painted with mascara and kohl, just as his lips were shiny with lip gloss that I knew tasted of chocolate. One Beta even peeled slices of apple for Amadeus, plopping them into his plush mouth…which honestly didn't make me crave to replace those slices with my lips, which tingled at the memory of his chocolate tasting ones...

Yep, my panties were officially a lying inferno.

Even dressed in his full-length gloves and satin top and tights, Amadeus looked more naked than the other Betas who he presided over like one wickedly alluring devil.

Emperor rolled his eyes. "The oversexed one will be insufferable now."

"Maybe you're just jealous that he's being worshiped?" I bumped Emperor's shoulder.

"How surprising that a witch can't tell the difference between worship and admiration. The Prince of the Gods is their icon: A Beta who was picked to become a prince by his kingdom, rather than being nothing but ignored servants." He sighed. "I suppose we must let him have his moment."

"As if I'd steal his celebrity experience." I watched

as a Beta with curly gray hair lifted a goblet of wine to Amadeus' lips, then as my burningly beautiful Charm licked at the rim, before swallowing down his long alabaster neck with enough elegance that I almost had a *coming untouched* moment.

Emperor's speculative look told me that he knew.

"Why's Moon not with him?" I glanced from one couple to the other, who shifted between stroking dicks and tits in sensuous waves of pale skin. My stomach churned at the thought of what might've happened to Moon, my first Charm and Prince of the Wilds. Was he in more danger than I was, returning to his own kingdom as the **REJECT** that the Omega Training Center had once marked him? "What on earth have the asshole Alphas done to him?"

When golden nails curled into my shoulder, I flinched. "*Woah*, you may be a gorgeous prince, but your massage technique needs some serious practice."

"Again, you notice the gorgeous." Emperor smirked. The nails dug more deeply into my shoulder, and I winced. "But firstly, let me point out that massage techniques were never on my curriculum, and secondly... I'm *not* moving my hand."

I turned to stare at Emperor who paled. When I tried to twirl around, however, I found that the claws had sunk into my shoulder and yanked me stumbling and falling onto my ass in the middle of the swaying Betas.

The Betas yelped in shock and scattered because a

Wolf Charmer crashing the party brought down their mood, go figure.

Amadeus' mouth hung open waiting for a slice of apple, before snapping shut. Then he fluttered his *Jesus, they should be illegal* long eyelashes at me.

"I know that my sexy behind's stamped as your property," his tongue curled behind his teeth, "but did you have to make such a dramatic entrance?"

"Nay, pretty Be, but your Countess does." The owner of those *seriously hadn't been trying to give me a massage* claws swaggered into the midst of the Betas, who shrank back. "And I'll teach you your proper place once I'm done with the Charmer."

Lyall was a warrior with lighter eyes than other Alphas...*and also Moon's ex-girlfriend.* So, not awkward at all.

I tilted my head. "Didn't I already kick your ass?"

Lyall examined her claws, as if deciding whether to file them. "Try and kick it now, on my fangs, *I dare you.*" My eyes widened. She seriously didn't realize how much stress I'd been under this last week, which needed a target...or that she was offering up her ass. "You call the Om *Moon* like any Omega can have a name, yet you're unworthy to own him. Why do you shame him? Even your own family know that you're no Wolf Charmer, or you wouldn't have been sent here."

I took a slow breath, whilst I quivered with rage.

"Trash talk," I edged my fingers towards a pot of red

paint that the Betas had used to daub the walls of the tent, "I respect that. But also, technically the House of Blood aren't related to me, unless you count them as future in-laws. So, if this is your *how the mighty are fallen* gloat session, go ahead, just get the facts right." She stared down at me, blinking. I grinned, whilst curling my hand more firmly around the paint. "I mean it, go for it. *Kick my ass.*"

"Silence, cub," Lyall spluttered. "You had your chance with the Om who'd been promised as *my* Wolf Bitten, and he could've lost his pelt because of your witch *in-laws.*"

"Wow, that one hit home, I mean you're seriously wrecking me here." When I mock grimaced, Amadeus giggled. "You know what would truly wreck me?"

I beckoned Lyall closer, and her brow furrowed, as she leaned closer.

The collective gasp from the Betas was so worth it, when I hurled the paint over Lyall's face.

For a moment, she didn't even move in shock, whilst the paint dripped from the end of her nose. Then Emperor laughed, lounging next to Amadeus like he only needed popcorn to enjoy the show.

At last, Lyall snarled, launching herself on top of me.

Holy hell she was large, heavy, and powerful... Plus, why did I forget that without my magic, I could barely fight off a kitten, let alone a wolf shifter? Except, that *stress* had morphed into rage and grappling with Lyall was as good therapy as breathing exercises or a yoga session in Corpse Pose.

Okami shot out of my pocket, biting Lyall on the ass, whilst she yelped and tried to swat him. I knew from painful experience that even his silken bites smarted.

I didn't have my shadows but I could still be a pain in the ass.

Lyall growled, smearing her hand through the paint on her face, before deliberately rubbing it into *my* face, so that we'd match. I squirmed against the squelching feel of her palm, wrestling to escape from underneath her.

"Throw in some glittery costumes, and I'd pay to watch this," Emperor said dreamily.

"Sexist," I hollered.

He shrugged. "Absolutely not. I'd pay more if it was Moon and you."

"I'd pay even more if it was Moon, you, me…and the Wolf Charmer." Beta's eyes glittered with excitement.

Emperor pointed at Lyall. "Sorry, but you've been voted out."

"This is how you allow your Oms and Bes to talk?" Lyall slammed me back against the floor in horror. "You're daft to think that you can control any of your men. What kind of arrogant witch are you to come swaggering into our world? I've craved to care for the Prince of the Wilds, loving him as a perfect Om should be, ever since we were wee kids. Because of you, however, he'll suffer."

I blanched, as my breathing because ragged. I couldn't deny it because Moon could be suffering *right now* because of my choices. I hated that I hadn't been able to protect him.

"I don't want to control my guys," I gritted out. "We're equals—"

"Silence, lest you be flayed!" At Princess Morag's booming command, the music cut off and the Betas fell onto their knees, trembling.

Lyall and I looked up from our position entangled on the floor, covered in paint like naughty kids who'd been caught…literally…red-handed.

Morag strode through the flap in the tent in a layered leather dress that looked like fur with the same pointy and calculating face that I remembered. Her hair hung in stormy waves around her shoulders. When she studied me, I almost caught the twitch of a smile, before she masked it.

"Playtime's over," Morag announced, "although it looks like you had more fun with furless than I would've expected, Lyall."

Lyall flushed, snatching her hand away from the unfortunate position that it'd ended up in, cupping my tit in our struggle. I shoved her away and pulled myself up onto my knees. Okami settled on my shoulder, sticking his nose in the air like he'd singlehandedly won the battle.

"Aye, right," Lyall muttered, not meeting my eye. "I hate the witch. She stole my—"

"Nay, Om wasn't yours for a long time," Morag snapped. Then her expression gentled, as she glanced between us. "Both of you love my brother in your own way. Fur and fangs, I've pushed his behind to act more like a perfect Omega, but he's always rebelled. I never considered that it'd lead to his execution, until tonight."

Lyall's stricken expression must've mirrored mine.

When I glanced at Amadeus, I saw that he'd leapt up, and Emperor clutched him close to his chest in distress.

"If you want him to survive my ma's rage, you'll both…" When Morag wrapped her arms around herself, I was shocked at the way her eyes gleamed. The last time that we'd been here, she hadn't even hugged Moon. I'd never considered that the way she treated him didn't mean she *hated* him. *Yep, witchy arrogance…* She slammed her hand against her thigh in frustration, before taking a hitching breath. "You'll leave off your feuding and do what's best for him. Lyall, ever since you were a cub, you've wanted to Wolf Bite my brother, even though you know that you scare him. It's an obsession."

Lyall opened her mouth as if to object, but Morag waved her to silence.

"And Wolf Charmer, my ma thinks that you're unworthy because the witches abandoned you." Morag's smile was all fangs. "Om told me that you only lost your place with the House of Blood because you protected him. I could never like a single skin…but know that at least I now don't want to rip out your throat."

I swallowed. "That's just peachy."

"You both love him," Morag said more quietly, "please, will you not work together this once to save him?"

Lyall and I shot each other self-conscious glances, before we nodded at the same time.

Morag let out a breath, before her shoulders slumped. "It's time to meet with the queen. There's nothing I can do about the state of you." She eyed me critically. At least the crimson could pass as war paint… maybe. "I can't be arsed to clean you up, but I don't imagine it'll matter, since you're even more likely to be executed than my brother."

I swayed, caught by Emperor and Beta who'd darted to my side. "Don't you think you should've led with that?"

Morag shrugged. "Nay, I don't, furless. Why do I care if *you* die? Come on, Queen Rhona will be even more furious if she's kept waiting."

Amadeus wound his arms around my waist, and

Emperor squeezed my fingers between his, as I followed Morag out of the tent of pretty Betas on unsteady legs towards a meeting with the queen. Now I had to save Moon from death, whilst facing my own execution.

CHAPTER 2

When I stared at the monstrous Alpha with fangs studding her dress like armor and a glove with silver claws clutched around Moon's throat, I forgot that I was knelt on the forest floor surrounded by shifters eager to execute me. Instead, I craved to kill any of them who'd hurt my Charm, especially the one who was now sizzling finger marks into his pale skin.

I'd never been bloodthirsty or possessive before Wolf Biting Moon, but marrying into werewolf royalty would do that to you, go figure.

Morag had shoved me to my knees in the glade next to Amadeus and Emperor, whilst Lyall had stood behind us in warrior stance.

Now, Lyall couldn't look away from Moon, just the same as me. You know, having to work with the ex to save your guy sucked but not as much as knowing that if it didn't work, those claws would take off his curly head.

I shivered, despite the waves of heat from the spitting campfire, dragging my mom's cape closer around me. The woodsmoke stung my nostrils. My crimson shadows raged inside to be free, but I still couldn't reach them like the high tide of an ocean. The fresh night air after the intoxicating incense inside the Beta's tent was like a slap to the face.

Moon was naked, as if everyone had equal gawking rights over his dick. His long limbs were crouched over to try and ease the pressure on his seared throat, and his moon blond curls hung into his golden eyes, which were flecked with silver. Despite his humiliation in front of the predatory court of Alphas — dark-haired women just like the Omegas were blond men — he tilted his chin, shooting me a defiant grin.

Okay, he was still my rebel Omega, who in the moonlight wasn't merely pretty... he was *beautiful.*

My breath caught, and I clutched my hands in my lap because I wasn't visiting the Kingdom of the Wilds, as I had been last time, as official Liaison of the House of Seasons. Instead, I'd been gift wrapped for the wolves along with my Charms to be their chew toys because I'd discovered too much about the murder of a mage called Kolby, the risk of a second Wolf War, and a magical weapon.

There was no way that I'd allow my hot rebel prince to die for me.

I glowered at the Queen of the Alphas, Rhona, who was tensed on the log bench, coiled like she was ready to strike, simmering with rage. The firelight danced across the crown of fangs in her inky hair and the necklace at her throat.

Moon's dad knelt as beautiful and silent as last time, but now he no longer looked like the smug and perfect consort, rather he was ashen and anguished. He edged his fingers in stealthy movements to stroke his son's ankle in comfort, hidden from the queen's sight.

Hey, facing death could bring you closer to your parents, who knew. Maybe I could throw us into even greater danger, and Moon would get a word...let's dream big here...*a whole sentence* with his dad.

"Don't execute him," Lyall and I burst out at the same time.

Then we wore matching blushes, *freaking fabulous*.

Rhona's gaze swung between us. "Aye, I see how it is. Have you two kissed and made up then? You've decided to wear matching war paint like charm bracelets...?" When she leaned forward, I fought not to recoil.

Lyall scrubbed at the paint on her face in disgust. "Nay, there's been no kissing. This is just..."

"You choosing crimson to match the Charmer's foul magic...?" Rhona's voice was sharp as a blade.

Lyall froze: a rabbit caught in the wolf's jaws. "Fur and fangs, *never.*"

I was used to feeling like the charity case in East Hampton, tagging along to my billionaire cousins' social events with the elitist set but I'd never truly squirmed before, whilst the tips of my ears shaded the same crimson, at the sensation of being the *villain.*

Rhona's lips curled, as she scrutinized me. "Even now, you swagger in here like you can make demands, single skin. Aye right, like I haven't been caught in this dance with the witches for centuries. They found you unworthy, and now you're mine." She touched the fangs around her neck, whilst her eyes narrowed. "You once pinned me with your shadows to the ceiling of my own Wild Hall." When her hand tightened to a fist, the fangs sliced into her palm, and blood seeped out. At least she was dedicated to her hatred of me. "But where's your power now?"

I dropped my gaze, not wanting her to see how much that'd smarted. My shadows tickled deep inside; being unable to connect with them was like being blinded.

"Your son was sacrificed to me, I get it. If I was you, I'd be cranky about it as well." I forced myself to meet her gaze again. "But you're working way too hard to fulfill the dickhead mother-in-law cliché right now."

Rhona's mouth tightened into a thin line. "And you,

wee Charmer, are already the monster that we always knew would lead to our son's death."

"*Woah*, chill out." I launched myself up at the same time as Emperor and Amadeus, as if I still had my shadows wound around them. "There'll be no monsters, death, or other *An American Werewolf in London* style creepiness. Let's just discuss this like reasonable, rational…"

"Witches and werewolves?" Emperor quirked his brow.

"I'm not my mom," I burst out. Then I flushed, wetting my lips. "And I'm not this legendary great-grandmother of mine either, whatever the witching hell she did to you."

I didn't miss the way that every single shifter winced.

So, I knew that it'd been more along the lines of wading over corpses in the first Wolf War than a cuddling fest like I loved with Moon…and how much did I want to snatch Moon away from the giant with the silver claw and let him nuzzle into his favorite spot on my neck…?

"What she *did* to us?" I hadn't thought that Rhona's voice could sound any deadlier but I'd been wrong. "How about steal our independence, furless? Our lands, heritage, and freedom? Massacre us, before forcing these marks of our shame around our necks?" She hovered her hand over the collar, unable even to yank at it without the risk of the witches' spells woven into it, spiking her with poison.

I cringed. "Okay, if you want to put it like that…"

"Silence your daft tongue," Lyall hissed, shoving past me, "anymore of your furless style of help, and you'll have helped Om into his grave."

I paled, smiling apologetically at Moon. He winked back.

I ached with the need to kiss his pink lips. He was my virgin prince, yet even though he'd teased me in the most tempting ways, he'd never allowed me to kiss him. I couldn't die tonight without knowing that my Charm desired to kiss me as much as I desired him.

He did, didn't he?

When Moon's concerned gaze met mine, his brow furrowed in thought. Holy hell, in the midst of possibly our last hour on earth, he couldn't tell that I was having kissy thoughts, right…? Although, there was no way that he missed the way that my gaze dropped to his gorgeous dick.

And that's why clothes were invented.

"On the Alpha's word, let Om live," Lyall stroked her knuckles down Moon's cheek, and he flinched, "and I'll educate him."

"Even as cubs, you refused to dominate him, Countess. Then later, he refused to listen to you," Rhona scoffed. "What's changed?"

Lyall's gaze became hard, as her fingers slipped

beneath Moon's chin and gripped him hard. "I've learned my lesson. I know what happens if he can't be broken to become a proper prince and Omega. And I won't lose him again." When she traced her thumb over his lips like she was coaxing them to open for a kiss, I took a step towards them, but Emperor caught me by the elbow and held me back. "I know his worst nightmare."

"By my hide, you go too far." Morag twisted to her mom, as if the queen would stop Lyall, but she was merely looking thoughtful, even as Moon panted with fear.

What on earth was Lyall threatening to do to Moon?

"Do you swear by Moon Oath on risk of your life to bring my son to heel?" Rhona demanded.

Lyall's eyes widened, but she nodded.

On risk of her life...?

I didn't hate many people — the shifters who'd murdered my parents, my High School bullies, and Little Red Riding Hood (because what kind of asshole would mistake a wolf for their grandma?), but I came close to it with Lyall.

Yet she was prepared to gamble her life to save Moon, which meant that I grudgingly lowered her to just under my hate level for LRRH. After all, it was twisted and all kinds of wrong, but she must love Moon in her own way.

I wished that she could understand that love should

be equal and not end with one of you at the feet of the other.

"What about you, wee Charmer? Do you Moon Oath to put all your Charms in their place?" Rhona cast a disapproving glower at both Amadeus and Emperor who stood at my side, rather than kneeling at my feet.

My pulse thundered too loudly in my ears, as my heart thudded against my ribs. This was the choice that I'd always struggled with: run and hide in the wardrobe where the wolves couldn't gobble me up...or face danger and death.

As a kid, I'd chosen to run and hide, abandoning my parents to their deaths.

I'd never make that choice again.

I straightened my shoulders. "I take it that you've forgotten, but the guys who you sacrificed to become my Charms are your three kingdoms' *princes*. Their place is seriously none of my business. My partners are willing, your kingdoms are safe in our hands, and I'm not the same dickhead Wolf Charmer as the ones who came before me. I know that you don't believe me, but there's only one way I can prove it." I took a ragged breath. "If you Moon Oath or whatever not to harm my Charms, then kill me and have that *Braveheart* moment."

"Did our kinky session back in the tent quite literally blow your confused American mind?" Emperor hissed.

"Kinky?" Amadeus hooked his arms around my

neck, and I shivered at the sensation, as he pushed his hips against mine. "And I wasn't invited…?"

"You have my Moon Oath." For the first time, Rhona smiled; it wasn't an improvement. The other Alphas prowled closer, predatory. "Countess, as your reward for taking my son in hand, you have the honor of ridding us of terror. Free us from disgrace."

I'd been called more flattering things than *terror* or *disgrace.*

I twisted to Lyall who grinned at me, whilst her fangs grew, as well as her golden nails.

In my aunt's House of Seasons, Moon had partially shifted into his werewolf form, which had been far more terrifying (and hot), than simply a few fangs and claws. Yet I had the feeling that the witches were clueless as to how far all the wolves could still shift, even in their collars because those fangs and claws were still deadly.

When Lyall stalked towards me, it was clear that the temporary truce between us was off.

I tried to shake Amadeus away, but he clung like a wickedly sexy koala bear around my neck. When Emperor blocked Lyall with his broad shoulders, she slashed him across the cheek. He gasped, and I could see how he struggled not to attack her as one Alpha to another, forced to pretend that he was an Omega. He ducked his head but he still didn't step out of the way, shielding me with his arms out in his robes like the golden wings of a butterfly.

I pushed Emperor behind me. "Honestly, do you think that it'd make me happy to see the crazy ex gut you as well?" Then my expression softened, as I stroked Emperor's hair and feathered a light kiss behind his ear.

His gaze was fragile. "I can't lose you, Crimson."

"*We* can't lose you." Amadeus bit my lower lip, before twining his tongue with mine both tender and passionate, just like earlier in the tent I'd craved that he would; he tasted of rich chocolate and just as good as I'd imagined.

Black candle hexes, how I wished that I could capture Moon's lips as well. Yet the claw was too tight around his neck for him to even speak, and the only way that he could communicate was the gleam of tears in his agonized gaze.

"First the *terror...*" Lyall sliced through the front of my mom's cape wrenching it off my shoulders.

Shocked, I stared at her, as she held it up like a stolen mascot from an opposing team.

The glade suddenly fell to silence.

The other Alphas gaped at Lyall like they expected my mom to be resurrected and smite her for her insolence; despite her bully tactics, Lyall's hand still shook.

When no shadows wound through the trees to string Lyall up in punishment for daring to touch my cape, Lyall smirked at me, rubbing the sticky paint off her hands on it like it was a rag.

My eyes burned with tears. "Give that back."

"I don't think so. You once took what was mine, so now I'm taking what's yours." Lyall didn't look away from me as she dropped my cape on the muddy floor and stepped on it with her boot, just like I'd been expected to stand on Moon with mine.

I didn't need my shadows to see red. The cape had become my link to my mom and Charmer legacy. The wolves had stolen mom and now they were taking even her memory. If Amadeus hadn't been wound around me holding back my rage, I'd have been throwing myself into a fight, even without my powers.

"Trust me," Amadeus whispered, "I'm not only a pretty behind."

"What…?"

"Now for the *disgrace*." Lyall's grin widened around her fangs, as she stalked towards me, raising her claws.

Here was the vision of the wolf who'd haunted my nightmares over the last decade. I stumbled backwards, but Amadeus spun out of my arms towards Rhona. Then he swayed to the haunting music that bled out of the Beta's tent, teasing off his long gloves and revealing his tantalizing alabaster skin.

Okami slunk out of my pocket, slithering sensuously around Amadeus, who arched into his touch like they were lovers caught in private passion, rather than the sudden stars of a sinful show that had caught the Alphas in its thrall.

Every shifter desired Amadeus, and I was breathless

myself at the need to yank him back into my arms and slip my hand down his pants, until I could touch his cute ass and the **WCH** that he'd requested to be branded there, which proved that he was *my* Charm.

Okami flashed back-and-forth like the Dance of the Seven Veils, whilst Amadeus swayed towards Rhona. In the shimmering light of the moon, there was no doubting his incubus blood, as his ruby eyes glittered.

I might've wished that he only danced for me, but I wouldn't be that kind of possessive asshole. Plus, my *pretty Beta* had the sinful body and angelic eyes that my aunt had warned me about with the shifters, but I was also learning that I wouldn't want him as an enemy. His dance, body, and sexuality were his weapons, and boy, did he know how to use them.

Rhona panted, leaning forward with her hands on her knees and an expression of rapt attention like the rest of us had been spelled into non-existence. When Amadeus danced closer with a swing of his hips, she snatched his wrist like a snake clamping its fangs into its prey and hauled his slender body onto her knee.

And he let her.

Emperor growled.

"How can I please you?" Beta nestled his head against Rhona's chest. "Pleasure with sexy little me is far more fun than revenge."

Rhona laughed, although she still stroked his hair. "Nay, you can't bargain with a queen, Be. You were given to me, so I already own you. What if I simply take?"

I grabbed onto Emperor, stopping him from storming to save Amadeus.

Amadeus had asked me to *trust* him, and I wouldn't underestimate him. Emperor had spent his childhood protecting Amadeus. *Maybe he needed to learn that his friend had grown up...?*

When Emperor turned his betrayed gaze on me, I winced.

Okami wrapped himself around Rhona's hand, before she could get any naughty thoughts. Amadeus snickered, as she tried to flick her new silver glove off, even as he caressed his own gloveless hand down her cheek.

I shivered at the same time as Rhona did. The touch of an incubus' bare hand on skin was like every plea- sure, desire, and need flayed, whilst the incubus could read and manipulate them. Then they were able to bring you what you most desired, whilst your pleasure gorged them.

If an incubus failed to please you, they starved. Once fed, however, they were powerful...and *hold onto your flaming panties* hot.

Rhona's eyes rolled back, as she shuddered, clutching Amadeus closer and whimpering. The Alphas around her shifted uncomfortably, muttering.

Huh, even I hadn't been able to reduce her to *whim-*

pering with all my magic.

"Ma," Morag begged, reddening. "Will you leave off…"

"Don't you want my touch?" Amadeus murmured. "For me to please you like this?"

"*Aye*," Rhona rasped, humping against him.

"Then remember that I'm a Beta and not an Omega. Plus, I'm the *Prince of the Gods*." Amadeus' gaze was steely, as he pulled away his hand. Rhona blinked, looking at him with hazy eyes. "If you don't take anything from me, then I'll *give* you what you desire."

Rhona reached out to tuck a strand of Amadeus' hair behind his ear, studying him with a softer expression than I'd yet seen. "Does the daft Charmer know what she has in you?"

Amadeus peeked at me through his thick lashes, and my knees almost buckled at the heavy-lidded need in his gaze. "She's learning." Then he glanced at Moon. "Your son carried on about the Countess all the time. He wouldn't admit it, see, but he missed her."

My chest ached, as I hunched my shoulders. Why did it hurt so much, even though I knew that Amadeus was only lying to make things easier for Moon?

He was lying, right?

"He did…?" Lyall's eyes lit up, before she smiled encouragingly at Moon. "On my fangs, it can be like it always should've been before the *witches*. You'll be my Bitten as was promised."

I waved my hand in the air. "Hey, not to be the buzzkill, but he's already Bitten...by the *witch* over here."

"All Claims are broken by death," Lyall snarled.

Maybe I shouldn't have put my hand up and waved so enthusiastically...

"The Wolf Charmer won't be executed tonight," Rhona bellowed, stilling Lyall in shock. Then Rhona kissed the top of Amadeus' head. "I swore off revenge, which leaves me with the question: what to do with the witch and her final Charm?"

Okay, so not death, which is always freaking fabulous. But the sadistic way that the queen was examining Emperor and me made me squirm like she was imagining a long list of nasty options.

"A bath, snack, and a good night's sleep because I'm beat...?" I smiled winningly.

Rhona only scowled, before turning her attention to Emperor. "Since you were a cub, I've noticed you, Prince of the Alphas, fluttering around like a haughty butterfly. It's time an Alpha broke your wings."

I clutched my arms around Emperor's waist, whilst my trapped crimson raged to be free and able to cocoon him in its safety.

Yet Emperor merely arched his brow. "I already have a Chief Alpha, and she doesn't break my wings. She sets me free to fly."

Rhona snorted. "That's because she's an unworthy witch who doesn't know any better."

"Nothing but an unworthy witch, is it?" Amadeus cocked his head. "Then would it please you to toss them both in the Witches Well for the Unworthy? No witch has ever escaped, or those are the stories that *I've* heard."

Rhona smiled cruelly; her eyes blazed. "You heard right. Although, if it rains, they'll drown."

"*Witches in a well. Throw them in, throw them in. Witches in a well.*" The Alphas chanted, circling closer and closer.

I stared at Amadeus, even as I shook.

Why had he offered up a life-sentence as a punishment? If I found a way up from a prison that was *inescapable*, his sexy behind was in for a spanking.

I refused to beg and show how terrified I was of being trapped in both the water and dark, which were my nightmares, because I was *unworthy*.

This time, it was Emperor's arms tightening around me to stop me swaying with dizziness.

I'd been thrown to the wolves by the witches, and now I'd be thrown into a well to drown.

CHAPTER 3

In the blackness, I clung to Emperor, wrapping my legs around his waist like we were in a seriously adventurous sex position. Instead, we were shivering at the bottom of the narrow stone Witches Well (which I refused to even think was for the *Unworthy*), which crushed us together in a cruel parody of a lovers' embrace. Although, if I had to be trapped down a well with someone, Emperor was now top of my list because of his strong arms and the way that he licked and nuzzled at my neck to distract me from the gnawing hunger and thirst.

The only guy that could've knocked Emperor off the top spot was Moon because his cuddles were kind of addictive...like toasted marshmallow lattes.

Trust me, *addictive*.

Except, it hurt to think of Moon, whilst I rested my

arms around Emperor's neck in the dark, when I didn't know whether Lyall was hurting him. It was equally painful to think of what Amadeus was sacrificing with Queen Rhona to keep us alive down this well, rather than savaged at Lyall's fangs.

When I shifted in frustration, the water that rippled up to Emperor's middle splashed. I wrinkled my nose against its rotten egg stench. My clothes stuck to me, rubbing in uncomfortable — *intimate* — places.

I peered upward, but the well cover had been slammed with a resounding and far too ominous *clang,* after Emperor and I had been lowered in here by a rope that'd then been pulled up after us. The dickhead Alphas reassured me that the lid had tiny holes in it for air...and to let the rain pour through.

I'd never been frightened of stormy weather, until now. Morag had described how sluices would open from the side and drain the Wilds' rainwater into the well.

Drowning had always been my recurring nightmare.

Boy, was this not my week.

Emperor's fingers stroked down my back, before digging into the tension between my shoulder blades. Every touch was much more intense in the dark. The last time that I'd been trapped like this, it'd been in the wardrobe in my parents' bedroom, during the massacre in the House of Silver. I should've been terrified. Yet I was safe in my Charms' embrace, even if I ached, was chilled to the bone, and close to gnawing off my own arm in hunger…or Emperor's because at this point, I wasn't picky.

Yep, I'd best keep that last part to my witchy self.

I groaned, banging myself against the stone wall. I felt Emperor flinch against me. For the last…however long we'd been stuck down here…it was as if he was part of my body; his movements vibrated through me.

"Hey, were you holding out on me?" I licked his cheek. "I thought that you didn't know massage techniques?"

When Emperor paused, I squirmed, willing him to start up his delicious touch again. "Did I?" I could hear the grin in his voice, even if I couldn't see it. "I believe that I said it *wasn't taught on my curriculum*."

I huffed. "Honestly, it's my mistake. I should've known that a pampered prince had massages coming out of his ass…"

I jumped at the sudden swipe of his thumb down the hollow of my back. "I'm certain that you haven't forgotten how sweet a sight I made tied to your bed by my own kingdom. Massages were useful tools in my diplomacy, and I learned that they were much preferable to being on my knees or back."

"I'm sorry," I whispered.

"Why? You're the only one who unbound me, or have you forgotten that as well?"

My lip trembled, and I couldn't help the tears that had been threatening ever since Lyall had stolen my cape and desecrated mom's memory from falling. I knew that Emperor must've been able to feel the way that I was shaking.

He *hushed* me, resting our foreheads together; his scent of sweet honey washed over me. "It's hellish to be confined like this, but I've been caged on the night of the full moon my entire life. We'll survive this, or are you truly an unworthy Wolf Charmer?"

I bristled, stung. My shadows battled at the binding that wound around them like vines to show him just how *worthy* I was to have him as my Charm, and I could sense the binding begin to loosen. "Dude, I'm a rogue witch. Does your loser ass need a lesson in Charmer and Charm relations?"

Emperor rolled his hips against mine. "That's right, filthy little witch, *teach* your bad wolf."

I giggled. Oh, I got it, he wanted to piss me off. *Mission accomplished.* His way was more creative than most to take my mind off…*everything.*

"Come on," he hissed, "I can't do all the work here."

I sighed, before tightening my legs around his waist and making him gasp. "What a bad wolf you are. Now I've caught you, whatever shall I do with you?"

Emperor's breath was hot against my ear. "You could punish me…?"

I didn't miss the hopeful lilt or the way that the words curled warmth through me despite the chill.

I rolled my eyes. *How in the witching heavens could I role play discipline, when I couldn't even stand?*

Then I remembered the scars on Amadeus' back, and it wouldn't even have mattered if I'd had room to swing a bull whip, I wouldn't have struck my prince.

"How about if I think he's a *good wolf*?" I turned my head to catch Emperor's lips in a tender kiss. He shuddered, but I had the feeling that it'd been more at the *good wolf*, than the kiss. *Hey, a praise kink I could work with.* "And I only want to snuggle with the wickedly hot prince…?"

"Then I'd say…" Emperor's lips brushed against mine on each word. "…Damn you for making me hard in these tight wet pants."

I snickered. "I'm so not saying sorry."

Then I sighed, at last allowing myself to think about the House of Silver and the two angels and Moon's brother, Moth, who we'd left behind.

Zetta, who'd been created from the essence of all Wolf Charmers and had taken mom's appearance, was still in the house, yet she'd been the one to betray me to the witches. Ramiel, the warrior angel who was also an Addict under the control of the witches, was looking after Mischief.

Nope, I still couldn't think of Mischief lying unmoving in the nest of blankets like he was already dead…

I closed my eyes and took a shuddering breath.

Emperor stilled against me. "Crimson…?" He asked cautiously.

"Do you think Mischief is still alive?" I murmured. Emperor's breaths were suddenly as unsteady as my own. "Why on earth is his energy being drained? You know, Ramiel will be freaking out…in a quiet kind of way…that we haven't gone back to them. I'm gutted that they could think that we abandoned them." I bit my lip to hold back the sob. "Jesus, I can't bear not being able to use my magic. It's kind of like I don't even know what I am if…I'm not a witch. Mischief once told me that having his magic bound was like being shattered. Boy, was he not lying."

"Undo my shirt," Emperor commanded.

I sniffed. "Nope, the mood's officially killed, sexy."

"Although I won't argue the *sexy*," Emperor replied, "it may surprise you that I can think with more than my dick." I flushed, fumbling with the buttons of his shirt to push it open above his waistcoat. "Now reach inside and—"

"Pull out a rabbit?"

"More like a butterfly."

I brushed my fingers underneath Emperor's silky shirt to his chest, edging across to his shoulder. I shuddered, as the dark magic of the Purple Emperor butterfly that was tattooed on his skin nipped me, until I could trace its outline by touch alone. Emperor's heart *thud* —

thud — thudded beneath the slow sensual sweeps of my hand.

"So strange that only you and my sister have found beauty in my *Curse*." Emperor shook, pressing into my caresses. "Does it intrigue you? This Omega who was born wrong as an Alpha? The clever tattoo that uses magic on a wolf?"

My hand stilled. "I'm such a jerk. It's just that your ink—"

"Binds me," he said, softly, "repressing who I am. I *understand* your loss, but it's only temporary. When shall I be allowed to escape my cocoon?"

When I kissed his cheek, I startled at the taste of his salty tears. Then I licked their trail in comfort.

I swept my fingers lower, just above his heart and over the **WCH** that he'd chosen to have branded over the **OM** mark, until it looked like nothing but his own beautiful pattern, which belonged to him alone. His dick twitched against me through his pants, and I shivered.

"You've already broken out of the asshole Kingdom of the Alpha's cocoon by yourself. You're my Charm but you don't need me to fly." I smiled at his sharp intake of breath. "You're my Purple Emperor."

I *eeped* at the sudden violence of his kiss. Our teeth clacked, then he bit at my lip, before his tongue thrust into mine with desperation and longing. The sharp scent of liquorice overpowered the sweet honey, until I lost myself in it and the vibrations of Emperor's fierce growl. I didn't know whether I was being kissed or savaged.

When he pulled back, panting, he snarled, "You truly like to tempt me, don't you? Let us be clear on something, your magic will return, but you still have power without it. I don't care whether you're a witch, wolf or Queen of the Fae, you see me, even in the dark."

I jolted at his nibble to my ear, then his soft suck along its shell. My skin felt too tight and hot.

"May I...?" Emperor's hands skirted lower along my back towards my ass.

My eyes fluttered closed. "Holy hell, don't stop."

He chuckled, warm and intimate in my ear. Then he cupped my ass under the water. I arched, whilst I was a hundred times more sensitive to every brush of his fingertips because of the blackness.

Please, please, just touch me a little bit lower...

Suddenly, electric guitars and throbbing organ music burst from the well's walls. Emperor and I both screamed, clutching each other tighter in shock.

Were my guts seriously dancing to the loud pulse of The Animals "House of the Rising Sun"?

As the haunting voice howled out its dark warning of pain and regret, I shivered because boy, did I get those vibes right about now, which I guessed was the point of whoever was tormenting us. Then in a blaze of light that burned my retinas and made *me* howl, the walls were flooded with images repeated on loop all around us, so quickly that my stomach lurched.

Finally, the halos in my eyes faded, and I blinked to clear my vision.

"Don't watch," Emperor pleaded. "How charmingly quaint of the Wilds to taunt us with our powerlessness to save Moon because trapping us at the bottom of a well with the threat of being drowned, wasn't quite harsh enough."

"Moon...?" Yep, of course I looked.

Then I wished that I hadn't.

White walls, a padded box, and Moon battling even though he was whining with fear around the muzzle.

I stiffened at the sight of the muzzle because I knew that they traumatized Moon.

Did he hate them so much because he'd been muzzled like this as a kid?

Moon was being dragged by two Alphas in leather uniforms towards the box, whilst he struggled against them like it'd burn him. They threw him inside with less care than I'd ever seen an Omega treated and slammed down the lid, trapping him in the dark and plunging all three us of us once again into the black.

The skin on the back of my neck prickled at the sound of Moon's panted fear, as if he was suffering in the well alongside us. A bitter scent like juniper berries caught in my nostrils.

How could I even smell the inside of the box?

My hands clenched to fists, whilst my red snapped through yet another thread of its binding in rage.

"The dishonorable, pitiless savages..." Emperor snarled.

"*Duh*, we're on the same page here." I nipped the end of Emperor's nose, and slowly his breathing slowed. "Witch knows I hate what's being done to Moon, I just don't get why they've locked him in a box."

"That revolting smell is a chemical mix of Alpha scent, made many times stronger. Moon is muzzled and trapped with it in an attempt to break him into becoming more...compliant and less rebellious an Omega."

I snorted. "I call bullshit."

There was a silence; all I could hear was Moon's terrified breathing.

"Do you know Moon's greatest fear since I knew him as a child? The *Re-education Center*," Emperor spat. "It's the ultimate threat held over every Omega. How romantic Wolf Bitings are, when an Alpha may send their Omega for *correctional training* after Claiming, if they misbehave. The Re-education Center is hidden, isolated deep in the Wilds' woods, where only the harshest methods are employed. No one knows exactly what goes on there, and no one cares as long as their Omega is soft, simpering, and on their knees at the end of it."

If I hadn't been so frightened for Moon, I'd have

definitely stopped to analyze the *help, it was choking me* level of cynicism in Emperor's view of Alphas and Omegas...and Claiming.

"*Hmm,* so this is his *worst nightmare* then?" My throat was dry, and I struggled to swallow. "But it'd be easier to French kiss a frog and transform him into my fourth prince, than to help Moon from in here."

"Oh, now *that* I'd love to see." When Emperor pressed his thumb into the crease of my ass, I jumped. Serves me right for forgetting just what the wolves' torment had been interrupting. "Our sweet frog prince to corrupt."

"Or you could free the Om from the Re-education Center," Rhona's voice boomed from the dark. *Would they freaking stop making me jump before I pissed myself...* "Fur and fangs, it all rests on you, lass."

"What do I need to do?" I demanded.

"Break your Bitten bond," Rhona's voice was smug.

"Go to hell," I growled. "And he's not an Om: he's called *Moon.* Did your queenly ass forget that he's also your son?"

"I thought that you'd be a stubborn one." Rhona's voice had lost its smug edge. "You can't mean to let another Wolf Bite him by force...? The Alpha can take her pleasure from him, but he'll never be able to find joy from the bond, only pain. If you don't willingly break the bond, I'll allow Lyall off her leash..."

"In the name of the furless heavens," Emperor

roared, "you wouldn't permit such a sacrilege on your kingdom's own prince."

"Nay, Omega, you've no idea what I'd *permit,*" Rhona's voice wound around the well like a noose. "No wolf from the Kingdom of the Alphas will ever give *me* orders."

The sound of Moon cut off, and the scent of berries faded. I trembled in Emperor's arms because it was like losing Moon all over again.

Had I messed it up? Should I've freed Moon?

When I opened my mouth to speak, however, Emperor adjusted me on his hips and whispered, "Don't say it. Moon would've killed us both or at least, taken back cuddling rights, which is just as bad, if you'd broken the bond. It's just…" Emperor sighed. "He's the magical Moon Child. I'm certain that he doesn't understand how special he is because he's been reviled for his difference. Yet if your bond isn't equal by the full moon, then you know that he'll die. So, is it…equal?"

"Am I jerk if I say that I can't tell?"

"You'd know, and I sense like a throbbing in the collar that's holding back my shift that we're getting close to the full moon. Of course, the Wilds unhelpfully didn't supply us with at least a calendar if not wi-fi access down here, so we could've kept track."

I laughed, even though I wanted to cry. "Cuddling rights or not, I have to break it. Jesus, I can't let Moon die."

I peered up at the lid of the well. I figured that maybe the queen or her guards had been lurking up there all the time, waiting for us to either give in or die.

My throat was too dry to even speak, or too thick with tears. I coughed to clear it. How could I get out the words that'd rip Moon away from me?

Would Moon ever forgive me for throwing him out of my pack?

Then something *thwapped* down through the black and hit me between the eyes.

I groaned, rubbing my head, before reaching out and grasping…*a rope.*

Huh, so these wolves were mind readers too, like that didn't make them creepily scarier…

"Honestly, the queen doesn't dick around when she gets her own way." I hauled myself off Emperor, wrapping my legs around the rope.

I'd sucked at gym in High School, but martial arts classes had at least taught me enough strength not to embarrass myself on a rope climb.

Not embarrass myself…*totally.*

"Werewolves aren't psychic." Emperor pushed on my ass, propelling me up the rope, as he climbed underneath me. "My guess is someone else awaits us."

And *that* wasn't ominous at all.

Clang — the lid was wrenched off, revealing moonlight and the pinprick of stars.

I hauled myself over the edge, collapsing on the

floor like a gasping, landed fish. Emperor leapt athletically over the side; although he was bedraggled like me, he looked ready to fight legions.

The cocky scorching hot asshole.

Then I let out a startled *oomph,* as a slender writhing contrast of alabaster skin, black hair, and ruby eyes, landed on top of me, kissing down my neck and rubbing his body against mine like it was the only way to mark me.

I laughed, clasping my arms around Amadeus' shoulders. "Good job on the rescuing. But it's a shame that you were the one who put us down there."

Amadeus stilled, pulling back to study me, until I squirmed. "It was the only place I could think of to stash you."

Emperor leaned against the tree, which had one end of the rope wound around it, before crossing his arms. Okami rested on his shoulder like a rider on his horse, wagging his tail at our rescue. I grinned to see him again and safe.

Moonbeams speared across Emperor's skin, until he glowed. When he shuddered, I remembered that he fed through their light. "*Stash?*"

Amadeus glanced at him from underneath his eyelashes. "*You* once stashed me in a wardrobe."

Emperor's brow arched. "Touché."

I traced Amadeus' wickedly pretty face; I'd been so

46

frightened that I wouldn't see it again. "I'm not rating the inescapable myth on this place."

He pouted. "What wolf would ever have helped a witch escape before?"

"What witch would be so epic that a wolf would want to save her…?"

"*Need* to save her." Amadeus touched my cheek gently with his gloved hand in a gesture that I'd learned was more intimate than the most passionate screw. "Please, can't you see that this is my pack too? Did you truly believe that I was nothing but a pretty Beta?"

I shook my head. In fact, I was beginning to think that Amadeus could be more dangerous than either of my other Charms.

I wet my dry lips. Let me count the freaking ways that I didn't want to know the answer to my next question but I still had to ask… "What about Queen Rhona? She was just mocking—"

"Only a recording, isn't it?" Amadeus pulled me onto my knees, before nuzzling against my neck with a contented sigh. "Would it please you to know why I'm sure?"

There was too much devil in the way that his lips curved against my neck.

"Okay, pleasure me."

Amadeus shuddered, and I knew that I was feeding him just from the words.

"I seduced her, until she couldn't even think beyond

her furry nose, then I slipped some sleeping herbs into her tea that you can't taste. I also considered slipping my claw across her neck but then I considered that you wouldn't want an interkingdom incident."

"Yep, l-let's keep m-murders to a minimum," I stuttered.

Okami howled, darting off Emperor's shoulder and wildly savaging a leaf, as if to prove that he was all warrior too…or that he disagreed on the murdering part.

Being around my Charms was bringing out the wild side in my magical wolf.

When I caught Emperor's gaze, however, it was cool like he wasn't shocked by what Amadeus had said, or at least was better at hiding it than me.

With his angelic face and sinful body, Amadeus was the perfect seducer, spy, and assassin.

I'd better remember that.

Had he been trained in more 007 skills than dancing? Was he meant to use those skills on *me*? *Had he already used them…?*

Then Amadeus drew back, and his smile became shy. The contrast was so sharp that it took my breath away. He pushed himself up and passed Emperor, pulling something out from behind the tree, before tossing it at me.

I yelped, throwing out my arms to catch… *mom's cape.*

My vision became blurry with tears, as my fingers

crushed into its velvety softness. It was torn, smeared with paint, and dirtied. It was just as scruffy as *I* always had been as a kid. Mom would've hated the state it was in, but to me it was *perfect*.

"Thank you," I murmured, "this pleases me very freaking much."

Amadeus glowed, even as he blushed. "What Little Red Riding Hood doesn't have their cape?"

I leveled him with a glare. "Don't compare me to the LLRH asshole who can't even see through a simple disguise."

Amadeus giggled. "I won't go comparing your sexy ass to the LLRH asshole. But you don't know what I had to barter to get that."

"I can guess," Emperor growled, "which means that you'd better hope you can run faster than me, Prince of the Gods."

Amadeus *eeped*, protectively covering his ass.

I prowled between them. "The only running we're doing now is to save our *Prince of the Wilds* from the Re-education Center. How long is it to the full moon?"

I peered at the bloated moon through the spiderweb of the metal lattice dome that hung over the Kingdom of the Wilds. The witches had made certain when they'd trapped and collared the wolves in their kingdoms behind the wall that they knew there was no escape back into the human world.

"Tomorrow night." Amadeus bit his lip.

I nodded, whilst my pulse pounded. "Then we'd better start running."

Even though I still didn't have my powers, I had to rescue Moon from the place that he'd always feared the most, before another Alpha forced him into the Wolf Bite.

Yet I only had one night and day to magically fulfil my bond with Moon, so that we became equals, or by the full moon tomorrow night, he'd die.

CHAPTER 4

I hunkered at the edge of the wall, whilst my thighs burned from the trek through the wood and my temples thudded. Dawn washed the sky clean of the night.

I hadn't imagined that a Re-education Center for Omegas would look like a prison, but then, I'd never dreamed that the wolves would've buried their own Omegas in a Borstal for Bad Wolves, which was isolated in a glade that could only be reached on foot...or paw.

It's kind of like the dick Alphas didn't want their brainwashed victims to escape.

I shuddered at the thought of Moon being dragged here and left somewhere behind the wall in the white arched building. Worse, that an Alpha could be planning to Wolf Bite him.

Tonight, the full moon would rise. If I didn't work out a way to bond magically with him as a Moon Child before then, he'd die.

Yep, this would be a *son of witch load* of pressure day.

Emperor crouched next to me with Amadeus plastered over his back, biting hard enough at his neck to make me wince. Emperor, on the other hand, didn't even flinch.

My Charms shone with strength: Emperor fed on the moonlight, and Amadeus, on the pleasure that he was giving Emperor. It was only me who was starving and weak with my powers still trapped.

I patted my pocket, edging my fingers in to check that Okami was safe. I'd insisted that he keep quiet throughout the rescue, and he'd made enough noise about *that* on the journey here. He whined, licking at my fingers with his silky tongue.

Then I peeked through a crack in the wall at the Re-education Center, whilst rubbing at the leaves that were caught in my hair; mom would've had a fit at the savage creature I'd become.

A line of naked Omegas knelt on the hard ground in front of the center, even though it was the sort of time only overzealous personal trainers or army cadets on punishment were out of bed. They tended to a straggly flowerbed with only their hands, whilst an Alpha guard in a matching uniform to the ones worn in the Omega

Training Center marched up and down, swinging a silver tipped cane.

I stiffened. Did they have those uniforms on bulk order or were all the centers run by the same assholes? Did the Alphas control the Omegas both before they were Claimed and then after, if they weren't as *perfect* as advertised?

When a teenage Omega with honey blond hair, raised his shaking hand to his forehead to wipe the sweat from his eyes, the Alpha snarled, whacking her cane sizzling across his shoulders. He whimpered and bent back to his task.

I hadn't known that I'd leapt up, until Emperor yanked me down again.

"I'm certain that you'll agree *stealth* is the shrewdest choice." He arched an unimpressed eyebrow. "Unless you wish to trigger *yourself* the very war between witches and werewolves that we've been fighting to avoid?"

I huffed. "*Duh*, I wasn't about to just jump in there without a plan."

Emperor's second eyebrow raised, until he stared at me with an expression of incredulity. *Snooty...sexy... asshole.* "How exciting, we have a plan. *Surprise me.*" Then he yipped, as Amadeus bit down for real on his neck. He shot me a sheepish grin. "Sorry, but this is a diplomatic nightmare. You witches artificially bound our three kingdoms together, and I won't let you be proved right that we're *beasts*. What do you think will happen if a prince from the Gods and another from the Alphas, kidnap the heir to the Wilds? Let's not worry about the witches, we could spark war between the kingdoms."

"This is Moon," I murmured, "isn't he worth that risk?"

I didn't miss the glance between Emperor and Amadeus. I fought not to shift, uncomfortable that they'd known each other for centuries as kids before me. But then they both nodded.

I swallowed. "Then screw diplomacy. I'm saving my Charm."

Suddenly, Emperor yelped, jumping into my arms and squashing me against the wall. I let out a startled *oomph*, as the air was pushed out of me.

Our gazes met, and Emperor blushed a pretty shade of pink.

"Aw, if you have a thing for sitting in my lap, you only had to ask." Emperor flushed an even deeper pink, although he didn't move off my lap, which made me thrum with desire, despite the danger inside the center. "Plus, kind of not *stealthy* with the yelping."

"There was a damned *spider*," Emperor hissed, shuddering. "I...panicked."

"He has this *thing*." Amadeus rolled his eyes, even though he squinted in the sun like it hurt his eyes.

Did incubi not go out in the sun like vampires?

Amadeus draped himself over my shoulder with his chin rested on his steepled hands.

I had to stop myself shivering at Amadeus' casual touch because I was surrounded now in the delicious honey and chocolate scent of my Charms and it sang to my Wolf Charmer powers.

Inside me, more of Ivy from the House of Blood's binding spell snapped like weeds sliced down by my shadows. I concentrated, struggling to pull them all free, but they ached, still trapped.

I banged my head against the wall. Huh, I'd add that to the list of Non-helpful Responses to Stress, especially when you have a headache.

I groaned. "Okay, I *don't* have a plan. Criminal mastermind wasn't on my resume, whilst I was running my freaking art gallery." I met Emperor's gaze. "Plus... a *thing*?"

Amadeus smirked. "Not only his cock, see, but also he's afraid of—"

"Don't say that word," Emperor gritted out, smoothing down his robes. "just...don't. Let's simply put it that I'm not fond of things that scuttle."

I smothered my grin. "Like the big ass spider on your shoulder?"

Emperor's haughty cool disappeared, as he squeaked, falling backwards off my lap and smacking at his shoulder in panic.

Panic...kind of like we needed as a smokescreen so

that we could sneak into the center. Even the brave Prince of the Alphas was scared of spiders, go figure.

But was there more behind his phobia?

I watched Emperor thoughtfully, whilst Amadeus slapped his hand over his mouth to muffle his laugh.

Finally, Emperor lay still on his back scowling at me. "Ha-ha, I believe that my sides have split with the hilarity."

Amadeus grinned, laying on top of him to mouth at his neck. "You're so easy."

"Not as easy as you." Emperor lightly brushed his hand over Amadeus' clothed dick, and he gasped, biting his lip.

"If it pleases you," Amadeus murmured.

Yet I stared down at my palms, willing myself to remember a skill that I'd barely used since I was a teenager.

When I'd first been learning my magic, I'd discovered that I could control animals. I'd practiced first on insects and then rodents.

I'd taught my cousin's mouse to ballet dance for her birthday; she'd been so excited that she'd barely slept that night, but her uncle had been furious, banning me from controlling animals again. Afterward, I'd cried alone in my room and I'd never missed my mom and dad so much. I figured that for my uncle, it was too close to me becoming a Wolf Charmer like his murdered sister.

Except, *that was what I'd been.*

It'd also been why I'd accepted my aunt's insistence at first that wolves were no more than animals. Honestly, I'd thought that they were just a bigger mouse to make dance.

Boy, had I been wrong.

But could I still command insects, whilst my crimson was bound?

"Bees first, dicks later." I pressed my palms to the ground. "Oh, and possibly some rats if we need them."

"Did I miss the memo on the *Doctor Doolittle and the Werewolves* remake?" Emperor raised his hand.

I sucked in a breath as I felt the coiling energy within me stretch outward, snaking through the earth, before shooting up into the domed sky in bloody streaks. I stared into the morning sky, waiting…*hoping*…that it'd work.

Please, please, please…

Emperor and Amadeus sat up in excited anticipation.

The morning was still and silent. I lowered my head, pressing my lips tightly together.

Hex a mage's dick, what on earth would we do now…?

Emperor stroked my shoulder. It felt more like understanding than pity.

Bzzz — I jolted at the sudden vibration of thousands of bees' wings.

I glanced up, as the sky above the wood darkened with a swarm of bees. Then I grinned, dragging my Charms to their feet.

Amadeus stared at me wildly. "You've no idea how much I crave to shag you right now, my wicked witch."

"If we survive today…" I caught his lips with mine, as they sparked with his own sweet power, "…you can screw me any way that you desire."

"Now, *that's* the type of promise I like. Until then," Emperor caught my arm, before boosting me onto his shoulder and then the top of the wall, "up you go."

Below in the courtyard, everything was screams, running, and panic.

I'd directed the bees to only attack Alphas, and they flew through the barred windows into the center on their mission. The Omegas crushed themselves against the walls in bewildered fright, but they weren't stung.

The honey blond Omega was watching the guard who'd tormented him, whilst she rolled around howling, with his arms crossed and a *revenge is sweet* smirk. As Emperor boosted Amadeus onto the wall, before being hauled up himself, the Omega met my eye. I raised my finger to my mouth in the universal *shhh* gesture, and he nodded with a wink.

So, there were other epic Omegas…? Why did that make it so much harder to only rescue Moon?

I dropped down on the other side of the Re-education Center, looking up at the high arched building, which had silver bars on the windows. In the midst of the chaos, the Alphas hadn't noticed us yet.

But they would.

"How will we find Moon?" Amadeus asked.

I quivered, as Moon's magic sang out to me, just as it had on the first day that I'd met him in the Omega Training Center. If I hadn't chosen him as my Charm, he'd have been executed…or *put down*, as Stella cutely called it. Yet I'd picked him because of the silver, which had drawn me to him — the magical Moon Child.

My heart ached at the need to hold Moon and make him mine again. When I sprinted towards the building's main door, I heard Emperor's holler behind me, but I was lost to Moon's magic, which stole my breath away with my cravings.

Moon was my Bitten: I could taste his blood on my tongue, imagine the feel of my teeth in his neck and the soft tickle of his curls.

He was my first Charm and Omega…*I was his*.

My shadows stormed in raging tsunami to burst free and join with his magic. My cheeks were suddenly wet, and I hadn't even known that I'd started crying. When an Alpha snatched at my elbow, I focused passing bees to sting her ass. She yowled, falling away from me. I followed Moon's trail like a will-o'-the-wisp to the room behind a gleaming door. It lay beyond a bank of abandoned monitors. Then I stopped in shock.

The monitors showed footage of an opulent bathroom, which reminded me of the one that the wolves had granted to me in the Wilds, after I'd Wolf Bitten Moon. There was a marble bath and a pile of fluffy towels. Massage oils were ranked around the steaming water and rose petals floated on top.

It should've been romantic.

Except for how it was *Moon* who was naked apart from his leather collar in the water, holding himself with a terrible stiffness, whilst his gaze was dead and blank.

I *knew* how much Moon hated baths. When I sniffed the heavy floral scent, I also knew that it was freaking *ylang ylang* in that oil…the type, which they used in the Omega Training Center.

I trembled at the memory of Moth's punishment: the way that the guard had massaged him with ylang ylang oil, before dunking him into ice-cold water to *cleanse* him.

Worse, was the messed-up fact that it was *Lyall* kneeling next to the bath and whispering to Moon like he was her lover.

Holy hell, I was going to hurl.

"By my fur, when you're mine, I'll bathe you every day, Om." Lyall smiled with a tenderness that shocked me, as she drizzled more oil onto her fingers and rubbed them together to warm it because the oil being too freaking cold was going to be what distressed Moon. Then she looked down bashfully like she was the one who'd been stripped. "I was always too weak to treat you like your ma wanted. You should serve me, but instead…" She reached out to massage Moon's shoulders, and he flinched. She scowled. "Enough of that. Why don't you cherish my care? Other Alphas would have you shivering your behind off in cold water." She leaned closer, wiping the oil down his neck, even as he whimpered. "*I love you.*"

She vibrated with such anguish that if she hadn't been trying to take away a member of my pack, I'd have pitied the bitch.

Yep, no pitying the asshole Alpha.

"But you're not my Charmer." At last Moon met Lyall's gaze, and his eyes blazed.

I grinned, until Lyall gripped Moon's curls yanking back his head, but she only tipped water onto his hair, before working in scented shampoo.

I glanced at Amadeus and Emperor who'd darted in behind me and were staring horrified at the monitor as well, then I nodded at the door.

Emperor's hands were clenched, but he shook his head. "A magical trap," he whispered, "which we have also at the Alpha Academies. Without express permission, there's no way to break through, unless your magic…?"

I booted the bank of monitors in frustration. The screens flickered.

"Your precious Charmer is unworthy, just as you're the *reject* that you always were, even as a cub." In contrast to the viciousness of her words, Lyall stroked the shampoo gently through Moon's hair.

"Aye, right. Then why do you want me?" Moon demanded, although his voice was rough with tears.

Then he yelped, as Lyall tugged him back and dunked him under the water.

Amadeus whined.

When Lyall pulled Moon back up again, she smiled sweetly. "There, isn't that better? Just trying to make sure that the shampoo doesn't sting your beautiful eyes." Then she leaned closer. "And I want you, wee Om, because you've always been mine — my promised prince. Stop your fussing. If you'd been with the Charmer for any longer, the witch would've become bored of all your trouble, then she'd have thrown you back as a reject again." I hated how Moon flinched, whilst I couldn't call bullshit. "Does she even know that you're a freak of a Moon Child?"

I stormed towards the door, quivering at her casual cruelty and prejudice. Sweat dripped down the back of my neck, as I prickled with fever.

Suddenly, my Charmer powers, which were as enraged as I was, broke free of the last bindings, which snapped like twanging guitar strings. I swayed, steadied by Amadeus, whilst my crimson shadows surged through me more powerful than ever before.

Hey, maybe they'd needed a vacation to reenergize...?

I fought back the wild laugh at the thrill of the shadows, before they exploded out of me in a billowing sea. My Charms moaned at the ecstasy, as they were caught in the waves of pleasure, joy, and dark desire for control. I craved to catch every shifter in Wolf Kingdom in the shadows' hold and make them dance.

I twirled, painting the room crimson.

Could I paint the world red...?

Then Emperor grabbed my hand. "Your eyes... they've transformed to silver."

I stumbled over my feet, slamming into the door. Only the Wolf Charmer line had silver eyes.

Seriously, that was one way to bring a girl down.

I twisted towards the door, sliding my questing shadows that thrummed in their freedom against its magic, which snapped back. I fought through the pain with the thought of Moon on the other side.

I gritted my teeth, threading my red deeper into the mechanisms of the door, which shot electric bursts back.

What if it still wouldn't break?

Come on, Crimson, you can do this...

Who cared if I didn't know a damn thing about being the kind of witch that my English aunt and her covens wanted? I was who *Moon* wanted, and honestly, since the covens had thrown me to the wolves, they could go to hell.

I clenched my jaw, crashing my shadows down in a tidal wave on the door. With a shrieking creak, it splintered into shards. I howled, leaping over the ruins of the door into the intoxicating haze of the bathroom. Moon sat up, splashing the water out of the tub in shock. Lyall merely twisted to me, however, with a raised eyebrow.

"Get away from *my* Moon Child, Countess. I'd never reject his gorgeous ass. I want him just as he is." I stalked towards Lyall, whilst my shadows washed over the floors and ceiling, until we were all shaded in crimson.

Moon smirked at Lyall. "*She's* my Charmer."

Lyall's nostrils flared. "Nay, witch's bitch, because a wolf's bite is stronger than a Charmer's. And I intend to save you from her single skin influence."

Then her fangs grew.

Moon's eyes widened in terror. I screamed, throwing myself towards Lyall to stop her Wolf Biting Moon, but she'd already sunk her teeth into his throat.

CHAPTER 5

I didn't know that I'd be able to experience my Charms' pain like it was my own, but when Lyall savaged Moon's throat right over my own Wolf Bite, severing my Claim, I howled.

Agony swept through me — Moon's own, entwining around mine — whilst my shadows trembled with it. I dropped to my knees on the marble bathroom floor, cradling my arms around my head.

Then suddenly, Moon's silver tugged at my red. I lowered my arms, until my gaze met Moon's, even though Lyall was still licking over her bite, savoring his blood with a smug satisfaction that filled me with a shuddering urge to *kick her ass.*

Emperor and Amadeus prowled closer, growling.

Then, despite the fact that Moon was naked apart from his collar, bitten, and shaking, he lifted his chin, which in any other Omega would've looked like he was offering his neck submissively.

Yet in Moon…?

Okay, so that's what princely defiance looked like.

I shivered, as his magic thrummed with rage, stirring my own into beating waves that darkened the floor to a bloody sea. I could feel his silver struggling against the influence of the collar. I flinched because his anguish at the way that it forced back his shift, controlling him in the most primal and cruel way, vibrated through me as well.

How in the witching heavens couldn't the covens see how freaking wrong it was to hold such power over every wolf?

The only way to save Moon before the full moon was to show that I trusted him as my equal. I wished that I could remove his collar. Yet Moon had told me that it was *impossible,* which in my uncle's business where I'd combined tech and magic had always been my favorite game. I *wrecked* impossible's ass (in the non-kinky way), unless, you know, I *didn't*…like with the dark magic that resisted me in the collar.

I narrowed my eyes; if I couldn't remove it, then I'd find another way around it.

Watch out, collar, it was time to have your leather ass wrecked.

When my red stroked Moon's silver, it sighed, entwining with mine. I steadied my breathing. Then for the first time, I allowed Moon's magic to meld with my own.

Moon's lips parted, as his breath hitched; his gaze was suddenly raw with disbelief. Joined and equal, our magic slipped inside the snake-like collar, which glimmered, as if it was alive, questing through the mechanism. The ancient magics inside lashed us, whilst Moon and I jumped at the sting, united.

I bit my lip, unable to look away from Moon's burning amber gaze. I trembled with the terror that the silver would shoot out and poison him.

Our magic pushed further and further against the furious collar's resistance. Nope, there was no way to remove it...but Moon and I grinned at the same time with the realization that now Moon's magic had seeped through the collar, I could force his shift...but *he* could also take it over and stop a transformation or turn himself back.

My uncle had always taught me to search for loopholes in deals.

I'd never violate Moon in a shift again or control him. Now he'd be able to transform almost like a free wolf. His pupils were blown, and his face was flushed with joy.

He'd be my equal.

Lyall paused in the licking of her bite, frowning as she glanced up at Moon's sudden change. "Do you still not know your place, Om?"

I yanked my shadows out of the collar, requesting a shift at the same time as Moon wound his magic around himself and seized control of his own transformation. He arched, before exploding in a spray of silver into a large white wolf.

This time, he was not only sinfully beautiful in wolf form but *deadly*. His fur glittered like pearls with water droplets, as his silky ears pressed to his head and his golden eyes glowed.

How was it possible that the danger of his snarl and fangs didn't terrify me, but flooded me with awe and pride?

Moon shook his head, forcing Lyall to fall back and wild water droplets to spray across the bathroom.

Lyall reached a trembling hand towards his fur. "Goddess Moon, you've grown beautiful," she whispered. Moon's hackles raised, bristling his fur, until he looked twice as large again. His lips curled back into a ferocious snarl. "Nay, don't think that you can dominate *me*. I'm still your Alpha."

Moon's paw shot out; his claws gleamed.

Lyall shrieked as she was pinned over the edge of the bath. Then Moon sank his teeth into her neck, savaging her throat.

How was that for a breakup?

Blood swirled into the water, turning it red. Lyall's arms and legs spasmed. When Moon finally raised his scarlet jaws, turning to look at me through his butterfly lashes for approval, I should've been shaking in my witchy boots. Instead, I smiled, thrilling on the sensation of *my* Wolf Bite, which settled back into place on Lyall's death. Moon had chosen me by reclaiming it.

I raised my hand against the tidal wave *splash* of water, as Moon leaped out of the bath, then paraded towards me with his head high and his tail lifted.

Yep, he was definitely in Alpha headspace.

Moon pushed his snout against my thigh, and I stroked the soft fur behind his ear, just like I'd craved to do ever since he'd shifted. My shadows caressed down his back and along his tail, whilst he quivered, sensitive to my touch in this form, panting.

"Your name is Moon," I whispered, resting my chin on his head, "and that asshole was never your Alpha. You're my Moon Child, the same as I'm your Wolf Charmer. We need each other."

Holy hell it was true. I felt it deep in my victorious shadows, which tangled with his silver now in a thrilling dance. He was what I'd always been missing — his power was part of me.

Then why were witches and werewolves enemies?

I shook with delayed shock because if this hadn't worked and I'd been unable to wreck impossible's ass, then by the full moon, my Charm would've died.

I couldn't lose somebody that I loved again.

Boil and bubble, I did love Moon.

He didn't need to know that, right?

Emperor stalked closer with Amadeus slinking at his side. "I hope you understand that was spectacularly dangerous." He cocked his head. "And like something I'd do. It appears that my friend has become a real little prince." He opened his arms with a smirk. "I still expect a cuddle though."

Moon's eyes narrowed, as he growled. Moon might've forgiven Emperor for whatever had driven them apart as kids, although I doubted even that, but Emperor wasn't in the *cuddle zone* just yet.

Didn't he realize how close he was to being savaged?

When Moon took one prowling step towards Emperor's welcoming arms, I snatched his tail. Moon blinked at me, then he launched himself at Emperor, shaking himself and spraying water all over Emperor's suit and robes.

Emperor howled in outrage. "How charming," he grumbled. "I'd only just dried out from the well. *True princes* have more refinement and—"

"Your hair's dripping into your eyes." Amadeus laughed. "You look like a drowned golden rat."

"*My hair…?*" Emperor stormed to the bathroom's mirror, molding his locks back into place, frantically

Amadeus's smile was wicked. "I always wondered if I'd please him more, see, if I just held up a mirror in front of my face."

I spluttered with laughter, whilst I hunkered down in front of Moon.

Moon whined, as I slipped my arms around his neck. Then he shuddered at the sensation of my red, which stroked through his fur.

In a spray of silver, he transformed back into a man.

Moon and I lay together in the puddles on the marble floor, whilst his skin was wet against the palms of my hands.

Moon wiped his mouth to clean away Lyall's blood, grimacing. "Fur and fangs, she even tastes as bad as I always dreaded she would."

I nipped at his top lip. "Dude, I don't want you to taste of anyone but me." I blushed. "Wait, I mean…"

He bit my lower lip, and I groaned as he licked at my blood. Would he kiss me at last?

Holy hell, please…

I licked him, trying to coax his tongue with mine, but he drew back.

Why…?

His lips were almost touching me; I needed to feel them.

I groaned, gripping his curls. I was desperate to feel him even closer, as desire coiled through me. I panted, nudging my thigh between his, and…

A dramatic cough.

Reluctantly, I pulled back to look up into Amadeus' teasing face.

"Is this an orgy?" Amadeus stretched, showing a tantalizing strip of alabaster stomach. He peeked at me, assessing my reaction. "You take us to all the romantic places…"

Well, that was one way to slap the haze of the joining with my Moon Child right out of me.

I stared around at the crime scene — in the middle of the Re-education Center — and blanched. So did Moon who whined. How much effort had it taken for him to rise up like that against an Alpha, let alone one who'd Bitten him?

What in the witching heavens made him so special?

Except, I knew that he was because I could feel it singing through my magic. If I was honest, I always had, which was why I'd picked him out in the Omega Training Center as my first Charm; I just hadn't understood why.

Yet Moon had.

Moon pulled himself to his feet, yanking me after him. He hung his head, however, avoiding my gaze. "They'll hunt my daft behind now. *Nay, all of us.* I've murdered—"

"Hey, you defended yourself to break the dickhead's forced bond. Let them hunt us." My red raged, and I had to battle to pull it back inside. "This witch is ready."

Amadeus bounced on his toes with delight. "I knew that you'd corrupt me, see! This last year, the worst that I was thrown into isolation for was…" He wrinkled his nose. "...stealing a cookie and risking my perfect waistline."

Emperor sauntered back from the mirror, sliding his hands around Amadeus' waist and making him sigh in pleasure. "It *is* perfect."

Amadeus squirmed, pressing against Emperor. "Well, I have to work to look this sexy, mind. But now I'm accomplice to murder."

"Would it be too much trouble to ask you not to look so thrilled?" Emperor arched his brow, but Amadeus only giggled.

Then he wiggled his ass up and down like he was giving Emperor a lap dance, whilst singing "The Fun Lovin' Criminal" in the style of Marilyn Monroe.

Huh, so that wasn't something that I'd ever figured on seeing. Plus, Emperor's stuttered breath and wide-eyed expression...? *Priceless.*

"We're the bad boy princes," Amadeus smiled slyly.

And boy, did that make me want to taste his lips as much as Moon's and show him that I could be just as bad as any wolf.

Only, was the truth that it was as *good* as any wolf...?

"Truly bad to wolfie bone," Emperor agreed, dryly. Then he slipped away from Amadeus, after a final appreciative squeeze, and prowled to Moon. The two guys eyed each other, before Emperor dipped his head closer.

Wait, would Moon allow Emperor to kiss him?

Jealousy burned through me, even though I wasn't the type of possessive dick that said I owned Moon's lips but still…I wanted them first.

Okay, maybe I was possessive of those adorable lips, go figure.

Yet Emperor only kissed Moon gently on the cheek. "I'm relieved that you're safe now."

The way that Moon raised his gaze to Emperor's, before nuzzling against his neck in answer, you'd have thought that it'd been a poem wrapped in roses and chocolates.

Okay, wolf romance was weird.

I bumped Emperor's shoulder. "So, what's the plan now? Get out of the center and back to Stella?"

Emperor's brow furrowed. "You still only have until the full moon to convince your aunt that the House of Blood are responsible for the mage boy's death. Yet why should she believe the word of a wolf and the Blood's own mage son…? *You* are the rogue witch, and *we* are the disgraced princes. Yet if we bad wolves and witches can't convince your aunt that this boy Kolby wasn't killed by wolves, then there'll be a Second Wolf War." His jaw clenched. "How many shall die then?"

I marched to the shards of the doorway, booting them until they exploded to powder. "Then I'll have to prove that I'm *worthy*."

Moon dragged on a uniform of leather trousers and

top that were neatly piled by the towels. They must've belonged to the guards but by Hecate above, Moon in leather was hot enough to melt my panties…as was the glower that he shot at me; I shrank back. "Nay, you won't, furless. You only have to prove your worth to *yourself.* No one else. You once thought that I wasn't doing my duty by being in the **REJECT** cell. But I was, even if you hadn't chosen me, and I'd been executed." I gasped, but he shook his head. "Will you understand now? As a reject rebel prince, I *stand* for something to every other Omega. What are you, if you don't stand for something that matters? If you let something else…your aunt, past, or the role that you were born into…decide your worth…?" He strode up to me, gripping onto my shoulders hard enough for his claws to sink in. I stared at him, shaking at the strength of his words. I'd never expected that it'd be a werewolf who'd make me understand how little I'd ever thought of myself, rather what others needed from me, and how rarely I'd challenged the truth of how they saw the world. Moon rubbed his nose against mine, before saying, softly, "Who will you be, Crimson?"

"Yours," I whispered, glancing around at my three Charms. "I'll be the Wolf Charmer who protects her pack. I'll stand for pack, however I freaking can."

Moon's eyes sparkled. "Then let's move our behinds."

"Wait." I snatched his hand. "Can't we save the other Omegas too?"

I hated the idea of leaving them here to suffer like Moon. I remembered the Alpha whacking the teenager, and it chilled me.

Moon stiffened, then suddenly I had an armful of cuddling wolf. This was the snuggling goodness that I'd missed, as he nuzzled at his favorite position on my neck. "You've no idea how much I've dreamed of someone wishing that." Then he pulled back, and his eyes gleamed with tears, although he didn't let them fall. "But not like this. On Moon Oath, I swear, we'll rescue them...but only when it's certain to be every last one."

I shivered at the determination in his voice. There was no way of doubting him.

Okami poked his furry nose out of my pocket. "Aw, wolfie, you missed all the excitement."

Okami whined, affronted, before flying out to wind around Moon's neck above his collar like a shimmering scarf.

"I missed you too, Wolverine," Moon smirked.

When Okami bit him, he laughed indulgently like it'd been a hickey. *Maybe it was the wolf equivalent.*

I led the way out of the bathroom, weaving back through the now silent corridors, before peering into the courtyard.

That's when I got why it was so quiet

I grinned. Yep, my bees were epic warriors. They'd pinned the Alphas down in one corner, whilst the Omegas laughed and joked, watching their guards cower and howl.

That was called witchy karma, assholes.

I sauntered into the courtyard, waving at the bees. "Thanks, my fuzzy sweethearts."

The bees flew up in a humming swarm, looping the loop, before bowing and flying back like a storm cloud towards the line of the ancient wood.

The Alphas growled, scratching at their stings and staggering to their feet. I didn't give them the chance.

My shadows shot out like webs, hanging them, as if they were in hammocks between the arches. *Let them feel helpless prisoners for once, at least.*

The honey blond Omega clapped in delight.

When I hummed the Spiderman theme tune, I glanced at Emperor from underneath my eyelashes.

He raised an unimpressed eyebrow. "Really?"

I grinned, finger walking up his side. "Dude, these webs are in honor of you."

"How thoughtful," Emperor gritted out, batting away my hand. When my red finger walked up his inner thighs, his eyelids fluttered with desire. "Damn you, I'll deny with my dying breath that you just made that sexy."

I whispered hot against his ear, "But I did, right?"

Moon strode towards the Omegas, who circled him

with surprised delight. The moon's beams shone across his skin, whilst his magic swirled in pirouetting spirals.

Moon gazed at his gleaming palms in shock. When Emperor and Amadeus exchanged a secret glance, I realized that I was witnessing something extraordinary…and special enough to make Moon shake.

Then the Omega with honey blond hair tentatively stepped forward, touching his palm to Moon's — the one that I hadn't branded.

Moon straightened his shoulders, raising his gaze, whilst his eyelashes were matted wet, to meet the blazing pride in his fellow Omegas'.

"Moon Prince," the teenage Omega asserted with awe, before calling out in a fierce chant (where were the submissive Bitten Omegas now?), "*Moon Prince, Moon Prince…*"

The other Omegas took up the chant, which was dark, joyous, and uplifting:

Moon Prince. Moon Prince. Moon Prince…

The Omegas were taking turns to press their palms to Moon's, as if in allegiance. *Why did I ever forget that he was a prince?* Unless, you know, it was more even than that. It was *respect* that he'd earned not just because of his title, or even by magically being born the Moon Child but because he'd suffered for his people and they knew that he'd die for them.

That was loyalty.

"They love him," Amadeus breathed. "They don't hate him for being the Moon Child."

Shocked, I glanced at him. Emperor's face was tight like he was trying to hold back tears.

Who'd hated…or hurt…Moon for his magic?

When Moon's gaze caught mine, he swaggered towards me with a nod towards Emperor. I hadn't expected the way that Emperor snatched him, holding him hard around the neck.

Uh oh, Alpha alert…

"Enough of the war between us," Emperor commanded. "You've always been a magnificent Moon Child and *mine*. I shan't allow anyone to separate us again. How many times shall I apologize?"

"As many times as I need," Moon rasped, even though he melted under the insistent circling of Emperor's thumb along his neck. Then Moon grinned at me. "Don't worry, I've saved some of my wolf loving for you, Crimson."

I snorted but dived into the hug, throwing my arms around both Moon and Emperor. Their breaths gusted across my cheeks. Amadeus *whooped*, diving into our warm huddle, whilst the Omegas cheered.

"My pretty peach, I warned you not to be tricked by the shifters' sinful bodies and angelic eyes." I stumbled backwards out of the safety of my Charms' arms at Stella's bellowed rage.

I stared around wildly. *Holy hell, where was she?*

"My aunt hasn't found her way back into my freaking head? You can hear that too, right?" I asked.

The Omegas whimpered, huddling against the wall with fright.

My aunt had that effect on wolves.

"Unfortunately, loud and clear," Emperor replied.

"Don't you remember the fabulous heart-to-heart we had in the House of Seasons about Claiming your Charm and acting like a *traditional* Wolf Charmer?" Stella's voice shook the Re-education Center. I stumbled, whilst my crimson withdrew from the Alphas, letting them fall onto their howling asses as well. "Did you think that I wouldn't sense in my visions you leading a riot in one of my orderly centers? How's that becoming worthy?"

I clenched my jaw. "*Your* center?"

"Like witches don't own everything." I could almost hear her shrug. "I let the Wilds play at outlaws, but who do you think supplies so many willing Omegas? Wait, even I can't swing the *willing* part. They *smoothly* supply the animals, and luckily for the House of Blood, the Re-education Center has plenty of the most disobedient hotties for rougher play."

The honey blond Omega crouched down, clutching his arms around his knees, as he ducked his head.

I hated it.

"I don't think so. This center is closed for business."

I waved my hands at the skies like Stella could see me. "So, *shoo*."

"Interesting choice. A pretty little bird told me that you'd burned your bridges with the House of Blood and been thrown to the wolves…?" I flinched at Stella's smugness. "My delicious niece, even I can't allow that fate for you, although I am cross enough to take back your birthday present."

My gaze shot to Moon, who'd frozen. Stella had given him to me on my twenty-first birthday like he'd been no more than a glittery gift.

There was no way on earth she was taking him back.

"Ivy was wrong," Stella's voice became steely, "witches deal with their own problem kids. It's a thing. You're not a mage and you shouldn't have been thrown to the wolves. The House of Seasons upholds the ancient laws of the covens and it punishes criminals… like you."

When the air was flooded with the copper tang of blood that wound out of the quaking building itself, panic rushed through me. Stella was calling to me with the stink of blood magic, which would drag me back to the House of Seasons.

My three Charms gripped onto me, whilst I shook, even though I tried to push them away to save them, at least. Yet they grimly held on, refusing to let Stella summon me back to be judged alone.

My chest ached, even through my fear, that I had pack who'd never leave me.

Then the blood magic wound out of the arches like an infection and snatched my Charms and me, hurling us across a scarlet path with such force, that I screamed.

Perhaps, I'd already been judged and this was our execution…?

The fourth time that I'd ever traveled by the stench of blood magic, I closed my eyes and waited to die.

CHAPTER 6

When my eyes fluttered open, my dazed mind reeled with the shock that I *had* died.

I stared down at Oxford's city center with its domes and spires, which sparkled like jewels in the sun far below, whilst tiny humans scurried along the streets.

Huh, so I was an angel on a cloud...?

Yet I'd always thought that it'd hurt less in the afterlife; my fevered temples thudded, whilst my blood bubbled like Champagne. A copper tang was caught in my nostrils.

Hold up, bubbling Champagne and copper...blood magic....?

This wasn't a cloud but the floor of the Clocktower in the House of Seasons, whilst I was looking out through the glass clockface onto the city below. I must have a bitch of a concussion, although I also had a feeling that maybe angel duty would've been easier than whatever Stella had planned.

Still: *yey life…*

I groaned, rubbing my sore temples, as I shoved myself onto my knees. The room swam, and I swayed with dizziness.

I was going to hurl.

"Ah, you're awake, sleepyhead. Did you have sweet dreams of sinful shifters?" My head shot up at Stella's voice from across the room, then I bent over again, as lights flashed in front of my eyes. Stella *tutted*. "No puking in my fabulous house. My Omega has been working hard today, and with your constant screaming about wolf *rights*, it'd be mean of you to give him another chore. Unless you get off on the idea of watching him playing maid…?"

I peeked up through my blurred vision. Stella was sprawled in a metallic throne-like chair across the bronze Clocktower, which had in its middle the map of the three wolf kingdoms. Her ass must've been numb as witching hell. Her fiery curls spilled down over her bronze velvet dress, which made her appear like a mechanical doll, whilst her silvery gray eyes were too knowing.

Leashed at her feet was the Ambassador to Wolf Kingdom: the werewolf who'd once belonged to mom.

The Ambassador was barely more than a teenager and a pretty Omega with neat strawberry blond hair. Just like last time, he was dressed in only a pair of panties, although for variety now they were pink silk.

Yep, Stella respected the ambassadorial position.

I knew that she wouldn't believe me, but her mistake was to think that she could continue to treat the wolves with such disrespect without consequences. She was terrified of them and yet didn't know how to do more than shame or hurt them.

But hey, I was slumped on my ass, whilst my ears rang, trying not to throw up on my boots, so it wasn't like I was doing any better...*yet.*

Because I would.

"Screw you, like I get to choose if I lose my breakfast, which I didn't even get, by the way. You're the reason I feel like this," I panted. "Shouldn't you be taking me to hospital or something?"

"*Or something,*" Stella smirked. "I just pulled you out of the Wilds because you're a criminal." She leaned forward. "I only ever role-play as nurse."

"Holy hell, I'm not the criminal." I staggered to my feet. "When you dragged me here last time, you were all about me solving Kolby's murder by the full moon or... what was the threat...? Oh right, you'd go to war with the wolves again. *Hmm,* let's see, what's happening tonight...?"

I stumbled towards Stella, catching myself on the map of Wolf Kingdom to stop myself falling.

Stella adjusted her curls. "Don't stop now, I'm about to nibble my gorgeous nails off with anticipation."

My eyes narrowed. "It's the full moon. Trust me when I say that my Charms and I sacrificed to get you this intel. The mud on the mage's fingers matched the banks of the Thames behind the House of Blood."

Stella blinked. "Wow, I'm glad that I didn't destroy my nails because that was staggeringly disappointing."

Okay, not the reaction that I'd been hoping for.

I swiped my tongue anxiously over my lips. "How disappointing is the arsenal of Wolf Tamer that they're stockpiling?"

Yep, I was pulling out my own big guns now.

Stella tugged on the leash, and the Ambassador whimpered, although he shot me a sharp glance first, which reminded me of Amadeus' quick changes between submissive and steely. I guessed that news of the Wolf Tamer as a war weapon would be terrifying to any shifter.

"Don't tell me that you've been getting your knickers in a twist over that…?" Stella laughed; it chilled me like I was trapped in a sinister fairy tale. "Do you think that the Bloods make a single move I don't know about, despite their vulgar ambitions?"

My aunt knew…?

My fingers curled around the map. I stared down at the metal pillars that created the wall behind Oxford, whilst precious gems and riveted metal recreated Wolf

Kingdom. At the furthest edge were the bronze trees of the Wilds. Light reflected onto the entire kingdom from the glass towers of the Alphas. I traced my finger down the sparkling sapphires of the River Thames, which wound through the middle of the Gods.

The covens looked down on the wolves as nothing but glittering toys, just as they could look down through the clockface at the humans as nobodies whose fates could — literally with Stella's visions and powers — be woven.

Not now that this Witch Charmer was in town. Hey, I could pull off the cowboy look.

I swung to Stella. "Honestly, I'm over being jerked around. Just tell me where my Charms are, then you and I can have a conversation."

"Have you gone all mafia on me? How thrilling." Stella grinned, but her eyes sparked. "Your beasts are back in the House of Silver. Do you wish me to summon them here, so that you can have some sexy play first, since you're so worked up? I bet that incubus can do such wicked things with his mouth—"

"Don't finish that sentence."

Stella lifted her foot, examining the toe of her pointed boot like it held the answers to the best cocktail, how to paint like Michelangelo, and that guy skill of taking off your t-shirt one-handed. "You're always telling me *not to speak* or what's *acceptable* for witches nowadays." Her voice was dangerously soft. "Did you miss the speech where I explained that I'm in charge? Your *boss*, if we're going to be stuffy about this. The other covens fear me. Do we need to take this to the Justice Chamber?"

I stiffened, whilst my pulse pounded. Stella said *Justice Chamber* like *Head Teacher's Office*. Except, that was where the trials were held for rogue witches, and last time that I was judged, I'd been found wanting, before Lux had almost executed me.

I hurriedly shook my head. "Oh, I'm aware that I've broken some…okay, a lot…of archaic rules…"

Stella arched her brow. "You think?"

"But it's not like you gave me a crash course in how to be your Wolf Charmer." I faltered closer, whilst my vision cleared, and my crimson shadows held me up on their waves. "You threw me into this and just expected me to adapt. Well, this is who I am. I'm not changing for you or your weird ideas of *worthiness*. Maybe it's time somebody had big enough cojones to tell you that the treaties with the wolves are wrong. And they're not the only thing."

I wiped the back of my hand across my mouth. Boy, I'd just grown myself a pair of witchy cojones, although they shriveled in fear at the way that Stella leapt and her eyes flashed.

"Who are you to come back from America and judge us?" She thundered.

I grinned because that was an easy one. "I'm your

Wolf Charmer. You may be the boss, but I'm the most powerful witch, or did I miss that speech too? I know that my legacy counts for...everything, right? You've used all these scare tactics and threats, but I don't think that you were ever going to kill me. Perhaps you'd have murdered my Charms, but I'm untouchable."

Stella sighed, suddenly looking exhausted. I forgot that she was close to the same age as mom would've been if she'd lived. When Stella shuffled closer, I noticed the lines at her eyes and the pinched thinness of her lips beneath her makeup.

Stella reached to tuck a curl behind my ear, and I flinched. "Not because you're the Wolf Charmer, pretty peach, because you're my sister's child. I sent you away to keep you safe until your powers were strong enough. I called you back to have you by my side. How's it working out?"

"Messed-up with a side of screwed." I dodged back from her fingers that'd looked dangerously like they'd been about to stroke my cheek.

The attempt would've been as painful for Stella as it would've been for me.

"Why can't you see past the werewolves' cuddliness to their fangs?" Her gaze hardened. "When you should be playing with them, *they've* been playing with you." I startled, and her look became sly. "You think that the Charms belong to you? The princes have been working on you *together* to make you *their* witch. These beasts are centuries-old: don't you think that they've had time to plan how to use you?"

My eyes smarted, and I turned away my head.

Come on Crimson, hold it together...

It wasn't true, mage's balls on a stick, it *couldn't* be true.

But what if it was...?

Stella pressed closer. I struggled to wrench air in and out of my burning lungs, as she clutched my head between her hands and whispered hot and heavy as a painful secret, "Your mum died because I was jealous."

I tried to pull back, but she held on tightly. My red swirled around me in distressed eddies. "Wolves massacred my parents at a party. I remember..."

"I should've been there that night," Stella's voice was tear-tinged and confessional. Had she ever shared this with anyone else? *Holy hell, why did she have to tell me?* I didn't want to think about mom's death, not when I hadn't saved her. "But it was the ball held by my more beautiful, powerful, and successful sister — who'd even inherited the Wolf Charmer legacy, of course. Why not? She had everything else: idolized by the other covens, adored by our mum, and loved by Daniel." I jolted. *Stella had loved my dad, but he'd been chosen by my mom...?* After how things had gone down in my marriage contract to Aquilo, I was certain that it'd been mom doing the choosing. I knew what it was like to not meet mom's high expectations. Was that what it'd been like for Stella with both her own mom and sister? "The wards were down to allow in guests, and the were-wolves attacked. I still don't know how they evaded our tracking, only that we were distracted that night. But it was an assassination. Funny how I can weave Fate but I can't predict its ironies: your mum only held the ball to show off her new Charm. Maybe if I'd been there, then I'd be dead too…or maybe I could've…"

She twirled away from me, leaving me desperately sucking in breaths against the memories of that night. I dragged mom's cape around me. With surprising tender-ness, Stella carded her fingers through the Ambas-sador's hair.

"It's not *my* Charms' fault." I battled the shadows, as they burst through the Clocktower in a tidal wave of rage. "They didn't murder anyone."

"Didn't they?" Stella's hand tightened in the Ambas-sador's hair, and he whined. "You were meant to control them, not be tricked by them. Do you know why I didn't trust the Wilds to choose their own Tribute?"

My heart thudded against my ribs, as my throat was too tight for me to do more than shake my head.

"I interrogated every Omega who was gloriously unlucky enough to be in need of re-education for years." Stella prowled to the bronze skin of the wall, which peeled back to reveal a cage. She dragged it through with a yank. "I never found out the identity of the true killers but I did reveal that they were from the *Kingdom of the Wilds*. You going amongst them as Wolf Charmer was a test for both sides."

I'd dreamed for the last decade of discovering my parents' murderers. I'd painted pictures of my bloody revenge.

How much better would it be for real?

I trembled with both excitement and fear, whilst I wiped my sweating palms down my jeans.

Stella spun the cage through the air towards me, and I yelped. Then I stared down in shock at Moon's wide amber gaze.

"He's their *prince*." Stella slunk closer. "Take your vengeance on the wicked wolf. Control the crimson tide: *kill*."

My shadows whipped like a thousand tentacles around the cage with a *clang* — again, and again, and again — in fury at the shifters who'd stolen my childhood, forced me to be sent away amongst the non-magical, and even now could be conning me. Yet Moon didn't recoil or flinch from my red. Instead, he pushed closer like it was a caress. Despite the danger, his gaze was trusting.

The dumb...adorable...rebel who was too brave for his own asshole good.

"Go to hell," I hissed at Stella, clenching my fists.

I forced my red to stroke Moon's curls, sliding beneath his leather shirt.

Moon sighed and arched, shooting me a mischievous grin, as my shadows tweaked his nipples into peaks. He raised his eyebrow, before slamming his hands against the sides of the cage.

If he wanted to make a point about *love not war*, then my shadows were down with that.

At least, they were, until footsteps clattered on the staircase. I twisted around, winding my shadows out of the cage. I kind of wished that I could go back to the comforting craziness of just my aunt, when I was faced with the two witches of the House of Blood: Ivy and her daughter, Lux.

With their floor-length black dresses and midnight hair, as well as snobby expressions like Goth dolls, the Bloods had always freaked me out, especially as Lux had bullied me when I was a kid. Yet at least Ivy looked human now, even if the glare that she was sending me would've made Medusa proud because the last time that I'd seen her, she'd been transformed into the Blood Witch.

Or as I now called her: *Blood Bitch.*

She'd been bleeding from her eyeballs, all down her face, and… It'd been this whole *thing*. That's when she'd been furious that I'd failed her tests to become worthy as a Wolf Charmer and had thrown me to the wolves.

This wouldn't be tense at all then.

I couldn't help the flutter of hope, however, as I glanced over her shoulder. I hoped that she'd brought her son and Lux's twin, Aquilo, with her because I'd asked him to marry me in order to save him from his family. He was a mage and in a Traditional family like this that meant he should be grateful they hadn't killed him, merely arranged his marriage.

Had I made it clear how much I hated these archaic rules?

"I'm over your whole jerk move of throwing me to the wolves. There were harsh words said on both sides, so why don't you just hand over my fiancé, and I'll go chill out with some wedding planning in the House of Silver. You know, just me, my Charms, and *your son...?*" I bounced on my toes hopefully.

To my surprise, Lux glanced at her mom with almost the same hope as me. Maybe the risk of her brother dying had hit her harder than I could've guessed.

Ivy's eyes narrowed. "My goodness, why should you have anything to do with my wretched brat of a son?"

Moon growled. "Mind how you talk about the Charmer's intended. You know that the blood bracelet will kill him, if you don't let them marry. I thought that my ma was a cold-hearted—"

"An animal that believes it can mimic speech," Lux's arrogant gaze assessed Moon, "can't expect to be heard."

So, all the bully stuffing hadn't been knocked out of the Lux teddy bear.

"Then hear this, dickhead," I snarled, "I'm engaged to Aquilo, and you're bringing him out now, so I know that you haven't flayed him, or this is going to be another smackdown situation."

How in the witching heavens had I gone from hanging paintings in my gallery in East Hampton, to issuing gang style threats? Ones that apparently weren't that threatening because Lux merely continued to study me unblinkingly.

It was Stella who smiled with a spiteful gleam in her eye. "It looks like my niece is actually keen to see your son in panties. Perhaps, we don't need all these..." She waved her hand dismissively, "...wretched tests and trials. A husband's cock warming her bed is all it needs to remind her that she can't love beasts, just as they'll never love her."

I bit my tongue to stop myself telling her how much I loved my wolf princes because call me a romantic, but Moon deserved not to be caged when he heard me say it for the first time.

Ivy looked like she was biting her tongue as well, whilst she reddened. Aquilo was nothing but a power-play between the two covens. The House of Blood had attempted to dethrone the House of Seasons by marrying me to him secretly and using my power, so my aunt was putting them in their place now.

"*Chop, chop*; go fetch your naughty boy." Stella clapped her hands. "My niece is in need of some sweet loving."

Lux grimaced but ducked down the stairs again, whilst Ivy swept towards me, bringing with her the stench of blood.

"How bold you are!" *Was her lip trembling?* I missed the way that she'd hugged me, the first time that we'd met, as if the warmth had been drained out of her. "I hope you remember that Aquilo isn't like you; he's an innocent."

Aquilo was a pretty, snooty, surprisingly brave dick, but he wasn't an innocent. He'd helped his sister bully me as a kid, and I knew that even though he'd tried to help the wolves, he still had a cruel streak.

Stella danced around Moon's cage, humming Madonna's "Like a Virgin" with inappropriate glee. When Moon rattled the cage, she only burst into song with a wriggle of her hips.

"Don't get me wrong, he's been trained ready for his wife," Lux bit out, ignoring Stella. "He'll make you a superb husband. But he shan't live with you until the marriage day."

Stella broke off her song. "How quaintly old-fashioned of you. Do you think his honor needs protecting?"

When I heard footsteps on the stairs again, my heart beat painfully fast, as I became suddenly breathless.

Huh, I'd never expected that I'd have missed Aquilo...needed him...this much.

Lux led Aquilo into the chamber by his arm, and our gazes caught; his pale blue eyes burned with such cold intensity that I couldn't look away. Then Lux yanked him harder, and he stumbled. At last, I scanned him for injuries but it was impossible to tell through the black jeans and velvet shirt, which hung open to reveal the same blood moon pendant that bound his magic, hiding it.

His face was a cool mask. His mop of almost white hair hung into his eyes, as he ducked his head. He didn't even move towards me.

What had Ivy done to him?

I stroked my arms, desperate to touch him, even though I knew that he'd wriggle away from me like a skittish kitten. This close, I could sense the magical engagement thudding through my blood, and by the way that he rubbed at his wrist, I knew that he sensed it too.

When he peeked at his mom through his hair, she ordered, "Greet your fiancée, Aquilo. After all, you're to be married next week."

I grinned so widely that my mouth ached. Aquilo's eyebrow merely raised, which was his first expression, so I'd take it. Then he stiffly crossed the room, before leaning to press his lips to my cheek. His scent of crisp fresh linen made me shudder. Yet his hand that rested on my arm, whose wrist was banded by the scarlet blood bracelet, shook.

"Thank you for not dying," Aquilo whispered.

"It's what I'm here for."

When his twin hauled him back like the piece of property that males were treated as within witch families, I bristled. "Dude, we're all friends now. Ease up on the Gestapo impression."

"I'd forgotten," Stella's smile was predatory, "how much of a *mage lover* you were. After all, Aquilo will already have to share you with the one you have stashed as your sex slave at the House of Silver. Do you plan on opening up your kinky parties because I'd love a taste of that glittery god."

I gaped at her, at the same time as Ivy gasped. I thought that Zetta had liked Mischief, but she must've told Stella about him anyway...

The essence of the House of Silver was nothing but a spy.

What on earth could I do to protect Mischief, whilst he was too weak to protect himself?

Stella pulled a pouty face. "Oh no, is this another: *stop it, aunt Stella, you're embarrassing me,* moments? And Ivy, did you truly think that you could've hidden your son's magic from *me*?"

Then her eyes gleamed silver, and she levitated off the floor.

Aquilo dived across the chamber, ignoring his

mom's furious yelling, and clutched me in his arms to protect me from Stella's fury.

"Do you think that you can keep secrets from one who creates the very fabric of secrets?" Stella boomed.

The room quaked and groaned like the metal was being murdered. Aquilo dragged me down by the hand to the Ambassador who was still leashed to a metal ring in the floor and threw his arms around him as well.

I caught Moon's eye across the room, as his cage rattled.

The map of Wolf Kingdom shrieked, as it disappeared down into the floor in fear.

Stella was serious about showing me who was in charge and why it was that the other covens feared.

CHAPTER 7

In a witches' house that shook like it was made of no more than cards and any moment could fall, I was held firm in the cool arms of a mage, whilst a wolf nuzzled at my shoulder. The Ambassador and Aquilo might not be mine in the way that my Charms were, but I could feel my connection to them through my shadows.

How could I keep either safe from my aunt whose rage was tearing apart the House of Seasons? The ceiling warped, caving in, and I shrieked.

"When you were born, I made a promise to your mum because she'd already lost a child." Stella levitated towards me.

My mom had lost a child?

I'd never known that but then, I guessed that I'd

been too young to tell, before my parents had been killed.

Yet why had my uncle never told me?

My chest ached at the thought. Had it been a brother or a sister? Did they die in the womb, at birth, or after? Would they've been magical like me?

Was that why mom had fussed over me like I had to be perfect because she'd still been grieving for this other kid…and I could never make up for their loss?

I huddled in Aquila's hold. His hair fell like a soft white veil across my eyes, as his cheek pressed against mine. "How did she lose…?"

Stella ignored me. Her smile was devious. "Zetta was always the clever one. Do you know why? She sensed something *unique* about you even then."

Stella's eyes sparked, as she advanced like the world's creepiest Fairy Godmother.

I winced. Hey, I'd been called worse than *unique*. Except, Stella made it sound as much like *reject*, as if I'd been thrown in the cell along with Moon.

My eyes narrowed. "Whatever. I don't care about your pinky promises; you don't know me. Who's my favorite artist? When was I first beaten up in High School? What was my wackiest magical invention?"

Stella blinked, then she lowered to the floor, whilst the House of Seasons finally stopped shaking. The rumbling settled to a low growl. "Oh, so now you want to get chatty?"

I rolled my eyes, and Aquilo tightened his hold. I loved the fresh scent of him and his breath against my skin. "I rest my case." Then I turned my head, catching Aquilo's lips with mine in a chaste kiss, which still had him gasping. Lux snarled, crossing her arms. Aquilo's questioning gaze met mine. "I have my mage fiancé now, so that's me all straightened out. Unless, you have any more epic tantrums to throw, before sending my Charm and us home...?"

When the Ambassador nipped my shoulder in warning, I jumped. I gazed down into his anxious eyes in surprise, then stroked his hair to calm him.

Yep, he was right: *why on earth was I inciting the wicked witch of all seasons?*

I cringed, as Stella stalked towards me; her hair still gleamed like bronze wires. "Sorry, internal attitude adjustment complete. I just want my mage and wolf safe. All I want is my pack."

"*Pack?*" Stella hissed. "The wolves have infected you. We have Houses; we're not beasts. Your mum would be ashamed."

Witching heavens, I should've known that *pack* would be the wrong freaking word to use in a coven.

Stella's eyes gleamed, and the clockface shattered in a shower of glass. Ivy screamed, throwing herself over her daughter, as the shards sliced them. My red ballooned in a protective bubble around my *pack*, including Moon, who was still trapped in the cage.

Shakily, I dropped my shadows, drawing in ragged breaths. It was the Ambassador stroking *me* now, in tentative touches down my shoulders, whilst Aquilo held my hand in his, squeezing our fingers together rhythmically like it was a ward against my aunt.

"In the name of the Head Coven, will you control yourself!" Ivy wailed, quivering as she magically drew out the shards that were embedded in her daughter and herself, before smashing the glass against the far wall. I flinched. "You never could think clearly around either your niece or a Wolf Charmer. Either she fights by and for our side, or my goodness, I vote for the Justice Chamber."

"*Woah*, hold up a witching moment..." I shoved back from the Ambassador, dragging Aquilo to his feet next to me.

Stella patted at her hair with a sigh. "*Rage hair*. It's one of the worst consequences of dark magic, I swear."

Then she smiled at me like we were in the middle of a civilized conversation, rather than her magical freak out that would decide my fate. And how much did I hate that she had any control over that because shouldn't we all have control over our *own* fates?

When Stella strolled to Moon's cage, tapping on the bars, I stiffened. "Let's see if I can think about this clearly then, shall we?" She trailed her hand around the bars, and Moon growled at her. There was danger in the way that she merely smiled back. "*You* have a mage problem: a dying god. *Witches* have a wolf problem: wolves who we need to kill. *I* have a Wolf Tamer problem: no test subject for my improved stronger dose. Can you see how the answer to these three problems is the same?"

My breath hitched, and my grip tightened on Aquilo's hand.

Stella couldn't be seriously offering to test the Wolf Tamer, which could become the weapon that wiped out the wolves or subdued them once and for all, on *my* Charms? I'd rather be turned into one of the frozen gargoyle statues in the House of Blood's courtyard forever than allow her to turn my wolves into test subjects.

"Not a chance in hell," I snarled.

"How will me becoming your lab rat help Mischief?" Moon asked, quietly.

My eyes widened. *What on earth was he doing?*

I knew that Moon was used to sacrificing for the Omegas but would he now sacrifice for his god as well? Yet if my god suddenly appeared, even the non-worship royal prick style one, wouldn't I suffer for him too?

Stella gripped the cage bars, practically cooing in delight. "Not just a pretty face, are you, Omega?" Moon grimaced, swiping at Stella with his claws, but she dodged back. "Never you mind your hot little behind. I'll help stop the mage fading, as long as he serves as a slave to the House of Silver. And *you* swear to test the new dose of Wolf Tamer."

She slipped a needle that bubbled with silver out of her pocket. Moon became ashen, whining. I didn't blame him because last time she'd pulled out a needle like that, I'd stabbed him with it, leaving him in agony.

Who knew what this new one would do to him... maybe it'd even kill him.

Aquilo marched across the chamber. "You imagine that I'd allow you to poison him? I'm only a mage... male...to be married off, so you think that I don't know what damage that dose could do? You haven't used it on the Ambassador because you don't want to risk killing him. Sorry, were you trying to keep that *secret*?"

Aquilo struggled to rip the needle from Stella, but Lux caught him under his arms and dragged him back. To my surprise, she was gentle with him, even if her words weren't.

Lux hauled Aquilo to the side of the room. "The wind doesn't choose—"

"I'm not the wind." Aquilo shook himself free of his sister. His gaze was ice-cold. "*I'm the Charmer's pack.*"

Ivy drew in a panicked breath, but Lux merely nodded, studying her twin with an intent gaze. In anyone else, I'd have called it respect. In Lux...? Who in the witching world knew what the bully was thinking.

"I take it that you've been waiting for the right

moment to force me into this," I gritted out. "But it's not my choice. My guys *aren't* my slaves, no matter what you say, and I won't make this decision for Moon. If he wants to do this…no matter how much it'll hurt me… that's *his* choice."

I battled to meet Moon's gaze, even though I was struggling to breathe and desperate to claw back the words and demand that he refuse to go anywhere near that poison.

Tell Stella to go to hell. Stay with me. Say no, no, no…

Why couldn't I at least tell him that I loved him?

Moon ducked his head, but when he looked up again, his gaze was fierce and more regal than I'd ever seen it. "You know what I said about us being enemies, Crimson? I take it back. You're a fine rebel. I've made my choice: I can't let another Omega suffer in my place."

The way that Stella's face lit up was indecent.

I bit my lip to force down the tumble of words to convince him to change his mind. "You don't want to lose your own wolf, but you'll make me lose mine?" I sneered at Stella.

Stella glanced at the Ambassador; her expression softened. Then she shrugged. "Sexy credit where it's due: your hot prince is stronger than my Ambassador. He has a greater chance of surviving…not much, but every little counts, right?" She unclicked the lock to the cage, dragging open the bars. Moon reluctantly crawled out. "Don't you see it, pretty peach? This isn't about killing him. I could've done that whilst you were taking your nap." I shivered at her breezy smile. "I want to see how far I can paralyze, restrain, control...didn't you once say *bully*?" She chuckled. "How arrogantly sweet, just like your mum, that you crave to wield such powers alone with your shadows. It's time that you learned to share your toys."

When she tossed the needle at me, I fumbled and then caught it.

I glowered at the Wolf Tamer. Why couldn't I just make it go *poof* in a spray of glitter? It was a shame that real witchcraft wasn't like the movies, go figure.

Moon straightened his shoulders, before determinedly rolling back his leather shirtsleeve.

I hurriedly shook my head. "I don't think so. If we have to do this screwed-up experiment, then you're giving us privacy. I get to take Moon home with me."

Stella's gaze flickered between Moon and me, before she nodded. "After all, ideally a beast should die in its own witches' House."

What a surprise that they even had witch rules about killing Charms.

My cheek twitched, whilst I rubbed at my arms. My gaze, however, never left Moon's.

I'd told him that he'd had the choice about the Wolf Tamer. I couldn't take it back, no matter how desperate I was to never let the needle break his skin. Yet now we had to return to the House of Silver to inject him with the Wolf Tamer to save the Ambassador and Mischief, but at the same time help the witches develop a weapon to defeat the werewolves in a war.

It was also an experiment that could kill Moon.

AMONGST THE CRIMSON SATIN OF MY FOUR-POSTER BED in the House of Silver, Moon lay in pale beauty, propped amongst the pillows. The scent of honeysuckle curled intoxicatingly around the sun dappled room. If I couldn't save my Charm, I could at least carry out the experiment in comfort and at home, amongst those who loved him.

There was no ever-witching way that I'd admit I was preparing for Moon to die, even though the needle weighed heavy in my hand.

Huh, a witch could cast a Self-Delusion Spell on herself.

I bit my tongue to keep the same fierce expression as Moon, who was determinedly not looking at me or the needle, which I hurriedly clasped behind my back.

I hadn't even been brave enough to explore up into the attic and check whether Mischief was still unconscious or had…faded.

Yep, not thinking of *dying* because I couldn't take both god and Charm leaving me at the same time. I'd survived my parents and being the one left behind sucked. I knew that it was selfish but sometimes, dying was the easy part.

It was surviving that hurt.

I'd already snatched the wolf fur pelt off the bed because the last thing Moon had needed was to have to snuggle under one of his murdered family. I'd wrenched open the window, whilst my red had whipped around me in fury to hurl the hated thing out, but Emperor had stilled me.

"We respect the gesture," he'd curled his hand around mine, before gently taking the pelt from me, "perhaps you could respect the dead?"

I'd blushed, as he'd drawn his thumb down the fur like a private blessing, in the same way that he'd done to the stone wolves in the Blood's courtyard. Then he'd carefully folded the pelt and stowed it out of sight in the wardrobe, which I'd once hidden in to save myself from the wolves.

Now, I watched how Emperor curled on one side of the bed with Moon, stroking his mess of curls. It caught at me, until my chest ached, that Emperor would've tidied Moon's hair in the same way for school. Unless, you know, he was trying to get him to look his best for his funeral.

I tightened my hold around the Wolf Tamer; the glass dug into my palm.

Moon turned into Emperor's touch with desperate longing. Why had Moon denied himself this closeness? What could've been so bad to divide the two princes?

At last it appeared that Emperor had been welcomed back into the cuddle zone. But it kind of spooked me how Moon allowed Emperor to caress him now like whatever had happened in the past no longer mattered because if this was Moon's last few moments, then he'd take what he wanted.

And that meant Moon didn't expect to survive this.

My shadows spun around me, faster and faster, whilst the world swayed.

I wouldn't let my Charm die…I couldn't…

Amadeus nestled on the other side of Moon with his arms wound around his waist and his head rested on his shoulder. Amadeus' eyes were more red-rimmed than mine, and he hadn't even spoken since we'd returned with news of Moon's choice. Okami nestled on his shoulder like he sensed that he needed the most comforting, even if he'd never admit it.

Yet neither of the other two princes had tried to talk Moon out of it. Maybe there was something in this royalty gig that I didn't understand?

Reluctantly, I stumbled closer to the bed, raising the needle. Moon flinched, then held himself entirely still. Amadeus growled, refusing to let go of Moon.

"My, what a big prick you have." Mischief's silky voice wound from behind me.

Mischief was alive...

I twisted to him with a grin that made my cheeks ache; Mischief's scowl was just as wide. *Yet I didn't care because he was alive and well enough to kick my ass.*

"Why, I ask, would you be so foolish as to consider murdering one of my subjects?" Mischief's long silver hair hung over his face, whilst his violet wings were outstretched.

He was pallid, and there were hollows under his eyes, but he was still the prettiest man that I'd ever seen.

And I still had wing envy.

I flushed. "I should've known that Zetta would've told on us. It's epic to see your gorgeous ass out of bed."

Zetta was the essence of all the Wolf Charmers who'd gone before me in this house. Stella had created her as a ward to protect me. She was a spy, pest, and probably more dangerous than Stella herself.

Mischief's hands circled like he was trying to summon his silver magic and failing. He hissed in frustration. "Do you imagine that your compliments shall reduce my rage? I look like death or at least, her hot bitch."

I blinked. "Still, hot, right?"

Mischief sniffed, suddenly looking vulnerable and

as unwell as I was certain he truly was. "You left us, witch girl."

Now it was my turn to pale. When I'd been trapped in the well, I'd been torn apart by the thought that Mischief and Ramiel would've thought that we'd abandoned them. "Dude, I'm sorry. I got back to you as soon as I could. You know you talked to me about the responsibility of royalty…? I get that now. It's just, Wolf Charmers have it too."

Mischief studied me seriously for a long moment, before nodding. His gaze became steely once more. "Oh, I remember who you are again: a witch. They *poison* and control. I believed you different, which was my mistake. Yet you shan't do it in my name. I won't allow—"

"Stop your fussing," Moon said, softly. "This way, the witches will save your godly behind."

"Why do people always insist on *saving* me?" Mischief howled.

When he tried to stalk to the bed, however, his knees buckled, and he stumbled to the floor. His breathing was harsh, as his eyes closed.

Holy hell, why did he always have to push himself so hard?

"I told you, no more of this stiff upper lip crap." I crouched next to him, wiping his hair back from his feverish forehead. "Should you even be out of bed?"

"I'm not an invalid," Mischief snapped, before his

eyes fluttered closed, and he groaned. Then he opened his eyes again with difficulty. "I admit, I'm possibly invalid adjacent."

"*Dying* adjacent is more accurate." Ramiel swooped into the room on pale violet wings, wafting in the scent of nutmeg that made me shiver.

Ramiel's fairy tale pink hair hung over his face, as he bent to hug Mischief, before pulling him back onto his feet, whilst supporting him with his wings. His large violet eyes gleamed.

Mischief sighed. "Oh, goodie, it's mother hen come to wrap me up in feathers again."

Ramiel circled his thumb along Mischief's hip. "Would you prefer Daddy angel come to put you over my knee for rudeness again?"

Mischief reddened. "Will you never understand the concept of *overshare*?"

Moon held out his hand to Mischief. "Come on, we're all getting in a last nuzzle. I've reserved you a space."

Mischief curtly shook his head. Then he shuddered, as Ramiel's hand inched across his ass in warning.

Moon smiled. *I wished that I had his courage.* "I can cut off your cuddle supply…"

At last, Mischief shakily returned his smile. Ramiel helped him to lie over Moon, cocooning him in his feathers, whilst Ramiel lazily lay out across the end of his bed with his long lean limbs like a pink-haired cat.

My crimson arched over the bed, stroking and caressing, connecting all my pack with pleasure, even though I was the one holding the needle.

Moon wrapped his arms around Mischief's neck. "Fur and fangs, you're my god. How can I not save you?"

Mischief turned away his face but he couldn't hide the tears that were wet down his cheeks. "It should be *I* saving *you*. Pray, how can you forgive my weakness?"

Moon turned Mischief's face back to his own, tenderly kissing the tears from his cheeks. "Goddess Moon, there's nothing to forgive." He cocked his head. "This is my time, that's all, to save my people, pack, and family."

Mischief snorted. "What are you...little me?"

"Less of the little."

Mischief brushed his hand across Moon's — *yep, those leather trousers were seriously tight* — pants. "I assure you that I can tell."

Awkwardly, I perched on the edge of the bed, and my guys stiffened.

I couldn't do this without telling Moon how I felt, even though this was less romantic even than my marriage proposal to Aquilo. I didn't appear to be the chocolates and roses style witch, more the deadly injection and imminent death type.

But Moon was my adorable First Charm, and there was nothing more romantic than the feeling that you were going to lose someone who mattered as much to you as breath itself.

"Hey, I know that I should've said it before but…" I met Moon's gaze. *Why was this so hard?* When his tongue darted out to moisten his lips, I couldn't look away. *Please, please…let him kiss me.* "I love you."

Moon's eyes widened. Then he grinned. "Aye, and I love you. Sorry, is this a big moment in the witch world? We're your Charms, can't you tell that we love you?"

Amadeus slapped Moon's stomach. "Play nice," he warned, although his voice was thick with tears.

I didn't know whether to thrill with joy or shudder with despair because I was loved, but I had to risk the prince who loved me.

Moon offered his bared arm to me without even hesitating.

It was me who hesitated.

Come on, Crimson, you can do this. Just push in the needle. Push it in, push, push…

A bundle of moon-blond curls and Omega fury bowled into me, throwing me off the bed. Moth, Moon's teenage brother and younger prince, had been skulking in the shadows of the room so silently that I'd forgotten he was there. Terrified that the Wolf Tamer would inject him by mistake — and there was no way he'd survive something that could kill a grown wolf — I struggled to dodge his cub-sized claws and extended fangs, whilst not hurting him.

"Stay back," I hollered at my guys.

Moth lunged at me, and the needle brushed his throat. I hissed, whilst my pulse pounded.

I'd promised myself not to use my shadows to control but…

My red burst out, wrapping around the flailing wolf. It pinned his arms gently to the sides, before dragging him up to stand against the wall. Fat tears dripped from Moth's eyes, but when I tried to stroke his hair to calm him, he flinched away.

It was hard to remember that he wasn't Moon.

"You know better than this, Moth. All that matters is you're safe, remember?" Moon's gaze flickered between his brother and me. "Just close your eyes, and when it's over, I'll—"

"*Lies*," Moth sobbed. "The witch has laid you out on your deathbed." He scowled at the rest of my pack. "They all know it."

Emperor raised himself on his elbow. "Whatever happens, I'll protect you, Moth. I swear, I'll always be there for you…"

"My brother told about you," Moth snarled, struggling against my red. "You made the same promise to him. Then you abandoned him." Emperor's face crumpled, and he blanched. I'd never seen the cocky prince so devastated. "Wolves from the Kingdom of the

Alphas are all the same. None of you are from the Wilds. How can I trust you? You say that you love him, but then you're *killing* him..."

"Nay, enough of that. It's done," Moon commanded like a true prince. Then his gaze gentled. "You can trust Crimson. She's the only furless witch who isn't a bastard." Then he yelled up at the ceiling, "I know you're watching, Zetta. Take my brother into another room and keep him safe."

"*No, no, no...*" Moth wailed, as he was dragged backwards through the wall, which melted like a glimmering puddle.

The wall sealed again behind him, shutting him out.

The silence was like a noose.

I shuffled to the bed, tucking the needle into my pocket, before I couldn't hold back the tears. In a flurry of feathers, tattoos, and curls my pack tangled together in a pile, nuzzling, licking, and stroking.

Amadeus feathered kisses down Moon's jawline, whilst Mischief cuddled him tightly as if he never meant to let go. Ramiel tenderly lifted his hand to brush his knuckles across the back of Moon's cheek, whilst meeting his gaze with an intense, burning gaze like one warrior to the other. Emperor nipped Moon's neck, before sucking on it hard enough to mark it in a claiming that made him whine; my shadows seethed at the challenge. Yet I understood Emperor's need as an Alpha and I wouldn't deny it.

At last, I kissed along Moon's cheeks and forehead, whilst he nuzzled into my neck, licking and sniffing. Then I hovered over his lips, brushing them lightly with mine.

They almost touched...

"Time to tame me, Charmer: I'm the crimson tide," he murmured; his breath ghosted across my lips.

Then he turned his neck, baring his throat for the needle, rather than his arm, in the ultimate submission.

I shuddered, drawing back and pulling out the needle. I caressed his throat; the artery fluttered underneath. The skin was warm beneath me and so alive.

Harder, just a harder push and...

The sharp metal pricked Moon's neck, and the bubbling silver drained into him. For a moment, he blinked up at me.

Then Moon screamed, arching in agony.

The other Charms held down Moon's arms, whilst the angels dived to hold his legs, as he wildly thrashed on the bed. Still he strained against them.

Moon's magic snapped out, stinging my red in his pain, and I hissed, caught in his wide-eyed panic. His connection to me strengthened. I could feel his magic, power, and the wolf inside. Just as I could feel how it was being submerged, forced back, and subdued.

I howled at the pain, violation, and loss.

Holy hell, what had I done?

Suddenly, Moon fell still.

Breathing hard, I stared down at him. His eyes were closed, and he was waxy, silent, and motionless.

Why couldn't I feel him anymore? Why the freaking hell couldn't I feel his magic? Why couldn't I feel....*anything*?

Moth had been right. It did look like a deathbed, and I'd been the one to kill Moon.

CHAPTER 8

I was a Wolf Charmer, sprawled in bed with three Claimed werewolves, an angel, and a god. But honestly, all I cared about was the guy I loved who lay next to me like he'd been cursed under a wicked witch's spell.

And *I* was the witch who'd poisoned him.

Except, this wasn't a fairy tale because in a fairy tale, Moon would awake on a kiss.

I pressed my lips more firmly to Moon's mouth like this kiss would count as our first one, and it'd stir him back to life. Although, I knew that it *wouldn't* count as our first kiss because Moon couldn't feel it, and it had no magical powers to awaken him.

I still imagined Moon's arms raising to clasp around my neck, as his amber eyes fluttered open to stare into mine with love, loyalty, and wonder at our kiss, whilst his tongue pushed up to press between my parted lips with equal desperation as my own.

I imagined that I'd brought him back to life, when in fact he remained lifeless beneath me.

Fairy tale kisses were the same bullshit as LLRH, who knew?

It was my crimson shadows that held onto Moon's life, magic, and the wolf inside, even though the connection trembled like the thinnest silk thread. His soft fur brushed against my shadows, specter-like; I could sense him huddled in wolf form with his ears pressed against his head, whilst he whined, bound by the toxic silver as if he was in chains, just like my shadows had been by Stella's magic.

Had they developed the Wolf Tamer from the same magic?

Okami sniffled in my jeans' pocket, refusing to come out. I knew that the bond he'd experienced with Moon, who'd been the first wolf that he'd ever met, was special and deeper than I'd ever expected. Okami had been my creation, and before he'd become friends with my Charms, maybe I *had* treated him like just another piece of magic and tech, even though I loved him. But now I understood that my Wolf Charmer magic had truly given him life, which sucked when it came to facing death.

It'd been kind of humiliating to admit (and not something that I'd ever write in a Witch Manual for

Wolf Care), but it'd been Amadeus who'd saved Moon's life and not by methods that would've been coven approved.

Although, maybe Stella would've been okay with it, since she was kinkier than me.

"You're his Charmer," Emperor had insisted, "and our adorable and precious Omega here is the *Moon Child*. What charming covens we have in Oxford that they force you to experiment on wolves, yet neglect to teach you about your bond with us. Do you wish him to be lost and not try *everything* to find him? I trust you with our pack. Don't make me regret that."

I'd shivered at the intensity of his growl.

So, Moon was simply lost beneath the Wolf Tamer and needed me to bring him home…?

Nope, there'd be no abandoning or regretting. I'd battled the magic binding my shadows and I'd battle to bring the guy that I loved home too, even if he was a wolf.

Would my mom be ashamed of me for loving a werewolf?

Weirdly, I hadn't cared anymore whether she'd have hated my choice in boyfriend. I'd always wondered if my choices were living up to the name of the House of Silver. But now, when I could lose someone that I loved again, I could see how petty and unimportant that was.

Hey, did I get my rebel badge yet?

I'd wiped at my eyes. As long as Moon would be

there to pin the badge onto me, it didn't matter if it read *Rebel*, *Rogue,* or *Asshole.*

Please…come back to me…

Yet when I'd coiled my crimson around Moon, before curling it around his whispers of magic, following its flow to discover his wolf deep inside, I'd been overwhelmed by a sweet silver fog that had stung like a swarm of bees.

Yep, I hadn't missed the irony.

I'd howled, falling back into Emperor's strong arms. He'd held me to his chest, whilst I'd shuddered in shock.

"The son of a bitch poison is still hurting him." I'd understood the way that Emperor had stiffened because the same rage whipped my crimson like an enraged octopus around the four-poster. "I can't break through it."

Amadeus had slipped his hands around my waist, easing me away from Emperor and onto my back next to Moon. Then he'd hovered over me with a predatory smile. I'd stared back at him, confused.

When in the witching heavens had I become his prey?

"You need to try again, see, whilst your bond is strengthened by another Charm." Amadeus' lips had sucked on mine; my pulse had fluttered in my throat. The taste and scent of chocolate had spiraled my desire, until I'd tingled, and my hands had clenched in the sheets. "And if it pleases you, I need to strengthen my power with your desire."

"Command him, witch." Mischief had rested in Ramiel's wings at the end of the bed; his gaze had been masterful and dark.

As an incubus, Amadeus didn't simply feed from giving pleasure, his power grew from it, especially if he was fulfilling your deepest desire. I'd known that I should ask for something more intimate than a foot rub to save Moon, but I'd blushed because I hadn't been used to asking guys like this and I hadn't wanted to just be one more asshole who used Amadeus' nature against him, even though I had the weird feeling that *he* was using *me*.

Huh, having scorching-hot guys offering to act out your secret fantasies wasn't as sexy as you'd think.

Amadeus' smile had faltered, before he'd raised his gloved hand to my cheek and whispered, "Let me pleasure you...*there*."

He'd glanced down with a significant arch of his brow, and holy hell, if I'd thought that my cheeks were flaming before, they'd been on fire now.

Because Amadeus had already known what I'd most craved from him, when I'd first seen him dancing at his Claiming. His glove had been torn, and he'd accidentally touched me with his bare finger, which was how incubi read your darkest, hidden, and secret desires.

Incubi read inside what you'd never told anyone, or

even admitted to others, so that they'd know how to please you. Perhaps, even to control you through your pleasure, as Amadeus had with Rhona.

Amadeus was delicate, talented, and *pretty*.

But what if he was also the deadliest of my Charms?

I'd realized how little I knew about incubi, Betas, the fanatical worshipers of the Kingdom of the Gods or even Amadeus himself.

Okay, there'd be no forgetting from now on that he had fangs, as well as a dick.

But the way that Amadeus had traced his hands up my inner thighs with a devilish smile, had made me honestly forget my own name. Amadeus' hair had brushed across my face in a dark waterfall, whilst his eyes glittered like rubies. Then he'd crawled down me, popping open the button of my jeans and sliding them down as well, along with my panties.

Okami had let out a protesting howl, darting out and curling to sleep on Moon's stomach.

Amadeus had peeked up at me through his long lashes, whilst stroking the crease between my thigh and hip. My skin had tingled at each stroke of his fingers, and I'd been desperate for him to touch me. He knew exactly *where* because this was my desire that he'd been acting out.

The teasing... beautiful...asshole.

He'd curled his tongue wickedly between his teeth,

before licking a trail down the center of my stomach towards just where we both quivered for him to be...

Then Amadeus had spent the next hour between my thighs.

I'd never known that pleasure could be so over-whelming that I could lose myself in it. Yet I'd moaned, thrashing on the waves that burst over me again and again, and my shadows had twitched and quivered the same as I had. They'd thrummed with energy. I'd thrust them back into Moon, fighting the silver haze.

The pleasure from Amadeus had blunted the pain from inside Moon. My red had twisted around the fog, choking it until it'd thinned, and I'd been able to *almost* reach Moon's wolf.

I'd gasped, and Amadeus had raised his head, licking his lips. His eyes had flamed. I'd never seen him with such strength.

He'd crawled back up me, murmuring, "Your plea-sure tastes delicious. Now, save my friend."

Yet Moon still hadn't woken up, and now I sat back, thumping a pillow in frustration; Emperor pulled it away from me.

"How about you don't commit pillow murder? And don't kiss Moon again." He plumped the pillow, placing it carefully under Moon to prop him higher. Then he cocked a haughty eyebrow. "Look, Moon could get himself in trouble in an empty room — and has. We'll find a way to bring him back."

It was Emperor's casual use of *we'll* that startled me. My shadows seethed, yet this was a pack, and I wasn't alone. None of us were anymore. After centuries, the wolves had found each other again, and I'd found them.

I just didn't have a witching clue what else I could do. And why *hadn't* someone invented a vet for supernaturals again…? I mean, it was a business opportunity.

I twisted my hands in my lap. "Jesus, it's just that he's still in pain, and at least, if we could stop that…"

Mischief scrambled out of Ramiel's hold, slinking to lay over Moon. He brushed his hand tenderly through Moon's curls. "I excel at taking pain. Lucky me, it's one of my Angelic Powers. Do you not yet perceive that I've been strutting around as a god, when I've been of little use to any of you but to take your pain?"

Ramiel's breath hitched. "Who would dare make you think that way? You're worth the world, Zophia."

"You were always too kind." Mischief's smile was sad. "Tell me again, pray, why a dying god shouldn't sacrifice himself one last time?"

Ramiel dived for Mischief at the same time as me, but he'd already pressed his hands to Moon's neck, where I'd stabbed in the needle. Mischief trembled, as his skin instantly became clammy and pale. Then he swayed and fell backwards into Ramiel's waiting arms.

"I can't even take all his pain…" Mischief's expression transformed to a terrible fury, as he spread his sparking wings. I shrank back. *Woah*, he looked every inch the ancient god that he was claiming to doubt. "Whoever is stealing my powers in their petty games hear this: they shall suffer thrice the agony of the foul fiends and tyrants who I've destroyed before."

Huh, that was one hell of a curse.

Ramiel brushed his wingtip down Mischief's cheek. "Hush, they'll fall by my sword, I swear."

Was it weird that I found that romantic?

Amadeus took a ragged breath, before touching Moon's cheek. "No one's taken *my* power. Look you, it's why I keep it secret. My mind blowing…kiss down there…" When Amadeus made kissy lips at me, I rolled my eyes, even if I crossed my legs. "…means that I can kiss Moon here…"

Amadeus hovered his lips above Moon's; Amadeus' translucent skin began to glow. My eyes widened, and I grinned, meeting Emperor's gaze. He looked just as excited and nervous as me, even kneeling forward to watch and clutching tight to the suit material on his knees, wrinkling it.

Hey, I *knew* how much this moment meant to him if he didn't even remember the damage to his suit in the midst of it.

Why didn't Amadeus let his lips touch Moon's?

Then I gasped at the ruby sparkles that whispered — *like life* — from Amadeus' mouth and into Moon's.

Suddenly, with a shuddering intake of breath, Moon's eyes snapped open.

My heart thudded so loudly in my ears that I could hardly hear. My eyes prickled with tears.

He was awake...Black cats dancing on a mage's dick...awake...

Moon yawned, before edging his hand to stroke over Okami's silky head, who jumped awake himself and was twirling around on Moon's stomach, howling in joy.

Moon's lip curled up as he turned his head to take in the group of wolves, angels, and one wildly grinning witch nestled around him. "So, I'm not dead then."

I spluttered with laughter, although it masked the desperate sob.

Amadeus tweaked the end of Moons nose, before sitting back on his heels. "I should bite you." His voice was suspiciously tight.

Moon rubbed Amadeus' arm. "Aye, you should." His gaze was soft. "On the furless heavens, thank you."

There was a moment's silence, before in a dance of feathers, soft skin, and pale limbs, my pack and I all tried to claim our snuggle time with Moon. I laughed, wriggling into the nest. Moon melted into my hold like we'd been apart for weeks, rather than hours.

Boy, did it feel like we had.

He nuzzled against my neck, licking and kissing down my jawline as if he meant to Wolf Bite me. "I was lost," his lips curved against the skin of my throat on each word; I shuddered at the intimacy of his touch and confession, "but you still found me."

For the first time, my Charms and I had the advantage. Stella had thought that the Wolf Tamer would kill or subdue Moon's wolf, yet my bond with my Charms and Amadeus' secret power had stopped the poison.

But what should I do with that advantage? I didn't want to hide terrified in the wardrobe and I was definite that my wolves would do anything to break free of their collars. I was the Wolf Charmer, and my pack were princes, angels, mages, and gods.

It was freaking time that we took back our legacies and our kingdoms.

Mischief's brow furrowed. "Tell me, is your happy face usually so hostile?"

I thrilled at the way that my dark smile made Mischief flinch; freaking out a god was a rush. "I'm just thinking about the ass kicking that we owe the Oxford covens."

"Dangerous as I'd suggest you *thinking* to be," Mischief smirked (okay, my smile only had limited intimidation value), "if it involves witches' asses being soundly kicked, then think away."

Ramiel raised his elegant hand. "Seconded."

"I have one question, our sexy little ball of incubus fun." When Emperor's hand clamped around Amadeus' elbow, he *eeped.* "What's with your magical kiss of life?

And I know: why didn't you sparkle Moon out of his personal hell straightaway? Wait, that's two questions. And oh look, how little I care."

Moon waved his hand. "Fur and fangs, why does it even matter? I'm fine now…"

"Do you know how many times you've said that, after we've hauled your pale bottom out of trouble?" Emperor snapped.

Amadeus ducked his head. "Please, I needed my power to be strong enough first." Well, that explained his gorging on *my* pleasure. Although, having been kept quivering on the edge of peaking for hours, before tipping over into the most intense orgasm of my life, I wasn't complaining. Unless, you know, it was about the *secrets* part of this because that was bad. "I thought it'd disgust you and I simply wanted my pack to desire me."

I looked at him blankly. "*Umm*, why would I be disgusted? Dude, it was hot."

Amadeus peeked at me like he was gauging my truthfulness. His cheeks and neck were flushed pink; he'd never looked more beautiful.

How could he ever think that he'd disgust me?

"Some incubi have the talent. I only wanted to please you and never shame you. I was meant to be only a pretty Beta — the *prettiest* Beta." His lip curled, as he glanced up. "My mongrel incubus blood was forgiven in my adoption so that I could be your prince."

"I believe I told you never to refer to yourself as

mongrel." Mischief raised his imperious eyebrow. "We are both aware just how strong your magic is. Plus, a mongrel can take down worlds."

Just for a moment, Amadeus' eyes flashed. Then he pulled at the bottom of his top, playing with a frayed thread. "The princess of my kingdom made me swear not to reveal it."

Emperor clenched his jaw, before his hold on Amadeus gentled. "Your sister dared to insist on a Moon Oath?"

"*Adopted* sister." Amdeus wrinkled his nose. "Don't go making Vala and me blood relatives."

Moon's gaze darkened. "You shouldn't have broken a Moon Oath for me. She can kill you now."

Amadeus smile was shaky. "Stop being Mr Bossy Pants. Like you get to risk your life for us, but I don't get to risk it for you?"

I blinked. "*Woah*, is your adopted sister that harsh a bitch? I mean, it wasn't like you were just showing off for a party trick. You were seriously being the hero."

Amadeus snorted. "You're sexy, Charmer, but you need a lesson in wolf politics." He clambered over Moon to me, before kissing down my neck.

I wet my lips. "Wolf politics is way more fun than the human kind."

Amadeus' huff of amusement gusted against my neck. "Just a demonstration, see? *This* is how close my pack was back on our island off the welsh coast before the Wolf War. We were so isolated that we'd never even seen a witch. We avoided the other wolf kingdoms. Then the war started, and we didn't think to fight because it had nothing to do with us, see?" His arms wound around me for comfort. "What did we know about anything outside this *closeness*?" When he wrenched away from me, the loss of his touch was painful. I got it then. *That* was what it'd been like for his pack to be dragged away from their island to their tiny home beside the Thames. "The survivors…what's left of us…we don't mix with the other wolves once we're out of school. Most would happily see the other kingdoms drown beneath the waves. Look you, Vala would be outraged that I'd broken an oath for a Wild."

"And a Wild would be outraged that I'm snuggling with a Beta from the Gods," Moon muttered.

"Whilst us from the Kingdom of the Alphas merely believe that we're superior to all the other wolves." Emperor grinned cockily. "An idea not without merit."

It'd never struck me so sharply that although the witches called it Wolf Kingdom, these wolves actually came from three different places across Britain, before the war.

"Well, let's just roll over and play good doggy for my aunt." I crossed my arms. "If you're not united, you'll always be leashed."

I didn't miss the way that my Charms exchanged a

glance. My guts churned. It looked like I was preaching to the centuries-old choir.

What did they have planned?

Moon nodded. "Aye, you're right, single skin. So, let's start with my brother. He'll be worrying his daft head off."

In the excitement of Moon's resurrection moment, I'd forgotten about Moth. The poor kid was probably stashed in a wardrobe somewhere, still cursing us out.

"Spooks," I hollered at the ceiling, "you can bring back Moth now. Hey, I know that you're listening."

Silence.

Okay, not pressing the freak out button yet...

I sighed. "Zetta, I'm sorry that I called you Spooks. Seriously, get Mini Moon's ass out here."

Suddenly, the temperature in the room dropped. Cold, damp, and moist. I shivered, whilst Ramiel enfolded Mischief in his wings. Okami whimpered, fluffing out his tail, as he flew to wind himself around my neck like a scarf.

Then the windows and doors opened and closed — *slam*.

I jumped. "I'm not loving the *Poltergeist* vibe. Why not stop creeping us out, and just tell us where you stuffed Moth?"

The bedposts burst into flames.

I fell off the bed, whilst Emperor hauled Amadeus and Moon free of the smoldering sheets, before battling through the blaze himself. Ramiel and Mischief coughed, swooping through the smoke.

I lay, clutching Okami, whilst he whined, staring wide-eyed, as the bed flared to ash like the tip of a cigarette *or a bonfire*.

To a witch, there was nothing more insulting than threatening her with a burning.

Zetta had just declared war.

CHAPTER 9

Dazed, I stared at the smoldering bed and scorched walls of my bedroom, which had now been transformed into a battleground.

I clutched Okami, as he hugged my throat. He growled at Zetta, even though she was still hiding from sight.

Zetta was the essence of the House of Silver and every Wolf Charmer who'd come before me. She wouldn't kill one of the Wolf Charmer line, right? Unless, I'd pissed off my ancestors enough with my modernization of their customs because let's face it: *their traditions sucked.*

My uncle had often faced opposition when he'd modernized his company. But then, he'd never risked burning.

I watched as my Charms warily prowled to their

feet. Ramiel dragged Mischief to the corner of the room, since his burst of flight had exhausted him. Moon held out his hand to me, helping me to my feet.

"I'm lady of this manor," I waved at the walls, hoping for once that Zetta would step through the skin like usual and this war would be over before it started, "stop dicking around or I'll find a way to exorcise your ass."

"Nay, you're neither a lady nor a girl." Moon nuzzled his cheek against mine, although his gaze was sharp. "You're a woman and a Charmer. *My Crimson.* No whispers from the past can stop you."

I scuffed my boot along the floor, whilst my mouth was dry. Hadn't I always been stopped by the past? My memories? *Mom?*

The cape was too heavy on my shoulders. Why didn't it feel like it was soothing me anymore, rather that it was smothering…?

Moon tipped up my chin; his fingers barely brushed my feverish skin. "Our pasts won't stop *us*."

I jerked, as suddenly nuclear alarm sirens wailed through the room. My guts clenched in terror at the alien sound, as I clasped my hands over my ears. Then the sirens cut off, and "Two Tribes Go to War" by Frankie Goes to Hollywood burst out, sung by the stone wolves whose mouths opened and closed in weird unison.

What kind of asshole used a symbolic burning, combined with electronic disco pop to declare war?

Yep, that'd be Zetta.

"Okay, we get it," I sighed. "You've moved on from the dancing with a naked Ramiel stage of our relationship to the wanting us blown up. It happens. Just tell us where Moth is, then we can get back to…whatever this is."

The walls blew a rude raspberry so enthusiastically — *and wetly* — that my hair whipped damply around my face.

I grimaced. *Now this was war.*

"Cease your inexcusable performance of ill manners, you intolerable creature," Mischief rasped.

Mischief's breath came in short pants, whilst his shoulders rose and fell too rapidly. He was dying, and I was certain that Zetta knew the truth behind that as well.

Zetta had tried to stop Ramiel and Mischief from investigating the mage's death, she was refusing to return Moth, and now she was threatening my Charms.

My gaze became flinty, as I swung my cape across one shoulder like I was the matador and she was the bull. If Zetta wanted to bring it, then I was done hiding from the bullies.

"Why are you ragging on us? I'm the Wolf Charmer, and this is my house." My eyes narrowed. "You either help us or you get out. *Whoops*, you can't. So, it looks like you're helping or dying, and it seems like you know what that'll be like, since you've watched Mischief."

I winced, as the growled hard rock of Godsmack's

"Cryin' Like a Bitch" exploded in a churning scream of electric guitars.

Well, that told me.

Emperor raised his eyebrow, smoothing down his golden locks. "Excuse me, are you perhaps suggesting that we'll be *crying like bitches*?"

Ramiel's gaze became steely. "Zetta wouldn't be so foolish. She knows that she's the only bitch in this house."

I gaped at my shy, softly spoken angel who looked anything but either of those things right now.

Remind me never to get on the wrong side of Mr Protective Angel.

Amadeus bounced on his toes in fighting stance, weaving to the dark harmonies of the heavy metal. "I told you that you were corrupting me. Please let me fight! I can school her."

The corners of Emperor's mouth twitched. "Of course you could. In the Gods, there's no doubt that they allowed their pampered prince to take part in brutal fisticuffs."

Amadeus scowled. "You've no idea what happened in the Gods."

Nope, that fact didn't freak me out at all.

"What is this: The *Fight Club* Mix Tape?" I hollered up at the ceiling like that'd encourage Zetta to finally show her asshole self. When it didn't, I booted the wall. "That's it, Spooks, I'm done being Miss Nice Witch. If you want a smack down…I mean it's not like I *want* one but…" I struggled to hold onto what Moon had told me: I was a Charmer who couldn't be held back by my past. "You know what, I kind of freaking do. You've been the pain in my ass too long. Let's take this one-on-one."

Zetta strolled through the wall, brushing a stray red curl casually behind her ear. It still hurt that she was wearing the ball gown that mom had worn on the night that she'd been murdered…*that Zetta had chosen to look like mom at all.*

"Wow, for a moment there, I thought that you'd never ask," Zetta smirked.

Mischief *thwapped* his wing against the floor, until I met his panicked gaze. "May I request that you hold off on playing Rambo? If this entity is the essence of your mother and this great-grandmother of yours, as well as every bad, bad witch to come before even her, then I'll hazard a guess that she does indeed intend to make us cry, like bitches or otherwise."

Zetta giggled. "The little god is always so much fun *and right.*"

Then she raised her hand, and cold air blasted me backwards.

Caught in a bubble that smelled of sweet honey-suckle, making my head swim, I sank through the door that had melted behind me. Then I tumbled across the house, yelping. I shielded my head with my hands as I landed at the top of the Elizabethan staircase. The evening sun bled through the wide windows, bathing the house in crimson.

It was almost the night of the full moon.

I hadn't proved the wolves' innocence or stopped the witches' development of the Wolf Tamer. I *had* saved my pack: no one could ever accuse me of being a pessimist.

Despite that, by the end of tonight, the Second Wolf War would be launched by the witches on the unprepared wolves who were my Charms' families.

It'd be a massacre, and that was me being an optimist about it.

Yet how could I defeat the entire Oxford covens, when I couldn't even take on Zetta?

My family's motto glowed on the wall:

Charm the wolves. Control the crimson tide.

I took a step towards it. Every single time that I'd walk down these stairs, mom would tap the motto, before reading it out. It'd become my nickname: Crimson Tide. My shadows flowed out of me, rippling over the wall and tracing the words.

I'd charmed the wolves, but how did I control the crimson tide?

What if it wasn't a bloody sea created by the wolves, after all? What if the crimson tide…*was me?*

My shadows thrummed with the truth of the revelation, which reached back to a time before the Head Coven had existed, or rules and diplomacy. Instead, to an ancient bond between Charmer and wolf, which was meant to be as equals like mine with the Moon Child, where the only danger was the seductive pull of my own shadows for *power*.

I paled, shrinking back. Okami rubbed his ears against my throat with a whine. Then I staggered, glancing down at my feet in surprise. The step beneath them was softening to melted silver.

I snarled. "Zetta, chill your ghost ass out. Stop sucking on my feet. I only want the truth. I shouldn't have hidden from it so long. What's my true legacy?"

"Charm the wolves. Control the crimson tide," chanted from the motto like a choir of school kids were trapped in the wall. I clutched my hands over my ears, whilst Okami whined. *"Charm the wolves. Control the crimson tide."*

Yep, so I needed a more direct approach that would appeal to the narcissist in Zetta.

"How do I become as epic as my great-grandmother?" I hollered over the chanting.

Then I shrieked, as a hole opened beneath me, sucking *all of me* down through its sparking mouth and spitting me into the dark cellar beneath, as had happened on the first day that I'd brought Omega home to the House of Silver.

I groaned, rubbing my ass, as I glanced up at the sign: **DISCIPLINE CELLAR**.

Freaking fabulous.

I trailed my shadows like fairy lights around the gloom, scrunching my nose at the stench of mold. The cellar's walls and ceiling gleamed in silver, and I shook my head at the reminder of the cages, muzzles, and punishment implements that mom had kept down here. Okay, not thinking about the *why* she had, but I wasn't vanilla enough to need a diagram to go with the paddles and canes. Only, I didn't think that safe words and limits had been involved with the Wolf Charmers who'd come before me and their wolves.

My breath hitched at the sight of *my* wolves hanging spread-eagled like pelts from the ceiling, which at least meant that they weren't touching the silver.

I shoved myself up, searching for a way to let them down.

Even chained, Emperor attempted for haughty. Honestly, he had a way of carrying off tied up but still in charge. "Funny fact: you didn't tell us that you had a dungeon in your cellar."

I reddened. "It's not mine…"

"Aye, a wolf dungeon," Moon added, narrowing his eyes.

I yanked at the chains, trying to free Moon. "Hello, *it's not mine.*"

"A kinky sex dungeon." Amadeus grinned, looking around with far too much excitement. When the other two Charms turned to glare at him, he pouted. "It could be…"

143

"For the love of Hecate, it's not mine, so strike me dead!" I howled.

Suddenly, bright light lit up the room, blinding me.

Honestly Hecate, that hadn't been an invitation...

I tripped backwards, crashing against the cage with a *clang*. When the light faded, I rubbed at my eyes. White spots danced in my vision, before it settled back into the dark. My crimson wove out, only to draw back in shock.

Zetta leaned over me, grinning. "Miss me?"

I shoved up, *whooshing* straight through her, which was unpleasantly chilly, before stalking to the other side of the cellar. "Like a mob and pitchforks."

Zetta twirled, pouting. "*Rude*. Shall we get to the striking dead part because that sounds fun."

I paled. "Jesus, why are you being such a hardass? All I want to know is—"

Zetta's gray eyes became flinty. "I can't decide if I care less about you want or what you say." She cocked her head. "Let's rank them equal and say that I simply *don't care*."

I dug my fingers into my palms. "Where are my angels?"

Zetta prowled closer. "I love it when you're all possessive." She shivered. "All that Wolf Charmer energy sends a chill down my spine."

My jaw clenched. "That's it. For the last time, stop looking like my mom."

Zetta pulled an exaggerated sad face. "You try your best for your kids…"

I launched myself at her, and she vanished. When I twisted back, she reappeared in Batman at his most dark and unrelenting.

"Don't you like to play at superheroes? Why won't you use your powers to rid this city of its filth?" Then she giggled, and boy, if I thought that I'd heard creepy things in this house before, it had nothing on *Batman giggling*.

"You're more of a masked vigilante," Moon called down as he swung in the chains.

"A playboy with issues…?" Emperor suggested.

Amadeus winked. "I'd have gone with *deluded detective*, but look at the muscles on him…"

Zetta spun furiously away from them, shrinking down into a tousled haired teenager in robes who adjusted his glasses. Harry Potter slunk towards me with the sexiness of a lap dancer.

I pointed at him, whilst I backed away. "Now I know you're screwing with me."

"Hermione, language," Harry chided, curling his tongue wickedly. Self-consciously, I patted at my frizzy hair, trying to make it lie straight in the way that it never would. "Come on, you *love* mages. You have that suckable Draco substitute all lined up for your bed. Whatever will Ron think? Or is screwing a bad Slytherin why you've chosen Aquilo? The thrill of the taboo?"

"Trust me, Aquilo isn't bad, and enough of the Slytherin bashing. Plus, you're the one wearing the skin of the humans' belief in the *good* mage."

Harry Potter covered his face with his hands and burst into sobs. "How could I've been so wrong, prejudiced, fill in your own boring blank?" He peeked up through his — *crocodile* — tears, and I crossed my arms. "It's almost like witches haven't been waging war with mages for centuries or being attacked by wolves."

I snorted. "When were you attacked by a wolf?"

Harry's robes bled into a scarlet hood, whilst a wicker basket now swung over a slender arm. I gaped at the asshole LLRH, as she slyly studied me back.

Yep, Zetta was going there…

"Let's get serious for a moment." LRRH swished her dress from side-to-side. "Red's my color, right?"

I turned my back on her, testing the chains that were holding my wolves again. "You had your chance. My *wolves* and me are breaking out."

"Don't hate on the Hood. You know why…?" A gust of honeysuckle scented air tumbled me across a stack of paddles that clattered beneath me. Zetta who was back wearing mom's skin glared down at me. "Because one day, the Hood will hate you back."

Except, this wasn't the mom of my childhood memories who'd fussed about the paint on my hands, taken me to play with Aquilo and Lux, or hugged me during thunderstorms. This was the terrifying warrior who I remembered from the mural in the House of Blood, who'd decimated the shifters in battle.

I hadn't wanted to know that this version of mom had been real. Yet hadn't I asked for the *truth*?

"Why are you fighting us?" I whispered.

Zetta's lips curled, whilst her eyes raged. "Why aren't you avenging *me*?"

My throat was too tight to swallow. I ducked my head, unable to meet her gaze.

Why in the witching-heavens couldn't she understand that I was desperate to avenge my parents? But I'd also learned since Claiming my Charms that there were other things, which were even more important.

When Zetta's hand hovered close to my cheek, for the first time, I craved its touch like she truly was mom, even though I *knew* that she wasn't.

Then she crooned into my ear, "Wolfie, wolfie, why do you run? Wolfie, wolfie, why do you hide? Wolfie, wolfie, why do you cry? *Because of the crimson the girl holds inside...*"

My stomach clenched, and I clutched my hand over my mouth.

That was mom's nursery rhyme.

Mom had touched my cheek, just like Zetta had tried to, and lulled me to sleep with that song every night. The rhyme had made me feel safe because I'd thought that mom had invented it just for me to keep away the wolves.

As the true horrifying meaning of the song crawled through me, I wished that I could believe nursery rhymes were nonsense and not based on truth.

Only, they were, right?

It was kind of weird to know that even as a kid, I was being trained to hunt and hurt wolves. Did the wolves sing the same thing to their kids, only their version was to teach them to *fear* Wolf Charmers?

Zetta's eyes sparkled cruelly. "Your aunt's not talented enough to cut the grade as a Charmer, so let her forgive your disgrace and live with your unworthiness if she likes. But I speak with one voice for the Wolf Charmers who've lived in the House of Silver. And they're *pissed.*"

Okami unwound from my neck, diving at Zetta and biting at thin air like he could tear her in two.

"Mom wouldn't kill me," I insisted, wishing that my lip wasn't trembling.

Maybe if I repeated it, I'd even convince myself.

"My favorite: a round of Mum Wouldn't." When Zetta pointed at the cage it was spotlighted like on a stage.

I gasped, dropping to my knees next to the bars.

The Ambassador was leashed, muzzled, and naked inside. His pale skin was purpled with welts and seared burns. I struggled to undo the door with shaking hands, whilst I was flooded with hot and cold at the same time.

"I'm done, Zetta. Your spook ass is dead." I rattled

the bars, but the Ambassador didn't raise his head.

"He's not here; it's a Wolf Charmer memory." Amadeus' voice was low and dangerous. The shock broke through my distress. "And she'll be dead on my fangs first."

"Why?" Zetta pressed her hand to her check in mock horror. "That was round one of Mum Wouldn't." When the Ambassador's image faded, I wished that I could've comforted him, even though it'd happened over a decade before. I shuddered at the thought of living in this house and not knowing the truth of what was happening. "How about upping the stakes? Great-Grandmother Wouldn't...? Because that's such a fun game to play in mixed witch and wolf company. Shall we see if we can all remain kissing friends afterward?"

"Nay, don't." Moon's panic startled me. I glanced over my shoulder, catching his eye. His curls fell into his eyes, as he shook his head. "You can't mean to show her like this. Crimson, it won't make you feel any better to know the truth in this way. You're not the same as your ancestors, just like *we're* not."

"Too late," Zetta singsonged.

Then the walls of the cellar fell away and my great-grandmother's memory exploded.

I spun around, unable even to speak.

The memory felt just as real as the Ambassador had done. But this time, I'd been dropped in the middle of a battleground or hell.

CHAPTER 10

I stepped alone into the middle of a war. Only, there was no rattle of gunfire, boom of explosions, or thunder of tanks. Instead, there was an eerie red that swallowed the world like it'd been transformed to Mars, which consumed even the sky. My own red cocooned itself around me, as if it could protect me from the crimson shadows in this past memory that washed over the ancient woods and the banks of the Thames.

Huh, that was what it was like to know that you'd only been a kid playing with your powers because these shadows that stormed with fury were my crimson shadows at their most terrifying.

They were the crimson tide and boy, were they *not* being controlled.

I paled, pressing the heels of my hands against my eyes like that would end the horror of the scene, but when I pulled my hands away again, nothing had changed: my great-grandmother was still alone on the hill beside the Thames, decimating the werewolves.

Shadows blustered in waves from my great-grandmother, whose arms were raised above her head. She wore a red-and-black ball gown disturbingly like the one that Zetta had encouraged me to wear on my first trip into the Kingdom of the Wilds. She was a cold beauty, surrounded by a red whirlpool, which swept up the wolves — Alphas, Betas, and Omegas.

I held my breath, clutching my arms around myself, as a sudden cold raised the hairs on the back of my neck. My own red wound around me in a cocoon like it could protect me from my ancestor.

What in the witching heavens would she do with the wolves now that she had them caught in her shadows?

My great-grandmother's eyes glinted cold silver, as she made the wolves spin through the air, like I'd once forced my cousin's mouse to dance.

Okay, now I got why my uncle had been so mad.

Animals and wolves weren't there for me to play with and *this* was where that thinking led: a Wolf Charmer dashing wolf after pretty wolf into the river and holding them under the water.

I cried out, whilst I stumbled to my knees.

I'd wanted to know the truth about my *legendary* great-grandmother. Now I knew. It turned out that what made her legendary in the witch world, and feared in the wolf, was genocide.

And I'd felt guilty about being the type of witch who'd Claim a werewolf and stuff him in a wardrobe.

"Isn't she magnificent?" Zetta crowed, blowing in my ear and making me jump. When she crouched next to me, watching the massacre with a dreamy expression, I glared at her. "The Crimson Hero of the Wolf War."

I shook my head, balling mom's cape over my mouth with my fist and turning my head to avoid seeing any more death or my bitch of a *hero* ancestor.

Zetta snickered. "You didn't think that the wolves respected you because of your quirky ideas and can-do attitude?" She examined my flushed neck, before snickering. "Oh, you did. Now that's what I call truly tragic. This...?" She waved her hand at my great-grandmother drowning my Charms' relatives like the Pied Piper had the rats of Hamlin. "Well, it's the witches' triumph in the final battle. Your Wolf Charmer line won them the war. Without the crimson shadows, who knows how long it would've dragged on. You wouldn't have wanted more witches to have died, surely?"

I shuddered. Why had I been haunted by nightmares of drowning, when the wolves were the ones to have suffered it?

Or had my shadows always held the guilt deep inside me...?

It wasn't me...not me...not me...

I curled into a ball, as if I could escape even my shadows, which trembled, distressed at my rejection. They pressed closer around me, stroking.

I didn't want to be touched, even though I knew that none of this was my fault or even my shadows' because they were *mine* and not the raging predators that had darkened this entire land to red. I could sense the hatred oozing from my great-grandmother's shadows: they were vindictive, bullying, and merciless.

Or as I called them: Dick Shadows.

My crimson, on the other hand, loved my Charms. They soothed, caressed, and brought them pleasure. Even though they vibrated with the need to control, they equally sang to *protect*.

I shoved myself to my feet, straightening my shoulders. Enough with the memory trip horror show. I *wasn't* this beautiful but terrifying ancestor. I was Crimson: a witch who'd been raised in America amongst the non-magical, who could mix a killer cocktail, run an epic art gallery, and love a pack of rebels.

But I couldn't murder wolves.

Weirdly, I didn't feel like I was missing out.

"Witches one. Wolves zero. I've got the score." I glared at Zetta. "Shut off this movie."

Zetta twirled a curl around her finger. "*Aww*, it's cute that you think you can still give me orders. We haven't got to the best bit yet."

I blinked, and instantly the scene flickered like it

was on fast-forward. I choked at the bitter taste in my mouth because I recognized the memory, only I'd been part of its ceremonial re-enactment to shame the wolves.

The surviving Omegas knelt on the banks of the river. Their blond heads were bowed, and they trembled, whilst my great-grandmother walked up and down their ranks with her mouth pressed in a hard line. I'd done the same thing in the Omega Training Center, when I'd picked Moon. The other Omegas had been quivering in fright then as well.

I hadn't understood their terror at the time, but holy hell did I now.

At the prettiest Omegas, my great-grandmother would stop, yanking the shifters' chins up with her red, so that they couldn't flinch away. When she'd make her choice, the Omega would whine in terror, before they'd be dragged behind her.

How many Omegas was she choosing…?

"You should've seen the size of her harem, which she kept down in these tunnels and cellar!" Zella smirked. "Every day another candy to sample."

I dry heaved. Then I sliced my hand through Stella in a karate chop. She squawked in protest.

"My wolves aren't my harem, they're my pack," I hissed.

Zella shrugged. "You say tomato, I say…" She leaned closer. "…*Too late*. Every Charmer recreates the sacrifice that the wolves agreed to, so that the war would end. Just like you did."

Why did she have to be right? But then, my Charms had gone through with it as well. Hadn't we all played our roles?

I shivered with the sense that I was missing something because my Charms didn't appear to be the types to meekly follow orders, no matter how tough the situation.

Would I've been just like my great-grandmother, mom, or Zetta with their casual cruelty, if I'd been raised in the House of Silver? Hecate's kiss, I hoped that I could've had the same courage as Aquilo to rebel against the prejudice.

Why hadn't I understood before just how kind Aquilo must be beneath his cold mask to have resisted hating the wolves? In fact, he treated them with respect and risked his life for them. I wished that he was by my side and not stuck with his snobbish family.

At last, Zetta blew at the blood-washed scene of terrified Omegas, and the silver walls of the Discipline Cellar molded back in its place. I turned around and then recoiled from the majestic statue of my great-grandmother with shadows coiling around her, which now stood in the corner of the cellar.

Then I looked up at my Charms who were still hanging from the ceiling by their wrists. They were ashen. Emperor was panting — his chest rising and falling far too fast — whilst his eyes were glassy. I didn't think that he even saw me anymore because the terrors of his childhood had been triggered.

For me, this had been an interactive history lesson, but for my Charms who'd been tiny kids during the Wolf War, this had been their *life*.

How much of the war had they witnessed?

Had they even been kneeling beside their conquered parents: the defeated royalty?

I strode to Emperor to stroke his side, but he flinched away from me, struggling to breathe.

"Give him some space, Crimson." Moon's gaze was steely, even though his words were soft. "He was there that day. He saw…"

I nodded, jerkily. Of course the traumatized wolf needed space from the Wolf Charmer who had the same powers as the witches who'd wiped out his people. I'd known that it'd happened…kind of…but seeing it like this was a whole other thing.

I felt the horror winding through my shadows, and I knew that I could never allow a Second Wolf War to happen.

But how could I stop it?

I got now why my princes had been prepared to sacrifice themselves as Tributes, as well as why the wolves offered their Omegas still to the witches to appease them.

Yet I had to end the cycle. These wolves weren't the

original fighters in the wars. Why should they pay for them?

"My aunt didn't want me back for all those schmaltzy reasons that she fed me, right?" I swung to Zetta, who'd wound her arms around the statue's middle, resting her head on my great-grandmother's chest like they were best buddies.

That's because Zetta contained her essence…

Zetta rolled her eyes. "Sorry, do you want me to talk about *feelings* here because I don't do that. Stella always had a sickening amount of emotion in her. So, maybe she thinks that she meant her tooth rotting confessions."

I snorted. "And what do you think?"

When Zetta prowled towards me, her eyes flashed as cold as my great-grandmother's. "I *know* that a Second Wolf War is coming, and Stella believes that you can win it for us again."

My guts churned. *Jesus, if my suspicions were right…* "And you don't," I said, flatly.

Zetta's eyes narrowed. "I believe in options."

"Like stealing Mischief's magic and those powerful Gateways in his head to use as some kind of magical bomb?" I guessed.

"*Ding! Ding!* At last she gets it." Zetta winked at me, whilst the walls exploded with applause. "The glittery god's magic in Stella's creations battle against the medicated beautiful beasts. Now *that's* a gladiator contest that I'd go and see. There's more than one way to skin a wolf."

My chest tightened with guilt.

How could I've left Mischief alone here with Zetta? All the time that he'd been getting worse, it'd been because of being trapped in the house with Zetta, *who was draining him of his magic.*

Hey, Mage Care was harder even than Wolf Care. For a mage, even a witch's house was toxic.

My mouth was tight, as my red snapped at Zetta like it could tear her apart. "Your spook ass was never created for my special protection, right? Stella placed you here to spy on me."

"Wait, don't forget I also manipulate you." Zetta screwed her face up, bawling her fists like a baby. "*Boo hoo, the mean old wolves killed my mommy. Boo hoo, whatever should I do?*"

"I'm not crying now," I hissed.

"The line of Wolf Charmers don't cry," my great-grandmother's voice wound from the statue, as savage and smoky as the shadows that coiled around her. I leaned protectively closer to my Charms, slipping my own crimson around them. "We charm the wolves and control the crimson tide. Are you not honored, girl?" The statues' eyes flashed silver. "*Wolfie, wolfie, why do you run? Wolfie, wolfie, why do you hide? Wolfie, wolfie, why do you cry? Because of the crimson the girl holds inside.*"

My gaze darted between my shaking wolves and the statue of my great-grandmother who was staring down at me in splendor.

Was this the part where I swore some kind of Charmer allegiance with a weird ritual and some seriously messed-up wolf flaying?

I didn't think so.

Zetta grinned. "Silenced for once. It's a miracle!" Her eyes shone with triumph. "This is your moment. Choose the House of Silver. Talk to your great-grandmother; don't be rude now."

I carefully raised my gaze to the statue's pitiless glare. Her lips curled.

I turned my back on her, listening to her howl of outrage. Coolly, I replied, "I don't talk to psycho war criminal *dicks*. I choose my pack."

Boy, that was satisfying.

Zetta gasped, before she flew around me at a dizzying speed. "Remember the options? I choose...to *kill* your pack."

Okay, maybe not satisfying enough to be worth dying for.

Suddenly, the walls and ceiling began to melt. Silver dripped like glimmering waterfalls. My Charms wailed and writhed in their chains, as droplets fell onto their shoulders, before trailing like tear tracks down their chests.

"Son of a bitch..." I snarled.

"Mum of one, actually," Zetta snickered. "This is your choice. I blame the Land of the Free and the non-magicals' obsession with equality, I truly do. A Wolf Charmer who won't control wolves is as ridiculous as your belief that these hot Charms won't kill." I clung onto Moon, working my shadows into the mechanism of the shackles, whilst he whined in pain. Zetta chuckled. "They're all *Jokers* plotting to watch you burn, but you're too soft to let me burn them for you."

A drop of silver sizzled onto Emperor's throat, and he groaned. When I glanced over, he shook his head. My Alpha prince would never allow me to help him before the Omegas that he'd sworn to protect.

"Amadeus first," Moon gasped.

"Keep quiet you," Amadeus whimpered, whilst silver licked down his wrists. "I can't spoil your track record of being the rescued one."

I couldn't help the smile. It looked like these Omegas and Betas protected each other the same as any Alpha.

"Hey, I'm rescuing all of you," I panted, wrapping my arms around Moon so that my shadows could work even more closely against the magic restraints.

My Charms' agony wracked through me as well, connecting us together. I could feel Moon's heart thudding in his chest; the quivering of his muscles against the strain, and his magic that coiled through me.

At last, the shackles opened with a *click*, and Moon

collapsed into my arms. His head rested on my shoulder just for a moment, and I ran my hand through his curls, wishing that I could allow him to nuzzle there and know that unlike the wolves in the vision, he wasn't drowned in the river or a kneeling Omega at the mercy of my great-grandmother.

Instead, I turned to Amadeus, thrusting my crimson into his restraints with even more force, whilst Moon wrapped himself around Amadeus' waist in comfort. The silver had seared Amadeus' shoulders, and he trembled at each new drop from the roof. When the shackles snapped open, Amadeus was caught by Moon and me.

I wrapped them both in my arms, floating on the joy of their touch and safety. Twisting to Emperor, who was struggling not to cry out but jerking at each burn, I threw my shadows with even greater strength at his chains, whilst my other Charms clutched him.

Zetta swaggered behind Emperor. Her eyes gleamed dangerously. "So close and yet…" She pointed up at the dripping ceiling, which frothed and foamed into a seething sea. "What happens when the tide comes in? Oh yes, it washes away the wicked wolves."

When she smiled, I knew that she meant to crash down the waves onto my Charms and drown them in silver.

CHAPTER 11

Trapped beneath the silver sea of the ceiling in the Discipline Cellar, I stared wildly, as it bulged above Zetta's head, then birthed a gilded angel whose wings beat with furious magic.

Holy hell, it was *Mischief* in truly godly form who hovered above Zetta. I realized that I'd never seen him acting the archduke before and sparking with righteous rage.

It was scorching-hot.

Yet why had he held back when we'd been fighting? And how much was it costing him to rescue us now? Unless, you know, he had more of a plan than to fright Zetta into letting us go?

My crimson wrenched at the shackles around Emperor, battling against the dark magic that bound him and hissing at its sting. Emperor twisted in his chains to dodge the dripping silver, whilst Amadeus and Moon snatched up paddles to hold over his shoulders and protect him.

Yep, I didn't miss the irony of their using the items that had once hurt wolves to protect a wolf prince.

Mischief landed in front of Zetta, whilst his wings remained outstretched and crackling. He spun disks between his hands, and I knew what it was like to have those hurled at me.

I'd expected Zetta to transform her loser ass into Dracula or Einstein, before pouting whether she still looked *fabulous*.

Instead, she recoiled, clutching her throat in a gesture that was so my *mom* in panic mode — like when I'd been a kid and I'd slipped on a branch in the ancient oak and almost fallen, or when I'd dropped an entire bottle of paint down my party dress — that my breath caught.

She wasn't mom. But she sure as witching hell looked like her.

My shadows gave a final yank, and the shackles around Emperor came free. Emperor groaned and dropped forwards, but Moon caught him. I hadn't seen Moon offer Emperor help before and I thought that Emperor would reject it by the way that he squirmed.

"Let me support your daft behind for once." Moon's smile was soft.

Emperor nodded, leaning into Moon's hold.

Amadeus' hand clasped mine. I wished that I could feel his skin, which was trapped beneath his gloves.

"You shouldn't be here." Zetta pointed a shaky finger at Mischief. "You, my glittery little god, should be dead."

Mischief's eyes flashed. "Why, I make an astoundingly sprightly zombie, do I not?" He twisted, flinging his disks at the statue of my great-grandmother.

Zetta screeched, stomping her feet, as the statue split down its middle with a deafening — *crack*.

Hey, so that's how legends were cut down to size or in this case, shattered to pieces, which were now bleeding.

Okay, *yuck*.

Zetta howled, "On the House of Silver and crimson tide, you'll die for that."

Mischief turned back to Zetta, prowling towards her. "Threats, why how original. Pray, did you think that it'd be easy to kill a god? I rather think you did." He raised an imperious eyebrow, studying Zetta like she was an interesting specimen. Then he moved so close that their noses would've been touching if Zetta hadn't been ghostly; his gaze darkened. "Senseless creature, did you not perceive that if you drain me of my magic, then it's stored within you, and I may drain it back?"

Zetta wailed, but before she could escape, Mischief thrust his hands into her guts. To my shock, she flickered like he was seriously touching her and holding her in place.

Amadeus's fingers tightened in mine, as Mischief's magic wound around Zetta, dragging his own power out of her. It burst like an imploding star out of her body, dragging her onto tiptoes, as she screamed. Mischief's face lit up in glory and triumph; his magic flooded back to him, wrenched free from its false vessel.

I laughed, flooded with joy that Mischief was safe from fading...*dying*...and that he'd been released from the prison of this house and Zetta.

I'd thought Mischief the prettiest man that I'd ever seen, when I'd first been attacked by him in this cellar a week ago. But now he had his magic back, he was more gorgeous than any guy had a right to be.

But then, he was an angel, right?

Zetta's pained gaze slipped to mine, and she raised her hand like I'd save her. I bit my tongue because this was the *entity* that would've killed my wolves and me. It was my past, Wolf Charmer legacy, and everything that I hated about the treatment of the wolves.

It wasn't mom, and I wouldn't be manipulated anymore.

My gaze hardened, and I nodded to Mischief.

Mischief's graceful hands slid up through Zetta to her head, which burst with a silver light. I squinted through the brightness.

Zetta screamed.

Then the House of Silver came tumbling down.

DAZED, I BLINKED MY EYES OPEN TO DARKNESS.

Then I coughed against the stone dust, scrabbling to free myself from the fallen masonry and roof beams. My head ached, and blood dribbled down my neck.

Frogs' toes, Mischief taking back his magic had pulled down the entire House of Silver that had been my family's home — the *Wolf Charmer's* home — for over four hundred years.

Despite losing my family, inheritance, and home, I hadn't felt this free since arriving back in England. Okay, apart from being trapped beneath the fallen rubble. Sometimes, it took destruction to create something new like in my art, go figure.

I wet my dry lips, before calling, "Hey, Charmer underground here."

Had my guys been hurt when the house collapsed?

When my breath came in too fast pants and my panic mounted, I wrapped myself in my soothing shadows.

My guys were okay... They had to be okay...

A chink of sky winked encouragingly down at me through the gloom. I edged my fingers around the beam above with my head, whilst my fingernails ripped, trying to wrench it aside. My red seethed at the confinement.

Suddenly, the beam was hauled away from above. I blinked against the light at the elegant hand that was being held out to me, before grasping it.

Then Ramiel was gently pulling me out of the rubble and swinging me into his arms. He wrapped his wings around me, and I gasped, as he tenderly held me. I breathed in his nutmeg scent and it meant safety...this, in the arms of an angel, was home.

"Are you hurt?" Ramiel asked, softly.

I shook my head.

"I believed that you wished no more stiff upper lip nonsense?" He licked up the trail of blood, which wound down my neck, delicately kissing over the graze.

I smiled. "Consider my lip limp."

Snuggling around in his wings, I glanced over the destruction. The House of Silver was in ruins. The smashed chandelier rested on top of it, whilst beams poked out like broken ribs. My brow furrowed: why was it glittering? Then I realized that it was the ruby floor of the ballroom.

It should've hurt me. Weirdly, it didn't. No matter how hard I'd tried, the House of Silver had never become my home again, only my pack's prison.

Emperor cradled Amadeus who had a bump on his head that matched my own. Moon was digging through the remains, chucking wood and cracked paintings over his shoulder.

Okami shoved his nose out of my pocket, before sneezing on the dust and burrowing back down again.

But where was Mischief?

My stomach twisted, as my eyes widened. Mischief had saved us all from Zetta, and I couldn't believe that the fates were cruel enough to allow him to die for it. Although, if those fates had been woven by Stella…

I struggled out of Ramiel's arms, diving onto the ruins. "Mischief…"

My guys leapt onto the wreckage with me, tossing stones aside, as well as rich fabrics. I shuddered at the sight of the wardrobe from my parents' bedroom cracked open to show its insides. My shadows washed across the craters, until it was reddened to an alien moon, trying to feel him out.

Where was he?

I bit back a sob. Mischief was a royal prick but he was *my* royal prick.

When the chandelier shook, I stumbled backwards, gashing my thigh on the fangs of a stone gargoyle. I hissed but never looked away from the chandelier.

Please, please, please…

Mischief burst out from the rubble, twirling into the evening sky with crackling wings, glorious and awe-inspiring. This was the dark splendor of Moon's god.

Mischief's magic erupted from him in a rainbow arc, whilst Moon's exploded up to meet his in a firework cascade above our heads. They were joined in a display of power; werewolves could never be simply beasts when they were descended from angelic gods.

Maybe my whistle wasn't honestly appropriate, but hey, Mischief made my heart pound. "Dude, that was freaking hot! Do you have a second for us mere mortals?"

Mischief sniffed, attempting to hide the way that the corners of his mouth twitched. His magic and Moon's faded, leaving behind it a glimmering trail. Moon quivered, shocked and joyous. Then Mischief swooped down to land next to Ramiel, who swept his wingtip down Mischief's cheek in greeting.

"At last you perceive my superior status, witch." Mischief clasped his hands smartly behind his back.

"Don't push it," I muttered.

Suddenly, Moon's eyes widened, and he dropped to his knees.

"Moth, moth, moth," Moon whispered, wiping a grimy hand down his thigh in agitation. He stared out over the destruction. "Where's my brother?"

My crimson whipped around in agitation, seeking Moth in the same way that it'd earlier sought Mischief.

"Whilst you were hanging around," Mischief rolled his eyes, "Ramiel and I were saving your brother." He waved airily towards the woods. "Oh, and stowing him a safe distance from the fight against his wishes. Feisty, isn't he?"

When I peered at the woods, which were tinged with

the first beams of the full moon, a small figure dashed towards us with bouncing blond curls and large eyes: *Moth*.

"*Brother*." Moon caught Moth in his arms, spinning him around.

Moth clasped his hand to the back of Moon's head like he was terrified that Moon would still drop dead from the injection if he let go. I didn't figure on my guilt in the Wolf Tamer affair going away soon. If Moth was like a regular teenager, he'd have already milked it for Netflix on tap and no curfew.

Huh, I guess an Omega prince from the Training Center hadn't ever watched Netflix and now didn't even have a home for the whole curfew thing.

I still reckoned that he'd milk the whole *pumping his brother with poison*, but after what he must've suffered being on his own and not knowing whether his brother was alive or not, he was owed that.

Who needed discipline anyway?

Mischief nuzzled his cheek into Ramiel's hand who purred. "Are we done with the mawkishness? That deplorable creature who was stealing my magic had hidden the cub in the attic like a damsel in a romance novel."

Moth ripped out of his brother's hold, baring his...*adorable*...fangs at Mischief.

Mischief sauntered to Moth, patting him on the head

with a level of condescension that made me wince. "Does the cub wish to thank his god now?"

If Mischief hadn't winked at me, I'd have thought he meant it.

"Chill out, Mini Moon. I can thank him for you." I grinned wickedly at Mischief.

Mischief took a step backwards. "What do you...?"

I stumbled on my gashed leg, drawing in a hissed breath. At least that gargoyle had taken his revenge on the Wolf Charmer line. Although with the way that the wound was stinging like a witch, I was considering taking back my non-discipline policy on all wolves.

"Have you forgotten the supposed limpness of your lip already?" Ramiel dove to my side, catching me in his wings.

I squirmed. "If my leg doesn't fall off, we'll count it as a win."

Ramiel's eyes narrowed.

Nope, I didn't like that look at all. I'd seen it just before Ramiel's hand had got all smacky on Mischief's ass.

Mischief snickered. "I advise allowing Ramiel to act out his mothering because he won't be happy until he's smothered you in love and attention. Sickening, isn't it?"

I poked my tongue out at him. Yep, it wasn't mature, but since I couldn't hug Mischief with as much fierce-ness as Moth had his brother because he was *alive* and safe from that dick Zetta, which is what I suspected he wanted to do with me as well beneath the shovel load of snark, it was the next best thing for both of us.

Emperor chuckled, stretching out on the lawns with Amadeus like they were any other romantic couple preparing to stargaze. Moon embraced his brother, snuggling onto Emperor's other shoulder. Emperor raised his eyebrow, but then smiled like everything had finally settled back to how it should always have been.

"Come on, you love all the smothering, right?" I countered.

Mischief blushed. "Silence your tongue. And no more than you do."

I grinned. "Well, *duh*."

When Ramiel crouched in front of me, touching over the wound with nimble fingers, I couldn't resist stroking through his soft hair. He peeked at me shyly through his bangs, and boy was it lucky that angels couldn't read minds because with him kneeling in front of me like that, I shuddered with the memory of how Amadeus' talented tongue had felt circling and licking between my thighs. When I flushed, so did Ramiel.

Wait, angels couldn't read minds, right...?

Amadeus giggled. "You're making our Charmer all hot and bothered. Either show her that an angel's kiss can take her to heaven faster than an incubus', or..." He tilted his head. "If it pleases there isn't an *or*...I love the sound of the first option too much."

Ramiel almost fell over his own wing in his haste to stand up. "I only meant to tend to you. I wouldn't ask more of my savior, when you've lost so much today."

When I looked at him sharply, he averted his gaze. Why did he always see me so clearly? I didn't doubt Mischief that Ramiel had been one of the cleverest angels.

My red slipped back inside me, coiling around me protectively.

Ramiel ripped off the bottom of his indigo harem pants, revealing his creamy calf in a move that was more sensuous for its care and innocence than Amadeus' at his most sexy. Then he bent over to tie it around the cut on my leg, although he was careful not to kneel again, and I was torn about whether I missed it. Then Ramiel led me to the lawns, helping me to lie down next to Amadeus, whilst I grimaced in pain.

Before Mischief could make a run for it, Ramiel swooped on him, entrapping him in his wings.

"*Sickening*, is it?" Ramiel's voice was hard.

Mischief pouted. "Why the cross face? Chocolate is sickening, and I'm quite the fan of that."

"Then I surely won't deprive you." Ramiel's eyes twinkled.

Mischief let out an outraged howl, as Ramiel rolled him onto the lawn and pinned him, feathering kisses over his cheeks, nose, and forehead.

Finally, Mischief melted underneath him with a muttered, "the indignity."

When Moth giggled, the rest of my pack snickered. Mischief might've just used up his godly credentials.

Emperor caught my eye, before nodding back at the wreckage that'd once been my home. "Well, that was all highly bracing."

I shuddered. My pack were hugging and collapsed on the lawns: safe….*for now.*

Yet Zetta had tried to murder us all.

My hands shook in shock. We'd almost been buried alive. What would we do, since nowhere was safe? How on earth could we survive?

CHAPTER 12

I hunched my shoulders, staring blankly back at where the House of Silver had once stood and the terrible visions from the past that Zetta had shown me. Now, there was only rubble with the bones of beams and floorboards jutting out. I glowered at mangled remains of the metal cage from the Discipline Cellar.

Holy hell, my Charms had witnessed the atrocities committed by my ancestors. How could they be lying here with me snuggled on the lawns? How could Amadeus be running his gloved hand up and down with teasing touches between my tits, until I thought that I'd growl at him just to caress my aching nubs, for the sake of Hecate?

"I'm not the same as them," I said in a small voice. "I'm not my great-grandmother or my mom."

I could sense that my guys had stilled but I didn't dare look over at them.

"Oh, but you are, witch girl." Mischief's sharp response shocked me into peeking at him. Mischief leaned up on his elbow, examining me intently. "Here's an idea: change what you are, rather than lying to yourself about what you're not. You shall always be a Wolf Charmer with the same fearsome power as your ancestors and the urge to abuse it. I've seen the struggle not to enjoy such control before."

I narrowed my eyes. "Archduke Asshole, I'm more into painting, donuts, and Amadeus' ass...not necessarily in that order...than abusing my crimson shadows."

"I do have a sexy behind." Amadeus wiggled his ass against my hip, and I shivered.

"Seconded," Emperor agreed.

"Do you need a third?" Moon called.

Mischief's eyes sparked. "Witless girl, the Glories of our world revel in dark amusements: pleasure and pain."

Cold flooded me. "I'm not like that."

"They desire to be the one collaring their lovers, whilst holding the leash and making those who have no choice but to follow them, crawl at their heels."

I reddened. Okay, put like that, I looked like a dick.

After all, my Charms were lying next to me on the

grass in their collars, and I didn't want to analyze the happy little daydream that Mischief's words had conjured that involved them naked and crawling…

"And there it is," Mischief said, softly.

I jolted. Fun negotiated roleplay in my daydreams aside, I never wanted my guys to either be leashed or crawl. I'd hated seeing them chained or muzzled. If I could break them free of their collars without poisoning them, then I'd do it right now.

Yet I couldn't deny that the Wolf Charmer power was inside me; without it, I'd never have been open to any of the covens' teachings. I pulled mom's cape more closely around myself, stroking my fingers through its velvety softness.

Mischief's expression gentled. "You see now? Your choice is whether to follow in the cruel footsteps of the House of Silver or to start afresh a new legacy."

A new legacy? One that could be built on Crimson Tide, rather than the House of Silver…?

"Who's ready for Crimson's pack?" I grinned.

Amadeus whooped, whilst Emperor and Moon howled in unison in a way that made my skin tingle.

I grinned, scrunching the cape tighter between my fingers. Then I frowned.

Zetta had made sure that I had mom's cape. Had she used it all this time to manipulate me by reminding me of my parents' deaths, as well as moms' shadow?

Furious, I pulled away from Amadeus, wrenching the cape off my shoulders.

During the werewolf attack and massacre, it had come to mean safety, but that was the lie. It meant a mom who I'd never truly known, a past that I didn't want to weigh me down, and a woman who I didn't want to become.

I leapt up, hurling the cape onto the rest of my old life that was I leaving behind. It landed on the rubble like a tear of blood.

Mischief pushed himself to his knees and inclined his head. "I shall admit that I was wrong to think you just another Glory. I'd be honored to be considered amongst your pack."

I took a steadying breath. "When were you going to spill that you're returning to the Realm of the Seraphim?" Ramiel let out a cry, clutching Mischief's shoulders like he couldn't leave if he only held onto him tight enough. Mischief ducked his head, whilst his wings drooped. "Those Gateways of yours are in your head again now, right? So, if that's how Zetta or the covens dragged you here, then that'd mean you could hike a ride back that way."

Mischief leveled me with a glare. "What a charming way to inform me that you've grown weary of my company. Would you also like to tell me not to let your witchy boot hit my angelic behind on the way out?"

I huffed. "You know that I want you to stay."

Mischief tapped his chin. "Do I? Why, thank you for informing me of what's inside my own head. Considering you're yet to inform me of that fact, I must be quite the psychic genius."

"Enough of that." Moon crawled across the tangle of wolves and angels to cradle Mischief, licking down his neck. Mischief arched into Moon's caresses. "Your godly behind is wanted and loved. Wasn't my dying a sufficient sacrifice to prove it?"

Mischief crumpled under Moon's scrutiny, offering a weak smile. "Quite sufficient."

Moon rubbed his nose against Mischief's. "Crimson's trying to say in her typical witchy way...or it could be American...I'm never sure..."

"Hey," I protested, "no ganging up against the American witch."

Moon shrugged. "Fur and fangs, what she means is: are you leaving us?"

Mischief squared his shoulders. "The Realm of the Seraphim is far from an easy land to reach without blood and...let's just say that without someone truly special to add into my own magic, I don't know whether it's possible for me to return." He gazed at me from underneath his eyelashes. "I apologize if you'd prefer me to lie but I ache for the family who I left behind and love." He closed his eyes and took a ragged breath. "I love them with such crushing intensity that it was only Ramiel's persistence that saved my life. I thought that my weakness and fading was perhaps from the loss of my lovers."

I fought back the growl in my throat, even if Amadeus hadn't managed to restrain his.

Mischief felt like *mine*, the same as my Charms and Addict angel. I'd found him in the Discipline Cellar on my first day in the House of Silver. He'd been part of this pack from the start.

Yet he wasn't because he already had a family.

"It's okay," I choked out, "I get it. You told me about them upfront, and how…whatever your lover's called…would never let you love a witch."

Mischief opened his eyes, before arching his brow. "Firstly, I believe that she would make an exception for you. You're choosing to make your own legacy, remember? And secondly, are you the psychic one now? Even were I able to return with a click of ruby slippers to the Realm of the Seraphim, I wouldn't go. Do you perceive why?"

I gaped at him. "Because Dorothy won't lend you the slippers, the dick?"

Mischief attempted a smile, but there was a sudden sadness and grief that shocked me, before he masked it. "Because I'm the Moon God and the shifters are my people. I've never hidden from my duty before and no matter the cost, I shan't now. Although the three king-

doms act like oafish infants fighting between themselves, rather than protecting each other from the enemy
who attacks them from without, I still must save them
from their own idiocy."

"That was rousing." Emperor flicked masonry off
his robes, feigning a yawn. "I hope my own battle
speeches as a prince are as inspiring."

Mischief's lips curled. "You can always hope."

"And you didn't wish to leave me." Ramiel shuffled
on his knees next to Mischief with a smile that was
painful in its pleading.

"And it would *destroy* me to ever leave you,"
Mischief murmured.

"I don't want to be the buzzkill who brings down the
romantic moment," Amadeus slunk to his feet, before
slipping his fingers under my chin and tilting my head
towards the woods, "but there are Fallen watching us."

"Dual?" Impatient, I stared out at the shadows flit-
ting between the trees, craning to catch a glimpse of the
vampire duke, whilst my stomach fluttered at the
thought.

Was it my fault that his punk ass was so divinely
hot? What would Dual's tongue piercing have felt like if
he'd done the same tricks as Amadeus…?

I caught myself, shaking my head. Dual was a
vampire duke and my enemy, wasn't he? The last time
that he'd been in this garden, Moon and I had humiliated him. Moon had the magical ability to mind control

both vampires and angels, although he hated to use it, as much as I was learning to hate the control of my crimson powers unless that control had been willingly gifted to me.

Dual would be less likely to kiss between my legs and more likely to sink his fangs into my neck.

Although, he'd been kind of offended when I'd asked him about the blood drinking last time and told me that he'd only taken from willing Blood Lovers in a way that'd made it sound dangerously sexy.

But then, vampires *were* dangerous, right?

Moon's mouth tightened. "By my hide, they're vultures circling at the destruction of the wards."

"Or they know something even greater is being destroyed tonight..." Emperor's gaze shot to mine.

The full moon was climbing into the sky; it hung like a death mask above the spears of the trees.

Moon prowled towards the wood. "Away with you! Didn't your duke tell you? I can control your daft behinds."

The vampires scattered, disappearing back into the wood. Wow, that was either reassuring or seriously terrifying.

I petted Amadeus, kissing down his neck, whilst he sighed. Then I smirked. "Aw, look at you, the Vampire Whisperer. Powerful Enough to Make a Vampire Piss His Pants; we should make it into your slogan."

Moon thrust out his chest, and boy, in his all-leather

outfit that was enough to make him the Charmer Whisperer as well. "Are you mocking me, madam?"

"*Duh*, you should know that I'm always mocking you, my Big Bad Omega. I'm also *praising* you because the Moon Child is badass."

Moon hooked his thumbs into his belt loops, catching my eye with a radiant smile. My breath stuttered at the pride that I'd caused by a single compliment, and I craved to make him smile like that again as often as possible.

"I'm afraid that although we've defeated Zetta and the vampires, we're perhaps too late to stop the war." Ramiel's gaze darted between Mischief and me. "I never halted my research into the mage boy's killing. It vexed me why the witches had set this particular full moon as the night that they'd spark war once again with the wolves, until I discovered—"

"*The Treaty*." Emperor launched himself up, gripping my elbow with an urgency that frightened me. "It's one hundred years since the Wolf Wars. This is the month that saw our defeat and the full moon that marks it. The quaint ritual to which we were bound is for all wolves who reside within Wolf Kingdom to be caged tonight as penance, even Alphas and royalty."

Chills made the hairs on my neck rise. Jesus, why had I had been raised with so little knowledge of my own world? I knew that my uncle had been trying to protect me, but you couldn't hide from these truths.

Had my aunt been planning this second war for years, simply waiting for the centennial, my own blossoming into my powers and this night, when the shifters would be at their most vulnerable?

Everything else had been a pretext.

And Stella had accused the wolves of being the *princes at diplomacy*. Yet *she* was the one who played games to hide the ways that she moved people around the board like pawns.

Amadeus' eyes glittered with fear. "My people…my kingdom…"

Emperor straightened his robes. "Mine too."

"Can I throw my hat into the kingdom ring?" Moon strode to join my circle of Charms.

I glanced between their determined faces. The Oxford covens were directly threatening Wolf Kingdom. My Charms would show that it didn't matter if they'd been sacrificed to a witch, they were still princes.

I shuddered at the thought that everything came back to Stella. From the moment that I'd stepped off the plane from America, I'd allowed myself to be led on the path that she'd set out, even when I'd tried to rebel. Trust me, it was hard to fight a witch who both saw fate and wove it. Yet Stella could only catch glimpses of what would come, and I wouldn't let her guide me anymore.

I might've been twenty-one when I'd arrived in England, but I'd still been a kid in this supernatural world. I'd taken wolf Tributes, become distracted by threats and a murder investigation that had only been set up as a justification for war and to convince me to fight by the House of Season's side. I'd done all that and trained my powers because I'd longed for approval and to become the Wolf Charmer that the covens wanted... that mom would've been proud of...okay, *that she could've been.*

But I wasn't a kid now. I'd never become mom and I praised the witching heavens for that.

It was time to step off Stella's path and forge my own one.

"Surely the witches would not be so dishonorable as to attack, before they even declare peace at an end?" Ramiel blanched. "If they were to launch an offensive tonight, it'd be little more than..."

"An ambush." Emperor was as pale as Ramiel.

"*Murder,*" Moon snarled.

"Stella once told me that you can't murder a wolf because to kill one is simply justice. I guess that she was setting up her defense for tonight's *justice* then." I stared at the moon, which hung deathly pale in the sky. If Stella attacked tonight, the wolves would be caged like pretty wrapped gifts for her to slaughter or inject with Wolf Tamer and subdue. *There was nobody to defend them, except me.* "Stella will be in the Justice Chamber." I glanced around at my guys who were watching me intently. "It's also a shrine like our witch's equivalent of your Goddess Moon. If she hasn't already gone to kick the wolves' asses, she'll be—"

"Oh, goodie, so we can stroll into the chamber where you're at your weakest and ensure that *our* asses take equal measure of the kicking." Mischief panted. I understood his fear of witches, knowing that they'd once held him prisoner and bound his magic. Ramiel placed a warning hand on his arm, but he shrugged it off. "Why, I ask, are you so keen on playing the martyr? Your shame, I wonder?" Moon growled. "Sorry, am I alone in hating this plan that appears little more than marching into the most powerful coven that has outwitted us at every turn? The one that has once committed genocide on the wolves and now wishes it on them again…and the same to us?"

"Hey, Sassy Dick, you're forgetting one thing," my shadows burst out in a glorious sea that lit up the night, "*I'm* the Wolf Charmer, *you're* a god, and *these* are angels and princes of the wolf kingdoms. And hey, whoever said I didn't have a plan…?"

Mischief's lips curled into a smile. "My apologies for underestimating you, witch."

I dragged my Charms closer, resting my head on the warmth of Emperor's shoulder. "Let's hope the asshole witches make the same mistake."

Tonight, the wolves would be caged to mark a hundred years since their defeat in the original Wolf War. Stella intended to break the Treaty and punish the shifters with the same poison that'd hurt Moon. If it didn't kill and subdue the shifters, it would still ignite a Second Wolf War, unless I could stop it.

Yet that meant facing Stella and risking my pack. It meant risking *everything*.

CHAPTER 13

When I burst through Stella's wards into the
Justice Chamber in the House of Seasons on a
wave of crimson, at last I felt like a witch in charge of
my own powers and fate. My pack stalked behind me —
wolves, Addicts, and mages — who by the witches'
rules should've been my enemy.

But hey, I sucked at following rules.

Plus, I wasn't simply a witch, I was the Wolf
Charmer. What was the point of being the last in a
magical line if you couldn't screw with tradition?

Stella had always had a way, however, of making me
feel less in control. Even now I stumbled, slipping on
the bronze floor because Stella hadn't even turned
around, as if I was no more than a kid storming in to
weep about the bully who'd pulled my hair. Of course,
she hadn't believed me when I'd been a real kid and had

finally found the courage to tearfully accuse the Blood twins of bullying, and trust me, Lux had done a lot more than pull my hair.

I glanced around the room that was like the inside of a cauldron with shadowy arches, checking that the platform with raised furry thrones was empty, unlike last time when I'd been judged *unworthy* by masked witches to be a Charmer and offered poison to drink. Wolf pelts hung from the walls. It was so hot that sweat prickled my skin.

The seats all around the chamber were hidden in gloom, and just for a moment, I thought that I saw something shift in the shadows. Then I blinked, and it settled. I stepped towards the movement, but at last, Stella waved her hand at me.

"What sort of manners do they teach in America? If you'd called to tell me that you were dropping by, I could've had the Ambassador prepare your favorite strawberries and Champagne." Still, Stella didn't look at me.

Mischief nodded at Ramiel, and then the angels circled around Stella, whilst my Charms and Moth moved closer to my sides.

Stella lit a black candle, balancing it on the altar in front of her with a hundred other candles, whose lights connected together like complex threads.

I paled. Huh, she hadn't been kidding about her whole *threads of fate* thing.

"Ivy smashed my phone, and I smashed mom's evil ring." I shrugged. "Sorry, I could've commanded a rat to drop by with a message. But seriously, I wouldn't want to send them somewhere that stinks as much as your coven."

When Amadeus snickered, Stella's back stiffened.

Finally, she turned around to face me. To my surprise, she looked amused. "Well, so much with the pleasantries. Truly, what sort of manners…?"

"I was making a point about corruption…you know, because I've found out your plans and…" I scuffed my boot against the floor. How did I say *you won't get away with it* without sounding like I was in a superhero movie? "I won't let you hurt the wolves."

Stella rolled her eyes. "I believe I got that, thank you. Oh, and don't worry, pretty peach. I was only playing the stern aunt before, of course I have food for you and your wicked but yummy hotties."

When she eyed Ramiel, he blushed, wrapping his wings defensively to cover his chest. When I strode towards him, yanking him by the elbow behind me, Stella laughed.

Why was she so calm? Where was her army or ranks of needles?

"So, you're the mage god who I've heard so much about." Stella's magic flared in her eyes like she craved to devour Mischief…*or his power*. "I can taste you from here. No wonder my niece wanted you all for herself."

Mischief's wings outstretched, whilst his silver crackled along them, and boy, did it taste just as scrumptious as Stella had said. I licked my lips, chasing it as surely as I knew my aunt was.

Hey, I was only human.

"I'd like to say what a pleasure it is to finally meet you." Mischief's smile was a dangerous feral thing that made me shiver. "But that would be a lie."

Stella flinched, before she forced herself to still. She laughed but it was falsely shrill. "Even gods can be taught their place, the same as wolves."

As if on cue, the Ambassador crawled through the bronze skin of the wall. He wore a white garter and panties outfit like it was his wedding night. Amadeus growled, and only Moon's hand on his chest stopped him from surging forward.

The Ambassador peeked at Amadeus, offering him a quick reassuring smile, like he wasn't the one on his knees struggling to carry a tray, which held a platter of strawberries and only one Champagne flute.

I frowned. *What was up with the mind games?*

Stella sighed as she snatched the Champagne and sipped it. "Delicious. I'm sorry, Crimson, but I don't have any such qualms about lying. You demolished four hundred years of history in the House of Silver. Don't you think that I witnessed such a major shift in the covens? You're a rogue, and they're not fed and watered, but judged and slaughtered."

Suddenly, bronze shadows snaked out of the ceiling in the coils of the Wolf Charmer Trap that could bind my powers.

I couldn't help recoiling, as the shadows wrapped around my wrists, dragging me onto tiptoe. I sucked in my breath at the sickening sensation of my crimson whipping back inside me. I'd only just had my magic returned, after Ivy had locked it away, and it hurt more than I'd expected to have it stolen so casually again.

Hey, don't flip out now...you can take this...

When I raised my chin to meet Stella's eye, I grinned because I *had* expected my powers to be stolen by the trap again. Witches had their traditions, laws, and punishments, which made them predictable. A rogue with a seriously scary but gorgeous god on her side, on the other hand, could have a few surprises up her Goth sleeve.

Mischief spun silver disks between his hands, whilst arching his brow. "My mistake, I thought that you were saying something important for a moment, then I realized that it was merely more bad guy rambling."

With a casual flick of his wrist, his silver shot out, slicing through the bronze shadows that shrieked like the cut off head of Medusa.

Emperor caught me, as I collapsed to the floor. My crimson burst from me, wild in its freedom.

Stella wailed in outrage almost as loudly as her defeated shadows, before hurling her glass at the

Ambassador. He cowered back, as the glass shattered on his head, slicing his cheek. Amadeus snarled, diving to the Ambassador and licking the trail of blood tenderly that'd dripped down like tears. The Ambassador nuzzled at his shoulder, and I wondered if he'd received any touch that had been sincerely gentle since he'd been Claimed by mom over a decade ago.

Then I remembered the way that the Ambassador had smiled at Aquilo, and Aquilo had rested his hand on his shoulder. Maybe my snooty but brave fiancé had been a secret friend to him, at least.

Jesus, I hoped so.

"A mage dares speak to me about *bad*?" Stella roared.

"I know, ironic, isn't it? Especially *me*, all things considered." Mischief hurled his magic like a lasso, and Stella squawked as it caught her around the throat, trapping her in a collar and leash. Then he shot out gleaming strands around her wrists…like hundreds of *threads*…before hauling her onto her tiptoes and suspending her from the ceiling, just like I'd been. He arched his brow. "But then, I do so appreciate irony."

Moon chuckled, although it was a dark sound that made me shiver with as much desire as Stella did with dread.

It was epic to see Stella leashed and collared, since I'd had to watch her humiliate the Ambassador and my own Charms. Amadeus pulled the Ambassador to stand next to him; the Ambassador stared at his witch captor, who was strung up and helpless, in awe.

I noticed that his head was no longer ducked or his gaze cast down. Unfortunately, so did Stella.

Stella's eyes narrowed. "I see now that I've been too soft...on all of you."

I snorted. "Unless that's British speak for *I'm a total hardass*: nope, you haven't."

Stella struggled against Mischief's magic. "Maybe you should *thank* the beasts for murdering your parents. You think that I'm a *hardass*?" Her laugh was brittle. When her gaze swung to the Ambassador, he shrank back, whilst Amadeus slipped his arms around his waist, shooting Stella a fierce glare. "Daniel was whipped almost as often as the cub for trying to protect him."

All of a sudden, I couldn't breathe.

Dad had known about the Ambassador and had tried to help him, but mom had hurt him because of that...? He'd been like Aquilo, but I'd never known...?

My knees buckled, and Moon caught me, pulling me against his chest. My eyelashes fluttered against his scratchy top, and if I kept focusing on that, then I didn't have to think how rarely I'd grieved dad, compared to mom.

Why?

Guilt settled heavy and cold in my guts because I knew the answer: because dad had been so quiet...I'd seen him so much less than mom…he hadn't made the decisions…

And because mom had been the Wolf Charmer, and dad had been under her control as much as her Charm.

Then I remembered that Stella had loved Daniel too. Did she hate me because of mom?

"You mum was brutal, ruthless, and terrified me even as a child." Stella scrutinized me. "My scheming and intelligence were never as prized as her raw power. You remind me of her."

My hands shook, as I bunched them in Moon's top.

"Silence your tongue," Mischief commanded. His expression was stony. "I'm under no delusion the damage that a mother can do. Yet I'm equally aware how hard the Charmer strives to be different."

Stella smiled like we were chatting over Champagne still. "Fabulous because so do I. My mother never recognized that cunning and intelligence could achieve as much as my sister's viciousness, but I've had long enough now to prove the winner there."

Emperor clenched his jaw. "You intend to break the Treaty tonight with the Wolf Tamer." *It wasn't a question.*

Stella sighed. "My luscious lips are sealed but…"

Suddenly, the air was filled with my moaned *ah, ah, ah*, followed by a shrieked *just like that, baby.*

My guys turned to look at me, apart from Amadeus who licked his lips with way too much smugness. I blushed so deeply that I must've matched my own shadows.

If there was a hell, then it was filled with poor bitches being forced to listen to a Greatest Hits of their own orgasms.

Okami darted out of my pocket barking in prankster delight, even though I knew that he couldn't be responsible this time. I'd insisted that he remain in my pocket, but he'd never been able to resist a joke.

Moon whispered hot against my ear, "Sounded like it was fun. How did I miss that?" When he pushed me back from his chest, smoothing my hair away from my forehead, I caught the hint of jealousy in his eyes. "I'm officially petitioning to be there next time."

Then he glowered over my shoulder at Emperor.

Emperor held up his hands. "Not guilty."

Then in the dark air between us, bronze letters curled:

Just a sexy new witch tone *wink* I miss our chats :(Ste X

Then the words popped like bubbles.

"Hey, you know what I miss?" I stormed to Stella, not knowing whether I wanted her to quail or continue with the same calmness that was driving me crazy. "Waffles with chocolate sauce. My cousins. Beaches with white sand and cocktail bars. And what I seriously wish that I missed...? Being caught in the middle of a supernatural war."

Ah, Ah, Ah…just like that, baby.

I clenched my fists, as once more, lettering curled into the air:

1 more night & u won't be! No more naughty wolves or war. SMILE! :) Ste X

"I said war not wolves," I gritted out.

Instantly, the walls of the chamber were filled with vision after vision of werewolf attacks. My stomach lurched at the dizzying speed, and behind me, Moth whimpered.

Yet I couldn't look away from the battles and massacres that'd been plucked from throughout history, before the Wolf War and the taming of the shifters. The werewolves looked more like the *beasts* in the witches' murals and how I'd painted them on the canvases that I'd sold: wild animals who tore apart whole villages of humans, whilst prowling the night.

Were any of these visions real?

I peered around at the faces of my Charms and the guys that I… Okay, I'd Wolf Bitten and Claimed them, what did it matter if I admitted in the privacy of my own mind that they were the guys that I *loved*? None of them would meet my eyes like I'd be ashamed of them, which meant that there was at least some truth in these visions.

Plus, I hadn't imagined my parents' murders.

Yet the wolves now weren't responsible for the crimes of their ancestors, just like I hadn't committed those of the past Wolf Charmers. If I could convince myself of that, then so should they.

Vampires, angels, wolves, and witches: none of us were teddy bears sprinkled in unicorn dust. Although, since Mischief could also shift into a unicorn, even they weren't sweet (although they *were* as cute as holy hell). We were all deadly, dangerous, and had as much right to the world as the non-magicals.

No injection created out of fear should be allowed to take away any of our power.

Ah, ah, ah...just like that baby.

When the bronze letters began to form again, I sliced through them with my red.

Stella blinked. "Now, there's ill-mannered, and there's simply rude."

"I don't think that you're getting it," I hissed. "I'm going to kick your ass, until I know that the wolves are safe. You're not my boss anymore."

Stella's smile was sly. "But I will be the beasts' boss. With the Wolf Tamer, I'll control their shifts and connection to the wolf part of their natures."

Moon had once demanded whether I'd had any idea how much power I had over him simply with the collar. When I'd first arrived, I hadn't had a clue but I did now.

Emperor crossed his arms. "Would you at least extend the courtesy of allowing us to choose our own deaths over extended and total slavery or would that be a kindness too far?"

"For the Prince of the Alphas," Stella's gaze flickered to the back of the chamber, "I could be merciful enough to offer death."

Ramiel's anxious gaze met mine. "Am I the only one who finds it worrisome how well she's taking her capture? Almost like she's wasting time or playing to an audience?"

"My, perhaps I judged you broken too soon, Addict." Stella's eyes flashed silver and a cage tumbled out of the ceiling, landing with a crash.

Trapped in the cage, Dual howled, landing on his ass. Then he crawled to the bars and sheepishly waved, although his eyes were just as soft and sexy as I remembered. His large gray wings were crushed inside the tiny space, and his military jacket in rainbow colors was torn.

I wished that I didn't crave to stroke his smooth ebony cheek to ease his pained wince, as he tried to shift on his knees. He wasn't one of my Charms, he was a vampire duke, even if he'd been captured by my aunt.

Is that why the vampires had been hanging around my house like a gang without their leader? *Had they been searching for their kidnapped duke?*

"Vampires have a weakness for heat." Stella grinned at Dual's flinch. "Don't make me go through all these trying threats to get you to release me because I can make that cage burn him to ash in a moment."

Dual paled but he didn't say anything. I guessed that

you didn't get to run a vampire court without serious balls. Although, since I knew almost nothing about vampires or their courts, it could take being a serious dick as well.

"I could just as easily burn *you* to ash," Mischief said, coldly.

Mischief's magic tightened around Stella, until she whimpered. In retaliation, she heated the bars of the cage, and Dual howled, curling his wings around himself.

"*Stop it*," Moth yelled, dropping to his knees in front of Dual, "she's hurting him because of you."

Ramiel frowned. "Why's it matter? He's only a Fallen."

"And I'm *only* a mage, and you're *only* an Addict," Mischief replied, harshly.

Mischief immediately cooled his own silver, and Stella pouted, before cooling the cage.

Dual sighed, falling forwards to rest his cheek against the bars. Moth tentatively reached to stroke him like I'd been desperate to do and as if his fangs weren't *just there…*

Moon tensed like he itched to snatch his little brother away from the vampire, even though *he* was the one who could mind control Dual.

Okami settled on Moth's shoulder, licking his cheek in approval.

Ramiel flushed. "I apologize. I meant that he's only a shameless flirt who last time threatened to *taste* you."

Dual grimaced, holding his chest. "*Ow*, the pink-haired assassin."

Emperor raised his eyebrow. "Duke Dual, I assume?"

Dual's face lit up. "A fan?" No one had the right to sound so sultry. "I'm touched."

Emperor's haughty expression trembled either with anger or an attempt to control his laugher; I thought that it was a little of both. "First you want to taste Mischief, and now you want to be touched by me. Vampires truly are minxes."

The rainbow beads that were threaded through Dual's braids *clicked*. "Don't act like you don't love it, Golden Boy."

Huh, stunned was an interesting expression on Emperor. I intended to make him look like that more often myself.

"What a peculiar lot you are." Stella wiggled her hands. "Free me."

Mischief hesitated, looking to me. I nodded.

When Mischief dragged back his magic from around her wrists and neck, Stella fell in a pile on the floor, rubbing at her neck. My Charms watched her with hard eyes, and it wasn't difficult to imagine how they felt, when their collars were still chafing around their own necks.

"I know that the Fallen's arse is divine," when Stella assessed me, I had the sinking feeling that I was in a secret test that I hadn't expected or studied for, "but even I didn't think that you'd risk so many beasts' lives for one fanged monster. Especially one who creeps around covens at night."

"Dude, *again*?" I rested my hands on my hips.

Dual fixed me an intense gaze that appeared to be willing me to understand. "What can I say? Maybe I have a thing for witches and *mages*."

My breath hitched at Dual's stress on the *mages*.

Was that code for Aquilo, or was it merely my wishful thinking? Had Dual been attempting to help Aquilo, when he'd been captured? But then, why would Aquilo have revealed to a Fallen that he was a mage?

Stella strolled to me, gripping my chin. "I needed to be certain, and it's clear now. Just look at you, brimming over with power and yukky non-magical morals. But it doesn't matter. I'm not your mum; I can accept different. Keep your zoo of mages, beasts, Addicts, and Fallen. So, you won't flay one of your own animals to pass the Wolf Charmer test...? Ivy was a fool to push you to that and end up having to throw you to the wolves. But I can be adaptable. If you skin a false one, then I'll let you live...and we'll talk about the whole defeating the Wolf Kingdom thing after, right?"

I blinked, glancing around at my guys like they

understood any better than me, but they looked just as confused.

Emperor shook his head.

False one...?

Ivy had tried to force me to flay Moon in Cosmos Tower, just as mom had flayed her first Charm, before she'd claimed the Ambassador to become accepted by the covens as official Wolf Charmer. I'd refused, leading to, you know, the whole *throwing to the wolves* business in the Wilds.

Did Stella mean it, however, about discussing the war like she'd even put a halt to that? Considering her whole stance on *lying*, I wasn't going with trusting her, but what if this once it was the truth?

My gaze crept to the pelts that hung on the walls. "It's kind of hard to believe that all I have to do is steal one of those furs, and you'll call off your whole crusade."

Stella gave a secretive smile as she slunk to the central throne, throwing herself down with the swagger of a war commander. Then she clicked her fingers, and reluctantly, the Ambassador crawled to kneel in front of her.

"A witch has to understand about sacrifice and protecting the world, pretty peach." Her fingers carded through the Ambassador's hair with surprising gentleness. "Were you always this slow to learn?"

Emperor bristled. "A *wolf* must understand the

precise same lessons. I assure you," his gaze swept across the other princes, "we were not slow learners."

Stella's lips pinched. "Where's a muzzle when you need one?" Her fingers tightened in the Ambassador's hair. "Either you become the Wolf Charmer our covens need, or we have no use for you."

I shook my head. "I don't want—"

"Well, tough," Stella snapped. "Did I want Daniel to be married to my bitch of a sister? Or to be ignored, just because the shadows rejected me?" Her smile was twisted, as she leaned forward. "The crimson shadows control all our fates. Shall we see if this is the time that you die?"

In a flash, which burst flashing lights across my eyes, the arena was spotlighted so brightly that I could only squint owlishly at Stella, who'd become shadowed on her throne. I rubbed my eyes against the back of my arm, and when I looked out again, I gasped.

The seats surrounding the chamber were ranked with witches from the Oxford covens.

I was such a dick: I knew that I shouldn't have ignored the movement that I'd seen in the shadows.

I backed up, whilst my guys encircled me. Amadeus clasped my hand, and I could feel the way that his fingers quivered even through his glove.

What must it feel like for a wolf to be surrounded in a witches' house by so many of their enemies?

Mischief swooped over us, whilst his wings sizzled

with wild magic: our god staking his protective claim. It thrilled me to sense his power and know that he'd risk himself to save us, whilst watching the way that the other witches flinched back.

Ivy and Lux stood at the back of the room with shuttered expressions.

So, they'd heard everything that we'd said?

All along, my aunt had been playing to the audience and using me to strengthen her own position over the other witches, which included Ivy and Lux.

Holy hell, I had to prove to the covens that I was stronger than both the Houses of Seasons and Blood or Aquilo would be the one to get his ass kicked...or whipped...in Ivy and Lux's rage.

I'd never forget the way that blood had wept from Ivy's eyes, nose, and ears, until she'd become like a blood doll. The Blood Witch was creepier than even my aunt.

I tilted my chin, outstaring the witches who eagerly watched the show like they were at the circus and I was the wolf tamer, of course.

Let the witchy assholes stare because I'd be taming *them* next.

Grrr — I startled at the rumbled growl from the pelts that hung on the walls, which echoed around the chamber.

The witches clapped and jumped up and down on their seats; the show was about to start.

Moon's steely stare caught mine, before he kissed me on the forehead; his lips were soft, and when he drew back, I could still feel the ghost of them. My tongue darted out like I could tempt him....*please, please, please*...just to press his lips to mine this time.

Instead, he turned away, sliding out his golden claws and fangs and dropping into fighting stance.

The pelts leapt from the walls, reforming through a hybrid of tech and magic that I recognized like I'd designed them myself, into a nightmare pack of mechanical wolves.

Then the mechanicals stalked towards my Charms and me, snapping their sharp bronze fangs.

CHAPTER 14

In all my dreams of being surrounded by wolves, which had haunted me since the murder of my parents, never once had those wolves been mechanical monsters.

It turned out that reality was more terrifying than nightmares, who knew?

Except perhaps the shifters had known all along that single skins had beasts hidden within them as well, even if they only ever showed one face.

The back of my neck was sticky with sweat in the sweltering heat of the Justice Chamber, and my heart thundered. My Charms and Ramiel formed a defensive circle around me, whilst Moon pushed his brother behind him. The wind from Mischief's violently beating wings gusted across my cheeks like breath.

The mechanical wolves growled.

I shook, as they prowled closer. Their eyes glowed, just like Moon's, yet freakishly *wrong*. They wore loosely over their bronze backs the white pelts of the *real* murdered Omegas, as if they were wolves trying to pass as sheep, and boy was that sickening on so many levels. I forced myself not to recoil.

They're not real...just bigass toys with lots and lots of fangs...

I glared at Stella, who lazily stared back from her throne.

Okay, in this circus, my aunt was the ringmaster, and the covens were the audience.

I refused to look out at the witches' excited faces. Stella had been so chilled, even strung up in her own House, because she'd been building to this grand finale, where I was the star. But hey, if the assholes wanted a show, then I'd give them one.

Let the dicks watch.

The Oxford covens would have ringside seats on a Wolf Charmer like they'd never seen before. I'd fight wolves *with* wolves. Honestly, I should send Stella a muffin basket for handing me the perfect opportunity to showcase my rebellion and the new world that I was forging.

When I grinned, Stella's smile faded. *It looked like she'd figured out that she wasn't the one in charge of the show anymore.*

My shadows built, before blasting out in a tidal wave at the mechanicals.

Nothing.

I blinked, biting my lip.

Huh, that was seriously not good.

I dragged my red back again, before once more washing it over the mechanicals to paralyze them.

Nothing, apart from the stinging bite of dark magic.

I swayed, and Emperor slipped his arm around my shoulders. His claws dug into my skin. When I glanced around at my Charms, their fangs were as long as the false wolves' teeth who were stalking us. Even in the midst of this horror, it made my skin tingle at their wicked beauty.

"Problem?" Emperor asked.

"Besides the killer toys?" My gaze darted to Emperor's. "I can't control them."

"Aye, because they're not wolves." Moon raised his eyebrow. "Do you still judge everything on how it looks? These are a *witch* invention, playing at wolf. Why would you have control over them?"

I flushed. Wow, I'd deserved that, but the snickers from our audience were a kick in my witchy behind.

Stella trailed her hand down the Ambassador's neck. He froze, allowing the caress. I didn't understand, however, the way that his gaze flicked with urgent pleading to Amadeus and then back to me.

What was he trying to tell me?

"Your Omega isn't just a pretty face, is he?" Stella pulled the Ambassador around to face her and then pushed him onto all fours. "Although, he has a far prettier behind." She chuckled at Moon's snarl. "Tech and magic combined has so many fabulous uses. Do you imagine that I never monitored you? Your uncle would send me reports: *genius*, he called you. I quite agree." She pressed her hand onto the Ambassador's forehead. "Surely you recognize the design?"

My chest tightened. "What did you say?"

"*Your design*. Don't you like it? This is only a game, after all. You merely need to snatch one pelt and you've saved your *harem* and the Fallen."

I was going to hurl...

Emperor tightened his claws in my shoulder to keep me standing. I flinched at the pain, but holy hell, did I need it. I recognized the mechanicals now because *I'd* been the dickhead to design them.

Yep, that was karma biting me in the ass.

Before I'd created Okami out of a sheet of silk to be my...if I even thought *pet*, Okami would kick my ass... to be *mine*, I'd planned a metal wolf that would be motored by magic. But it'd only been the size of a cat, which would've been kind of cute and not *terrifying*. I'd decided, however, that I wanted something that I could always carry with me, so that if I needed him, I could slip my hand in my pocket and know that I wasn't alone.

Okami had saved me from a dark place of grief and loneliness.

Now my own creation, however, had returned to devour me in a way that the true wolves in the Wilds hadn't, even when I'd been thrown to them.

Now *that* was irony.

"My, what a shocking surprise that you're responsible for these horrors." Mischief rolled his eyes. "May I request that we *fight* them now, before they attack?"

When Ramiel's wings swept forward, a rose gold sword curved into his hand; pink fire sizzled on its tip. Sometimes, when I wasn't with Ramiel, I forgot how beautiful he was. Then when I saw him, my breath caught in my throat, and I felt like a High School kid again with my first crush. Seeing Ramiel with this gorgeous sword in his hand — *a warrior angel* — reminded me that he was ancient, mighty, and *choosing* to battle for me.

I protected my pack, but they also protected me. I surged with pride, as well as fear, because I knew how powerful the mechanicals were.

I was the jerk who'd designed them.

When the wolves growled again, snapping their bronze fangs and circling even closer, Moon pushed in front of me, pulling me away from Emperor.

"Goddess Moon! You can't control the false wolves," Moon whispered, "but you can control *us*."

"I don't think so. I'm not proving these dicks right about my power. I won't control you," I hissed.

Moon licked up my cheek in reassurance, and I shivered. "Nay, we're all *willing* and *seriously enthusiastic. This consent that you rant on about...?* You have it, Crimson."

I glanced at my Charms. In turn they nodded, even Moth.

"And is my god willing?" Moon peeked up at Mischief through his curls with an aching desire.

Mischief snorted. "However could I resist such a look? Willing is stretching it but I shan't resist, if it means that we destroy these fiends."

"My sword is at your command." Ramiel bowed his head.

What on the witching earth did they mean?

Moon's silver magic wound around mine, crackling like popcorn. Its power entangled with my red, until I shuddered with the strength of the Moon Child. My legs almost buckled.

Woah, was that the effect of the full moon?

I gazed at Moon in awe. He was as powerful as me. If he wasn't an Omega and my Charm, but was respected as a true prince, I wouldn't want him as an enemy.

Our magic caressed each other's in delight at the joining, and we clasped each other lost in the joy. Until

Okami dived past me in a blur of silver, whining indignantly.

Okami was jealous that I'd invented another wolf, and not only him. *Did he think that he was less special now?*

I drew back from Moon, furious with Stella for hurting my silky prankster of a best friend.

Plus, Okami would get his fluffy ass kicked with his reckless solo mission.

I winced at Okami's howl.

Yep, his fluffy ass was being kicked...

Okami had dive bombed the leader of the mechanicals, who'd snapped his jaws down onto Okami's tail. Okami was wriggling to get away, but he was trapped. Tears streamed down his cheeks.

My shadows exploded out, winding around my Charms and Moth in a way that was different to any time I'd used them before. Now, they were tinged silver with Moon's magic: a mix of wolf and witch. They were there to control but only with consent, and that meant they'd strengthen, rather then weaken. These were my princes fighting at my side, rather than animals that I'd make dance.

I quivered with the intimate connection and joy. *This was true power.*

My wolves were now puppet-like, yet I could feel them through the bond, and they could feel me. It was weird but it felt like this was how I should always have been fighting with my Charms.

I sent Moon leaping at the lead mechanical, slashing his claws across his flank with a *clang*. The mechanical still didn't let go of Okami. Then the other mechanical attacked.

Emperor and Amadeus stood either side of me, snarling at the wolves who were stalking around me. Ramiel rushed the mechanicals with a sweep of his sword; the pink fire blazed out, catching the mechanicals' pelts on fire, until they looked like flaming candles. But they didn't slow their attack. In fact, twin nightmares slashed at Ramiel's wing, and he gasped in pain. Mischief shot out his spinning silver, lassoing the stragglers of the pack, before pinning them to the walls.

There were too many of these monsters. Even united, our energy was being divided.

All I needed was one pelt, right?

I threw Moon onto the lead mechanical's back; Moon savaged it, dragging at the pelt with his claws. I winced at Okami's whimpering, as he was jerked side to side by the mechanical. Then I wrapped my red tighter around Moon's magic.

Moon glanced up at me, before arching his silver towards the two angels: he was about to mind control them. Now I understood what Ramiel had meant about being at his *command*.

When Moon's magic pulled both angels towards us

and under its spell, I trembled with the thrill of their power linking with Moon's and mine.

There was no confusion, shouting, or mistakes. There was only the fluid battle of a united pack: *The Wolf Charmer and her Moon Child in battle.*

Moon dragged Mischief and Ramiel towards the lead mechanical, whilst using their fire power to create a path for my Charms, Moth, and me to sweep through as well.

I hadn't known that I had a performer in me, but becoming a gladiator had brought it out of me. My crimson coiled in ecstasy, as I launched Emperor, Amadeus, and Moth at the mechanical.

The weight of all my guys landing on it at once, pinned the mechanical down. Yet I'd designed these things, and I knew how strong they were. I smarted from the dark magic, every time that I tried to prise the pelt free, and my Charms had no more luck, as they ripped at it with their claws.

That thing wasn't coming free until the mechanical was dead... Okay, it was kind of dead already, so at least until I worked out how to turn it off.

Then I laughed because I remembered the one weakness in my toy that I'd never been able to improve: *it's neck.*

What was the bet that Stella hadn't worked that one out either?

My thoughts flowed through my magic to Moon,

who smiled. Then he caught Mischief's eye with as much respect as if he was kneeling once again on the ground for him.

Why did I ever forget that Mischief was also Moon's god?

Yep, that'd be because Mischief was also a royal prick...who in a spray of silver sparkles, transformed into a unicorn who was as large as a war horse.

With a neigh, Mischief reared up onto his hindlegs; his hooves glittered. His mane flowed like every girl's dream. I had to resist the urge to stroke it. His violet eyes were large and wild. He hadn't been joking before about his *powers not functioning at their optimum*, when he'd only shifted into a plushie sized unicorn. I understood why Moon was watching him with such wonder...*and love*.

Then a metallic light like liquid mercury, shot from his twisted horn towards the leader of the mechanicals. The light sliced through the weak join of its neck, cutting off its head.

Immediately, its body *clanked* to the floor, and every other growling monster collapsed as well. Their glowing eyes died, as their life was stolen along with their leader's.

Was it weird that I felt a teensy-weensy bit guilty?

I bent down, helping Okami to wriggle free of the now slack jaws of the mechanical. Then I held his soft body to my face, whilst he licked me in distress.

I ran my thumb over his damaged tail. "Battle wounds are freaking hot. Seriously, you look bad boy and dangerous now." Okami's ears perked up, and he nudged me with his nose, before spinning around like he could look at his own tail. He raised his chin proudly. I caught him, stroking down his back. He wasn't a toy like the mechanicals; he was pack. "How about a rest for the war hero?"

When Okami nodded, I slipped him into my pocket.

The audience of witches exploded into whooping applause behind me, and I tensed. Would they've cheered in the same way if I'd been killed too?

"Congratulations," Stella's voice wound smugly through the chamber, "I knew that a worthy Wolf Charmer lurked inside you. Come and mingle."

Once, her words would've meant *everything* to me. The witches who were now crowding out of their seats and eagerly around Stella to greet the new Wolf Charmer were the covens that I'd always wanted to accept me. But now, I knew that I was a leader.

What did being popular matter, when I had pack members to protect?

I ignored Stella, instead running my hand through Mischief's mane like I'd been craving to ever since he'd turning into the cutest killer unicorn. When he tossed his head with a snort, I petted his pink muzzle instead, and he calmed. His butterfly long lashes fluttered, before in a spray of silver he transformed back into his angelic self. I froze with my hand still petting him. He wrinkled his nose.

"Don't mind me, that's only my nose," he grumbled. I snatched my hand back. "Were you the girl who always wanted a pony?"

"Dude, I had *two* ponies and now I have a unicorn. Neat, huh?" I smirked.

"You also have an angel with a bleeding wing." Emperor slipped off his robes, before pressing them against the gashes in Ramiel's wing.

Ramiel blushed. "Don't soil your beautiful garments for my sake, prince. I shall heal."

Emperor wrapped the robes more tightly around Ramiel's wounds. "How interesting. I also thought that you could bleed out?"

But I didn't miss Emperor's wince. I'd never met anyone who had so much pride in their clothes...or hair. Yet he'd get blood on his robes for an angel...? Or was it that Ramiel was now part of his pack?

Mischief snatched my hand, pulling me towards Ramiel. "Let us see."

Emperor pulled away the robes. When I studied the claw marks, my eyes narrowed.

Please let me be wrong...please, please...

"By my hide, they match the ones on the murdered mage boy, Kolby." Moon's mouth was tight. "This is how the rotten bastards killed him. It's why there was no

scent of wolves and the pattern of attack was wrong…
but the claw marks…"

I nodded.

What could I say? *Sorry my aunt is a psychopath
who framed your kingdoms for the murder of a mage
boy, so that she'd have an excuse to start a war…?*

Honestly, maybe that would be a good start.

It chilled me how well Stella had planned tonight's
entertainment. Yet what she hadn't reckoned on was that
now she'd made me the official Wolf Charmer. I'd
passed the test. That made me the one and only, and
even though I'd started all of this not knowing a damn
thing about her witchy world, what I did know was this:
The Wolf Charmer had political clout.

Wolf Charmers could spark wars, win them, and
they could end them. So, now I could…*my way.*

I stared out at the sea of witches who were watching
me with expressions of curiosity, hostility, and *who the
hell does she think she is?*

Ivy and Lux stood either side of Stella's chair like
dark bodyguards. My stomach roiled at the thought that
my pack wasn't complete, not while my mage fiancé
was still trapped in the House of Blood.

Without him, I was still leashed.

I wet my dry lips, as I faced Ivy. "No Aquilo
tonight? Is he too busy washing his white hair to come
and see me?"

Moon elbowed me — *oomph*. I forgot that he was Aquilo's fanboy.

Ivy became rigid, holding the back of Stella's throne so hard that her fingers sank into the fur. "He's *dead*."

My vision blurred, and for a moment, I forgot how to breathe.

My knees buckled, and I fell to the floor. I clasped desperately at Moon, as he knelt next to me, whining and nuzzling against my neck. The Ambassador was weeping and rocking too beside Stella.

Aquilo couldn't be dead...it wasn't the end of the month...not dead...dead...dead...

I let out a scream, and my shadows burst from me in a torrent of tears that cast the chamber into a red twilight.

Had I been fighting the wrong battle tonight?

"Wow, you truly do like that snobby little Bloods boy," Stella laughed. I struggled to hear her over the red wailing through Moon's grief and mine. "Despite the fact that he's a mage, I guess that this proves it's the right match."

I blinked up at her through my matted eyelashes.

Say Aquilo's not dead...say it...say it...

"He's not dead." Lux studied me, although not with the cruelty that I'd expected. Then she added with an angry glance at her mom. "Although I believe that he wishes he was."

"You...*bitch*." I rose up with Moon growling at my

side.

My red lashed the walls now in furious waves. Attempting to kill me...? Weirdly, I was getting used to that. Throwing me to the wolves...? I'd come back stronger, leading my own pack. But tricking me that the guy I...had clearly becoming way fonder of than I'd known...that was a dick move.

I'd make these witches regret it.

Ivy's eyes glowed wine-red. "My goodness, you act like *you* didn't reject my home and guidance or *my son* didn't recklessly turn on his own mother. I offered him to the Rebel Academy, you know, but even they wouldn't take him with your magical engagement. You're bound to him by blood. I attempted to bind his magic with a branding—"

Stella wrapped a curl around her finger. "And you can thank me for stopping her. He's *yours* to brand; it's always a deeply intimate occasion. Just ask if you want ideas for what kinky fun to have afterward."

Mischief stalked towards them with his wings gleaming. "Desist your spiteful wittering. This is your Wolf Charmer: you shall respect her." The covens fell silent in shock, staring at him with wide eyes. Stella simply arched her brow. His smile at her was all death; holy hell, I hoped that he never smiled at me like that. "You tiny creatures believe that branding and binding others gives you the control. I promise that you shall learn by my hand how insignificant you truly are, and afterward, not one of you shall dare shatter a mage in such a way again. If you do," his wings spread in violet glory, "I shall shatter your world."

Stella slow clapped. "Well, that's me told."

Then she clicked her fingers, and the front of Dual's cage fell open. I glanced around, as the vampire crawled out, wincing at the pull on his muscles. He pushed himself to his feet, rolling his shoulders and stretching his wings out.

"Winners get rewards." Stella pointed at Dual. "Slaughter him, shag him, take him to a movie. He's yours."

Thanks, Aunt Stella, for turning me into the dick slaveowner again.

Dual raised his eyebrow. "Yeah, sorry but I don't do *owned.* I'm a duke and I run my own court. Now, if any of you sweeties are offering to be *mine…*"

He winked at Moon who pinked, before slinking towards me with a swing of his hips. Dual snatched my hand and raised it to his lips. Then his gaze met mine; it blazed with an intense sincerity that shocked me, as he tenderly kissed the back of my hand.

"Thank you," he murmured.

Then I e*eped,* as Dual spun me closer, cocooning me in his wings. His fangs grazed my neck. I shuddered, wrapped in the citrus scent, which was like blood oranges, of his warm wings. His feathers were soft, whilst his teeth made my skin tingle for more.

"You'll step away from our Charmer now," Moon's growl sliced through the passion of the moment, "or I'll make you. Remember how I can do that…?"

Dual's jaw clenched, and I winced.

When I'd first met Dual, I'd asked Moon to demonstrate his power to mind control vampires and angels on him. The demonstration had included forcing Dual to tell us his most secret sexual fantasy, and it'd turned out that becoming the Prince of the Wilds' Daddy Dom had been Dual's dream.

So, Moon could boot a guy in the balls…

Yet I wanted to know whether Dual truly did know Aquilo, and I couldn't help the way that I felt safe in the sparkling sweetness of his wings. Maybe his court wasn't such a bad option for a base. Except, was that how he lulled naïve assholes into become his Blood Lovers…?

I didn't need Moon to save me.

Instead, I yanked Dual's head back by his braids; he hissed but didn't struggle. Then I slowly lowered *my* mouth to *his* throat, and he didn't flinch but leaned towards me with a sigh. I bit down with my blunt teeth, before sucking a hickey to mark him.

I was standing in front of a coven of witches, having defeated mechanical monsters, with my pack of angels, mages, gods, and wolves at my side. Did Moon seriously think that I was frightened of one vampire?

He should be frightened of me.

Dual let out a breathy laugh. "Sorry, prince, but your *Charmer* doesn't appear to be in agreement." When I let go, he pressed his lips against my mouth as if he was going to kiss me, but instead whispered, "Blood and bones, you're as special as Aquilo says."

I jerked, but Dual held on tight with his wings, splaying his hand along the hollow of my back.

"As fun as it always is to watch a witch and a vampire getting it on," Stella pulled a face, "we do have a schedule to keep."

She snatched the Ambassador by the scruff of the neck, before pressing her hand over his collar. With a yowl, the Ambassador transformed into a silvery gray wolf. He was small and pretty with a sleek tail that he tucked between his legs, cowering before my aunt.

I pulled back from Dual, desperate to stroke the Ambassador and calm his desperate whimpering.

It was the night of the full moon. *The wolves could transform.* Were they scared to show their wolf forms to the witches?

Amadeus launched himself towards the Ambassador, even though Moon tried to hold him back. He skidded to his knees in front of him, stroking his sleek head. The Ambassador rubbed his cheek against Amadeus, whilst Amadeus hugged his neck.

Stella laughed. "Such devotion between princes. We should have the two play together."

I stiffened, glancing out at the other witches. They

appeared as anxious as me; their gazes darted between Stella and me like we were evenly matched boxers in a ring, and I'd been the underdog who'd suddenly surged back, so that they no longer knew who to bet on. I understood their insecure expressions now. The Wolf Charmer was revered, but the Bloods and Stella knew me as a kid, more than viewing me as some legendary figure.

But these other covens didn't.

I pulled away from Dual, puffing out my chest, as I sensed victory for the first time. "Seriously, stop acting like you're still the boss." I forced a cruel smile to dance across my face, just like I'd seen on Stella's so many times. *Hey, I could act like an asshole too.* "I'm the Wolf Charmer now. I decide what happens to my Charms *and* the wolves. There won't be a war tonight because I already control Wolf Kingdom. Look how I fought. All three princes, an angel, and a god under my shadows." I twisted back to Dual who with only a slight huff, dropped to his knees. "Even the Fallen Duke. Not bad going, since I've only been in Oxford for a week. Think what I could achieve in a year."

Excited mutterings swept through the audience — *I had them.*

Stella ran her hand down the Ambassador's back, yanking him closer to her by his tail. When he yelped, I remembered how sensitive Moon's tail had been in wolf form.

Amadeus scrambled to hold onto the Ambassador, but Stella fixed a muzzle that was shaped weirdly like a gas mask over the Ambassador's distressed face.

"And no more *muzzles*," I hissed.

Stella slumped back on her throne, whilst Ivy and Lux prowled either side of her. "You can't stop the war starting because *the war never stopped.* Do you want to know a secret, which was hidden from the Wolf Charmers?" When Stella smiled, I realized that my attempt hadn't been even close to her cruelty level. "The Treaty was never more than a ceasefire. But your great-grandmother was too taken by the sinful beauty of the beasts to kill them all; like you, she'd rather screw them, than put them down." Moon slipped his hand into mine; tremors ran through him, and I remembered how I'd found him in the **REJECT** cell, waiting to be terminated, if I hadn't chosen him. "Maybe it's a flaw in all Wolf Charmers. Your crimson shadows are a corruption that allow the beasts too close. But unlike your great-grandmother, mum, or you, the red isn't in me…and I can finish them."

When the Ambassador whined, I sniffed at the weirdly sweet scent that all of a sudden rose up from the floor.

"Fur and fangs, she's gassing us with the Wolf Tamer," Moon gasped.

Then I choked, as Stella's magic poisoned my pack with a cloud of toxic gas.

CHAPTER 15

I gagged on the silvery cloud that flooded the Justice
Chamber, holding my arm across my streaming
eyes. My nose wrinkled against the sweet scent of the
Wolf Tamer, which had been magically transformed into
a gas attack.

Where were the UN to enforce their ban on chemical
weapons, huh? Now I understood the Ambassador's
muzzle: *it actually had been a gas mask.*

My Charms, who were whining and staggering in
the chemical fog, however, didn't have masks to protect
them. *What if they'd already inhaled enough poison to
kill them?*

My heart lurched, as Moon staggered. His hand
slipped out of mine, and his eyelids fluttered. He was
being dragged down by the drug.

I couldn't lose him to the Wolf Tamer again...

"Jesus, get them out of here," I hollered at the angels.

"I can't…my wing." Ramiel's gashed wing drooped, as his agonized gaze rose to mine.

My aunt had stopped my angel flying…? Okay, now I was pissed.

Ramiel still dived to Emperor, as Emperor slumped over, cracking his head on the ground. To my surprise, Dual caught Moth and covered him with his body like he could shield him, just as the Ambassador whined and curled around Amadeus.

Mischief nodded, stretching out his wings and snatching Moon into his arms.

"Nay, h-hold on…not me…t-take my brother…" Moon slurred.

Mischief gritted his teeth, meeting my eye with flinty determination. Then his wings wrapped around Moon, who slumped like a rag doll, and swooped up with him to the high roof above the gas.

Safe.

Yet why had Mischief saved Moon, rather than this brother? If we survived, Moon would seriously sink his teeth into Mischief…and more likely his sweet ass than his throat.

My shadows burst out of me, wrapping around my remaining Charms and Moth, ready to pin them in sticky webs to the ceiling as well. I'd promised to never use my powers without consent but saving them had to be a loop hole, right?

Yet it was too late because they'd already collapsed like a series of fainting dominoes. Instantly, the gas dispersed, leaving nothing but its sickly scent behind... and the guys that I loved... No hex in the world would make me think *dead.*

Breathing hard, I dashed to Emperor, crouching next to him. I brushed my hand across his cold forehead; his cheek was purple and bruising where he'd fallen. I brushed his hair back because if he woke up with his hair messed-up, he'd be moaning for hours.

He was going to wake up.

I raised my shaky hand to his lips; my palm brushed their petal softness.

I felt a breath, then another, and another... ghost light but puffing across my palm.

I let out a laugh that was more of a sob, sitting back on my heels.

"Such drama over a beast, no matter how beautiful he is," Stella scoffed.

I stiffened. It was funny how you could forget that you had an audience when you thought that your Charms had been killed....*or honestly, not freaking funny at all.*

I stood, turning to face Stella. When I pointed at her, I noticed that my hand was no longer shaking. In fact, red hissed down it like a blade. "Trust me, I'm done dicking around with diplomacy or tricks. If you attack me, then I can live with it. But you attacked my wolves with their greatest fear, and that makes *me* your greatest fear."

Stella slunk out of the chair, stepping over Amadeus like he was litter. My jaw tightened.

Stella waggled her hands. "Oh, I'm quaking over here." Then she turned to the covens like this had all been a demonstration put on for them. *Woah, maybe it had.* "Look how effective the Wolf Tamer is in gas form! The beasts are incapacitated in a matter of moments but not killed. They wouldn't be able to run, even if they weren't caged tonight. I have Wolf Tamer missiles ready to launch at a word from me on the three kingdoms. This was just a small taster dose that I kept here to show you. How did you like the show, ladies?" She winked at the witches who applauded politely; Stella should've gone into sales.

"And the kids?" I gestured at Moth who was cradled by Dual; his moon-pale curls rested on Dual's dark shoulder. If Stella did this, she'd be committing genocide just like my great-grandmother. Did she think that would finally make her a legend as well, rather than simply another tyrannical asshole? *I had to stop her.* "I take it you don't care that you're not only gassing fighters but all the civilians too?"

"Every wolf is guilty; every wolf must pay," Stella snarled, stalking towards me. "Don't you get it yet? This is all your fault." She poked me in the chest on each word, quivering with rage. "If you hadn't been so weak, then tonight you and I would've reveled together in the centennial celebrations of the defeat of the wolves. Tonight would've been when we took vengeance — together. Why do you think I called you back to England?"

I shook my head, whilst blinking back tears. When I was younger and painted canvas after canvas of wolves arching in agony, I'd have done anything to be offered a night to avenge my parents' deaths. The offer of a place next to my aunt and with the covens as their Wolf Charmer, whilst exiled with the non-magical in America, had been my dream.

But now it was my nightmare.

I couldn't let it become every shifters' nightmare as well. I shuddered at the image of the caged wolves panicking as they choked on the gas, before collapsing — vulnerable to anything the witches chose to do.

Would the witches kill the Omegas who weren't perfect and pretty enough like last time?

I cocked my head. "It must suck for you that I don't give a damn about any of that. It's kind of like you don't get it yet: as your new Wolf Charmer, I outrank you." My grin was feral. "And I prefer the moonlight."

When I looked up, Mischief nodded. Still holding Moon tightly in his arms, silver magic burst from his beating wings, blasting through the walls of the chamber.

I shivered at the thrill of his magic, as it tingled through my crimson.

Maybe I do have a thing for powerful guys.

The witches shrieked and covered their heads. The beams of the full moon shone through like spears over the collapsed bodies of the mechanical wolves and onto my motionless pack. To my shock, despite being unconscious, my Charms and Moth shifted into their wolf forms.

Amadeus lay next to the Ambassador: two silver gray wolves like brothers. Amadeus was as elegantly beautiful in wolf form as he was a Beta, with fur that glimmered. I wished that I could see his eyes, but you know, he wasn't *free* in this form, he was trapped by the Wolf Tamer. The Ambassador whined, nudging Amadeus' muzzle in comfort.

A small wolf — Moth — was enfolded in Dual's arms; Dual's black hair fell like a veil over Moth's white fur.

Hold on…gray, white, and…

Emperor would be revealing his *black* Alpha fur to the world, which considering a male Alpha was seen as Cursed and killed on birth, wasn't a good thing. He'd been forced to hide this secret his entire life with the help of the butterfly tattoo on his chest and hair dye to pretend that he too was a *perfect Omega*, rather than an

Alpha. He'd spent every full moon caged where he couldn't be seen, at his mom's order because let's face it, she was a dickhead. Only his sister had saved him from being ripped apart at birth.

Honestly, my shadows longed to give her some kick up the ass parenting advice.

But now, as I stared in horror at Emperor who lay beneath Ramiel, I knew that he was only moment's from losing everything.

Smoking cauldrons, he was *hot* and all Alpha in his wolf form; he was powerful and large with jet black fur. He should've been the nightmares who'd stalked my dreams, but instead, through my Wolf Bitten bond with him, a wave of safety and home washed over me. I knew that he'd protect me, just like I'd always protect him.

Except, how could I do that?

I took a ragged breath, as I met Ramiel's eye. His look was questioning, but this was an angel who read as many books as Aquilo (I had a feeling that the two geeks would get on), and smart as he was, he nodded with understanding. He snatched the fur pelt that I'd prised from the leader of the mechanicals to prove myself a true Wolf Charmer, tucking it lovingly over Emperor to hide him.

I laughed shakily. "Jesus, when did my life become this complicated?"

Then I yelped, as Stella wound her hand through my

curls and yanked my head back in a move that I'd seen her perfect with the Ambassador.

"Let me take a guess, niece: about the time that you were tricked by the sinful bodies of the wolves?" Stella pulled me closer, and I grimaced. *Why had I never noticed the danger lurking in her eyes?* Her lips skimmed my cheek like a brand. "You're nothing but a wolf in witch clothing. Why would you wish to be as weak as them?"

When she pointed at my Charms, who lay suffering because of her cruel weapon, my red snapped in furious whips.

"Let me introduce you to the Moon Child." Mischief's voice was coolly mocking, as he landed next to me; the blast of air from his wings was like a shot of espresso. *Boy, did I need that right now.* "Call him weak, whilst he *devours* you."

I blinked in confusion, whilst Stella merely gave a smug smile, before shoving me away from her. Moon hadn't even transformed like the other wolves.

Then Mischief's gaze met mine, and I understood. Suddenly, my shadows in a rushing crimson tide washed out of me. I was caught in the grip of a wild passion, as Mischief crowded closer, holding Moon between us, whilst his wings cocooned me. I wanted…*needed*… them both. Their power and magic joined with mine. It spiraled in silver and red around the moon beams.

Whilst Mischief and I held him, Moon transformed

in a dazzling burst into a white wolf, which threw us staggering backwards. The softness of his fur and the weight of him had pushed against me in a way that was more intimate than any screw and more like a birthing.

I stared at Moon with as much awe as I saw reflected back to me on Mischief's face. Only, Mischief's expression had gentled: the royal prick was proud of his subject.

Stella was right to call Moon *sinfully* beautiful. But he was anything but weak. His fur gleamed, and his silky ears pressed to his head, as he growled deep in his throat.

Stella froze, becoming ashen. Some of the witches shrank back, scrambling behind chairs, whilst others like Ivy and Lux, watched impassively. It looked like they were waiting to see what side won. I guessed that they'd call it being pragmatic.

I called it being dicks.

At Stella's gasped sob, I realized just how real her terror was. It was enough to freeze her rational thought and magic. Mischief had known or understood.

What did he fear like that? I wanted to know so that I could curse it to ashes.

Moon's lips curled back, as he bared his fangs, and Stella whimpered. Could she've wanted to hurt, subdue, and kill the wolves out of this *fear*?

Stella tried to back away, but this time it was me grabbing her. I snatched her waist, and I almost couldn't breathe with the shock, as she clung to me like I was there to *save* her.

For a moment, the touch of her curls against my fluttering eyelashes and the scent of honeysuckle flooded me with the memory of mom.

Why did I have to be the Wolf Charmer? Why did the truth of my past, family, and legacy have to be so different to the lie that I'd spent the last twenty-one years believing?

My expression hardened, and I tossed Stella to the floor in front of Moon. This was *his* choice and royal judgment.

We were in the Justice Chamber, after all.

Moon's fur bristled, then he leapt on top of Stella, pinning her down with his claws. Stella's scream was cut off, as Moon savaged her throat. When blood spurted over his muzzle, he shook his head in disgust and stepped back. The kill had been swift, efficient, and merciful.

An execution for her crimes...and to save Wolf Kingdom.

My knees still buckled, and I snatched handfuls of Moon's fur to hold myself up. Dual prowled to my shoulder; his steel claws shot out, along with his fangs.

Ramiel's sword slid into his hand, as he joined Mischief in his gorgeous glory.

I adopted Emperor's brand of cockiness, as my gaze swept with deliberate iciness over the gathered covens.

They shifted uncomfortably, staring at their slaughtered leader wide-eyed. Although, I noticed that there weren't any tears. It kind of made me wonder whether my aunt had been as much of an asshole to the other witches as she'd been to me. Maybe some of these bad rules and traditions were just as unpopular with the other witches as well…?

"Am I weak now?" I raised my eyebrow. I'd never been the one in charge before but I was a fan of the respect that I was finally being afforded, as long as I could keep channeling the badass in me. I locked gazes with Lux who did no more than look back at me coldly. She didn't, however, challenge me. "What dickhead wants to call me weak next?"

Moon snarled, revealing his scarlet tipped fangs, on cue. A witch shrieked. Were they so terrified of the wolves because this generation had never even seen one in full wolf form? Or because they believed the lies and tales that their ancestors wove to justify their oppression?

Either way, I'd find a way to show them that wolves weren't the devil. Just, not today.

When I glanced at Ivy, however, I frowned. Her fists were clenched, as she quivered with rage.

Woah, she wasn't bleeding from her eyes again, was she…?

It looked like the Blood Witch was the only asshole prepared to call me and my pack out as weak. Considering that she'd also been the one to throw me to the wolves, I was more than ready to throw her to mine.

Except, Ivy magicked herself with blood magic faster than I could even follow to crouch in front of Moon. I gasped, as a curved silver knife slid into her hand, and she pressed it to his throat.

My heart beat wildly, as Ivy's red-wine gaze met mine. Her coppery stench made me gag.

"I — Ivy, of the House of Blood — *call you weak*," Ivy sneered. Her gaze darted over our audience. This was a powerplay. She thought that I'd cleared her competition, and finally she could become the boss. As my future mother-in-law, she'd be an even more terrifying leader of the Oxford covens than Stella had been. "Fall to your knees along with your creatures and crawl to the back of the chamber, where the Wolf Charmer trap will once again bind your powers. This time, however, I don't imagine that I'll ever allow you free use of them again, since you're a *murderer*…unless you wish me to slit the beast's throat and wear his beautiful pelt tonight."

I stiffened, whilst my pulse pounded.

Please, no, no, no…

Ivy twisted Moon's ear, and he yelped. The knife sliced deeper into his throat, beading it with blood.

CHAPTER 16

When Moon crouched low, pressing his own neck into the knife, I gasped. The blade sliced through his pelt, and he panted. I couldn't look away from the beading blood that matted his fur like a scarlet collar.

Honestly, was Moon offering his wolfie ass up as a sacrifice again? Yep, that wasn't happening.

I glanced around the pinched and pale faces of my guys who hadn't been gassed, whilst in wolf form. They were as frozen in shock as me because this was meant to be our moment of triumph with the Moon Child standing beside me. I'd make some noble speech about the danger of abusing power, witch and wolf unity, or you know, *let's all be friends now guys or my pack will rip out your throats* — because hey, I was new to both power and unity myself.

Instead, Ivy had a silver knife at Moon's neck and the threat of my magic being bound again. Why in ever-witching hell didn't Ivy understand what a sacrilege it was to bind another's magic?

I shivered, despite the heat of the Justice Chamber, chilled at the thought of losing my powers. My crimson shadows wailed, trembling; they crashed against the bronze walls like they could escape. Yet there was no way on earth that I was sacrificing one of my guys to save myself or my magic.

If I had to lose everything to prove to my Charms that they were worth more than they'd always been taught...*that I loved them*...then I would.

Holy hell, why did I have to lose everything...?

"Desist your foolish heroics, wolf," Mischief commanded. His hands shook, and his gaze darted between the knife and Ivy's head like he was weighing the chances of cutting it off, before she could kill Moon. *But then, she could move so fast...* Mischief vibrated with anguish. *Why hadn't I realized that Mischief loved Moon as much as I did?* "It's harder to live and fight, than to be the martyr who sacrifices and dies." He shuddered. "You do not have permission to die. Do you understand?"

I'd have laughed, except for the pain in Mischief's eyes and the deadly seriousness of his order.

Moon whined, and I found myself hoping that for the first time he'd listen to his god. Then Moon blinked in a way that could only be apology, before shoving himself harder onto the blade.

"Son of a bitch," I hissed, before dropping with a *clang* that made me a flinch onto my kneecaps. "Look, I'm falling to my knees. Does this make you all hot? I didn't think that you were kinky."

Ivy trilled with laughter. "My goodness, you know nothing about me. Seeing anyone on their knees is always a delight." I flushed. "Especially in company."

The other witches...

Hey, when the guy that you love is about to die for you, it's easy to forget that you have an audience.

I winced as I raised my gaze to the covens who were watching avidly. Yet their expressions weren't hostile like I'd expected. In fact, some were thoughtful and others even frowned at *Ivy*. Maybe I was closer to having friends amongst the witches than I'd thought.

After all, I was the official Wolf Charmer now, and the one thing I knew was to never underestimate the power that *title* held with the covens.

Ivy nodded at the angels. "Now your creatures."

To my surprise, Dual instantly fell to his knees. Did vampire dukes have experience in this position? His dark gaze hadn't left Moon's since he'd been in danger. It was kind of sweet how protective he was, even though he wasn't pack and would probably bite me for even thinking *sweet* about his masterful ass.

Mischief, however, sneered, "I haven't knelt for the

most powerful mages, emperors, or gods. I shall not kneel for a mere witch."

Ramiel wound his fingers through Mischief's hair, yanking him to his side, but his voice was soft. "You're not kneeling for a witch. You kneel for Moon."

Mischief's eyes sparked, as he steeled himself. Then he began to kneel. Ivy's grin grew, as she finally eased the knife at Moon's neck.

Suddenly, the room darkened. An icy wind blew across my cheeks, and I raised my hand across my eyes.

What in the witching heavens was happening?

Mischief leapt to his feet, before his knee had even touched the floor.

So, at least his *no kneeling* record was still intact. My inner child couldn't help blowing a raspberry at Ivy on his behalf, and oh boy, was my adult self tempted to do it for real.

Then I blinked up at the holes through the Justice Chamber that Mischief had blasted. Everything had fallen dark because the moonlight had been blocked by the gray winged vampires who were swarming through like feathered bats. They crawled down the walls or swooped above our heads: glorious, beautiful, and *terrifying*.

Male, young, and punk: they were like anarchy with fangs and claws.

Yep, I could see the witches weren't best buddies with them. Could I help it that I was just *a little bit* excited by the thought of seeing their court now? *Dual wouldn't be able to tell, right?*

Dual snatched me around the waist, pulling us both to our feet and twirling me. "I knew that my boys would come for me!"

I whooped. "Now that the fanged cavalry has arrived, we're all...wait, I want to say *saved,* but it could be *dead.* You are on our side, right?"

Dual chuckled, raising my hand to caress the back of it with his thumb, in a way that shouldn't have made me tingle, but in fact, sent tingles though my entire body.

Weirdly sexy vampire.

Dual pointed at the witches. "Time to clear the room, boys." His smile was wicked. "Have fun."

The vampires dived at the witches who shrieked.

"You can take that cowardly knife away now," Mischief's voice was tight, as he glared at Ivy. "You're outnumbered and outsmarted. Simply put, treacherous witch, you're *out*: out of luck, supporters, power, and if you do not desist from threatening the life of one so many times more worthy than yourself, you shall soon find yourself out of *life*."

Wow, even I shivered at the commanding danger of Mischief's words, as his wings spread behind him like a warning and his magic spun around him.

Ivy paled, and the knife at Moon's throat shook. She stared frantically at the remaining witches who battled the vampires with blasts of fire, whilst the vampires slashed and bit. The air was thick with magic; I choked on it. Yet scarlet dripped from Ivy's nose and ears in quivering rage, as most of the witches vanished in bubbling pops of blood magic. It must suck to leak like that as the Blood Witch; she couldn't have much of a poker face.

I didn't blame the witches for escaping. Their leader was savaged, vampires were on the war path, and their Wolf Charmer was...less than conventional. Hey, that's the type of pragmatism that even I couldn't call dickish.

Although, I could call it freaking gutless.

"Nothing has changed," Ivy whispered like a mantra to ward us away, "nothing."

I caught Lux's eye; she leaned against what had once been her executioner's throne. She wasn't battling the vampires but she wasn't helping her mom either.

Yep, pragmatism.

Then a blast of wind knocked me onto my ass, and I squinted up at the moonlight, which was streaming through the gaps. Someone was silhouetted in the light but they didn't have wings. Instead, they were caught in a miniature whirlwind that lifted them up and into the chamber.

It was beautiful.

The angel without wings' magic crackled across my own. Woah, that was one badass...*mage.*

A mop of white-blond hair falling over pale blue

eyes as cold as the ocean, tight black jeans and velvet top: *Aquilo*.

And he wasn't wearing the blood pendant that his mom forced him to, which seared his neck and restrained his magic, so that nobody would discover that he was a mage.

Huh, it looked like he'd decided to go public.

My heart clenched with the sudden realization: Aquilo had brought the vampires here. *He'd revealed his secret to save me.*

I took a step towards Aquilo without even knowing that I'd done it. I had a sudden breathless need to trace over the blood bracelet and know that he was mine, safe, and *alive*.

As he flew towards me, my throat tightened. Maybe if I'd grown up knowing another magical kid like him, I wouldn't have felt so alone. What would it've been like to have explored our new magic together, rather than both had to hide it? Our childhoods had been stolen from both of us, right? But I was determined that from now on, we'd be free and so would our magic.

When Dual slipped behind me, stroking my curls back, I shivered. The beads in his hair clacked across my neck, and his lips were hot on my ear.

"Are you surprised that your mage is the hero? Aquilo has sneaked out and sought sanctuary in my court for years." Dual swept his tongue down my neck.

"As I have Fallen, I swear that these witches don't deserve him."

"You're singing to the witchy choir here." I couldn't help the way that my red snapped possessively, however, at the thought that Aquilo had been...yep, I was leaving it at *friends*...with Dual. "You're a greedy vampire, you know that? First you want my Charms and now my future husband."

Dual's laugh gusted breath against my neck in a way that was so erotic it should've been illegal. Hey, for all I knew in witch law, *it was*. "What can I say? I'm a hedonist. The Fallen don't get hung up on little things like that." He wrapped his wings around me. They smelled tangy and sweet; I hungered to suck on his wingtip. "By my bones, don't be jealous. There's enough Daddy to go around for all three of you. Just think about it." *Wait, he was serious...?* I wrenched out of his wings to look at him. He studied me back, speculatively. "You'll be safer at my court."

I swallowed. He had a point, right? I couldn't believe that I'd trust him more than the witches who I'd known about my whole life or the werewolves. But Aquilo had gone to him — *had always gone to him* — and for him to feel safe amongst vampires, meant at least that they were safer than the witches.

And I didn't have a home anymore, now that the House of Silver was destroyed.

I glanced at Stella's mauled body. It wasn't like I

could ever bring myself to take over the House of Seasons.

Aquilo landed in front of his mom. His gaze fixed on the knife at Moon's throat. When he raised it finally to his mom's, his eyes were frozen ice.

"There shall be no more killing or flaying of Omegas," Aquilo's voice was low and dangerous.

Ivy's lips curled. "You'd give *me* orders?"

"Hasn't someone always?" Lux's voice wound deadly as a blade, as she prowled towards her mom.

Ivy's gaze glanced between her two twins in shock: dark and light haired, they stood together.

Aquilo gaped at his sister in equal surprise. Lux was an elitist bully who'd tormented me as a kid and Aquilo ever since she'd discovered that he was a mage. But the way that she'd *begged* Ivy to save Aquilo's life had woken her up to the truth that hurting him could mean his death, and she was a lot of asshole things, but at heart, she loved her brother.

It was just that she'd been raised to hate mages.

The Ambassador dashed towards Aquilo, leaping around him in joy, although his howl was muffled through his gas mask. I'd forgotten Aquilo's kindness to the Ambassador.

Now that Stella was dead, could I adopt the Ambassador?

I grinned because Amadeus would either *whoop* or possibly drop between my thighs and do that licking thing with his tongue that we both loved so much in celebration.

When we'd been kids, I'd thought Aquilo was a snooty bully who didn't have any friends but his sister. It turned out, however, that he was more popular than me.

It was weird that I kind of didn't mind that.

Ivy snorted. "Someone's keen for an early night without pudding. Enough, Lux. Grab your disgraceful brother, we're going home."

Lux's mask slipped, and her eyes flashed. "My brother is no disgrace. *I am* for not understanding it sooner."

Aquilo's eyes widened. Then his fingers lightly brushed against his sisters'. She startled, before brushing the back of her hand against Aquilo's.

I remembered how Lux had always protected Aquilo when he'd been little, before his magic had come in, like he was precious. Aquilo had called it *control*, rather than love.

Maybe this time it could be different?

I ached for Aquilo to have the chance for his sister to love him because I knew that he was desperate for it. I hated that I'd discovered the truth about my family but at least I knew that they'd always loved me.

Aquilo had never been loved.

Please, please…let him have this.

Blood streamed from Ivy's eyes like tears; her

cheeks were wet with scarlet. "You shame us by exposing your magic, *mage*," Ivy snarled. "Now I discover that I've raised a traitor as well...? I confined you to your room. I punished you. I—"

"I'm well aware of all that you've done, mother," Aquilo drawled. "I've worked hard every day of my life to exceed your expectations and yet it's made no difference to your *punishments*. I could spend my life achieving every goal that you set me and I wouldn't be able to live down the shame of what I am and was born to be….a mage."

"A *hot* mage," I added.

Aquilo's lips twitched like he was smothering a smile, and his chest and neck pinked in a way that made him even hotter. "It appears that my fiancée believes that I'm a *hot mage*. She also wishes me to be *free*." He ducked his head, but I didn't miss the way that his shoulders shook. Eddies of air wavered around him in sympathetic distress. "With her, the same as with the vampires, I don't feel ashamed. They make me determined not to hide what I am anymore." His gaze slid to Lux who scrutinized him with a sudden intensity. Then he flew to Ivy on a blast of wind. "I shan't be invisible."

"Then you'll be dead." Ivy's face was coated in blood in full Blood Witch mode, as she launched herself at her son.

Holy witching hell…no, no, no….

The knife flashed; moonlight caught gleaming silver

along its blade. I threw myself forward, at the same time as Lux, but I couldn't make it in time.

It was going to slit Aquilo's throat...

Only, then there was a flash of white, which launched itself up and between the knife and Aquilo. The blade sank with a sickening crunch into the side of the Omega...*into the Ambassador*...and Ivy staggered backwards, as Aquilo cradled the Ambassador down to the floor in his arms.

"I'm sorry, sorry, sorry..." Aquilo wept.

He clutched the Ambassador's bloody body to his face, whilst his white hair mingled with the Ambassador's white fur, as he bent over him.

The Ambassador struggled to raise his head to lick Aquilo's face, then he closed his eyes and became still.

Too still.

Hecate help me, the Ambassador had died in Aquilo's arms...died to save him.

My red cocooned around Aquilo, stroking him to sooth him. Yet death I understood. There was no comforting. Ivy had stolen a prince away, but it meant nothing to her because how many Omegas had she murdered?

Dual crouched next to Aquilo, gently touching his hand, whilst Moon whined mournfully and trotted over, before resting his head on the Ambassador's like a goodbye.

My eyes gleamed with tears, but I couldn't let

myself give in to grief. I had a Blood Witch's ass to kick.

When I turned to Ivy, I was surprised to find Lux at my side, and her look was one that I remembered from all those times that she'd bullied me, as well as the nightmares I'd suffered after. I'd never expected it to be directed at her mom.

Trying to kill her brother had been a dick move.

Ivy stumbled backwards, but Ramiel caught her firmly in his wings.

Ivy wailed, struggling against his grip. "Who do any of you think you are to go against our traditions and laws?"

My smile was all teeth. "I'm a painter who loves Jeff Buckley and fruity cocktails. Oh, *and I'm the freaking Wolf Charmer.*"

I smelled the coppery tang the moment before Ivy disappeared in a bubble of blood magic. Mischief howled in outrage.

Lux shrugged. "She can only hide, and I'm exceptional at Hide and Seek."

I made a choking noise in my throat, battling not to flinch. I'd spent many hours as a kid playing Hide and Seek in the House of Blood with Lux...only when she found me, that was when the pain started.

You know, maybe it was time that Ivy experienced her daughter's game.

I glanced at Aquilo, who was still rocking and cradling the Ambassador's body to his chest.

Who was I kidding? Ivy was more than overdue to meet the bully version of her daughter.

I stiffened, as out of the corner of my eye, I caught movement in the shadowy arches. I nodded at Mischief, and he spun disks between his hands, before swooping up to the ceiling. Dual stood, gesturing at his vampires to gather behind him.

I scanned the arches. I was high on the adrenaline of the fight, fear, and freaking grief of what I'd already lost.

Don't think about the Ambassador...don't think... How in the witching hell would I tell Amadeus that his prince had been killed...?

Whoever decided that now was a good time to mess with me would have their ass handed to them, and I wouldn't even bother with the sling.

When a gang of Alphas slouched into the chamber like raiding a witch's house was a chore, I gaped at them. I recognized them as Alphas from the Kingdom of the Gods: I remembered the way they'd looked like moonbeams in Wild Hall. They wore shimmering transparent dresses with platinum collars (just like Amadeus). Their black hair was identically caught onto the top of their heads with clips like crescent moons.

My brows furrowed. "Aren't all the wolves meant to be caged tonight?"

Dual snorted. "Your pretty incubus has you sitting on his lap as a pet already, has he?" I bristled, whilst my red danced as excited by the image Dual had conjured, as it was outraged. *Now was not the time for naughty kinkiness.* "There's always a danger to loving wolves."

I examined him, surprised by the deep melancholy lacing his words. That was experience speaking, and experience hurt like a bitch.

When Dual sauntered towards the Alphas with the vampires falling into rank behind him, I expected him to attack, but instead he shot me an apologetic wink over his shoulder. "This is where I leave you, Charmer. I'll take on witches but not werewolves."

The lead Alpha nodded at him with a sickly smile that didn't reach her eyes.

What did the wolves have on Dual? His sudden retreat smelled of blackmail more than cowardice, which was kind of sour like rancid milk.

I arched my brow. "I take it that we no longer have a home at your Court, *Daddy*?"

The lead Alpha scrunched her face up in disgust. "Yuck, keep your Fallen sex games to yourself."

Dual waggled his eyebrows. "Where would be the fun be in that?" Even I shriveled at the Alpha's venomous glare. Dual's wings drooped, and he cleared his throat. "The thing is that werewolves and my court have this *we don't bother you,* and *you don't bother us* thing going on. I can't mess that up for my people, especially now that the witch folk will be on our arses, and there's something far too precious riding on the deal for me to break it." He blew me a kiss, although there was something in his eyes that he seemed to be willing me to understand. "Until next time, witchy."

Precious…? Like diamonds, his vinyl collection, or a Blood Lover? I was going with Blood Lover, after his orgasmic praising of blood.

But would he abandon us over blood?

Yep, I truly didn't know a damn thing about vampires, only the way that I heated inside at Dual's touch and craved to be able to trust him.

Huh, well that impulse had bitten me in the ass.

"You can't go with the Fallen Duke." The Alpha waved a lazy hand; her dress shimmered in the light. The other Alphas encircled us, as if they were the shark gangs at my High School. I blinked. These Alphas were nothing like the ones in the Wilds. They didn't dominate with their strength because they didn't feel the need to: they were too self-assured. "You're coming with us to the Kingdom of the Gods."

Aquilo stiffened, finally looking up from the Ambassador. His eyes were red-rimmed but fearful. As a kid from the House of Blood (who'd been responsible for more Omega deaths than any other coven), he'd be in danger in Wolf Kingdom.

Lux shook her head. "My brother remains with me."

I snorted. "Seriously, do you ever think of anyone but yourself and your brother?"

Lux's gaze was icy. "Why? Should I?"

"If I don't marry Aquilo, he'll die," I gritted out. "He stays with me."

The lead Alpha sighed. "Whatever. But you're all cordially invited to the Kingdom of the Gods because Queen Banan wishes to meet her daughter-in-law, *yada yada.*"

I stiffened. "So, where we're at is that my own mother-in-law is kidnapping me?"

I jumped as the heavy metal of Ozzy Osbourne's "Bark at the Moon" burst in wild guitars from the Alpha's pocket. She held her finger up at me in the universal gesture to silence me, whilst she pulled out her iPhone.

I grimaced; it was just my luck to discover Alphas with a sense of humor.

Also, why was it now weirder for me to see someone chatting on an iPhone than it was to see vampires swooping in to fight witches?

My life was officially screwed.

The lead Alpha tapped her foot, as she hummed and nodded to whoever was clearly commanding her down the iPhone.

Who was pulling the Alphas' puppet strings?

At last, the lead Alpha swiped off her phone, before pointing it at me like a gun. "We're not lawless Wilds."

When Moon growled, her gaze swept over him mockingly. "This isn't a kidnapping: it's an invitation to our Lunar Shrine. We'll make sure that your Charms are treated and healed. By the light of the moon, let us honor you as guests. Haven't you overstayed your welcome with the witches?"

I crossed my arms. "Okay, maybe…"

That'd be a huge *yep with a dollop of whipped cream, sprinkles, and chocolate sauce on top.*

Where else could we go? My Charms were still unconscious, and I didn't know how to make certain that they awoke. Aquilo had burned every bridge to ash with his mom. I'd brought my own house tumbling down to rubble. Dual wouldn't…*or couldn't*…help us. The only family who I had left were in America and they were non-magicals. How could they understand any of this? Plus, werewolves weren't allowed to travel and it wasn't like they had passports.

Escaping had been the easy part; it was building a new life that was hard. Plus, I wanted to claim back the kingdoms for my Charms and help the Omegas. I couldn't do that by running away.

It looked like it was time to throw myself to the wolves again…but this time, I'd be leading them.

I took a deep breath. "You heal my Charms and don't kill my fiancé mage." The lead Alpha sighed like my demands were a hassle, but she nodded. "Let's start with the honoring."

"And the worship." The lead Alpha licked her lips, before staring at Mischief. She tapped her iPhone over her heart like she was texting a love message. Mischief arched an imperious brow, although he glanced at me in confusion. "*Our Moon God has returned.*"

Moon God, Moon God, Moon God...

The Alphas chanted in adoration that looked closer to wanting to jump Mischief and discover just how godly he was without his pants on, and I knew that he was *seriously* godly.

Mischief became ashen, backing away, whilst the Alphas circled around my pack and me.

The lead Alpha grinned. "Oh, and our Wolf Witch."

The Kingdom of the Gods was a land of fanatic moon worshipers, who'd decided that Mischief was their god and I was *their* witch. I'd go with them to save my Charms, but I had the churning sensation in my gut that their devotion made them more dangerous than even the Wilds.

CHAPTER 17

Waking up in the Lunar Shrine to the soft kiss of an angel to my inner wrist, a wolf to my neck, and an incubus to my lips, was exactly how I'd imagined the Kingdom of the Gods would be. Well, if I'd dreamed of it as a sort of half Wolf Charmer utopia and half divine reward.

I sighed, wriggling further into the softness of the deep satin cushions, hoping to encourage my lovers down to the good bits.

Woah, hold up one mage hexed minute, my Charms had been healed from the gas and transformed safely back into guys again...*naked* guys whose dicks were pressing eagerly like impatient puppies against me.

I fought not to giggle. It looked like *that* part of them wasn't leashed.

My Charms' clothes were neatly folded next to the

cushions, which meant that they'd transformed back and then had been stripped.

That wasn't creepy at all then.

The night before, the Alphas had marched my exhausted ass all the way back to the Kingdom of the Gods, which was besides the Thames. When I'd raised my hand like I was still a kid in class and asked how we wouldn't give the non-magicals a show that'd end up on social media, unless they, you know, thought we were the most convincing LARPers ever, the lead Alpha had grinned and told me that the angels had set up the spells and wards so that non-magicals couldn't see the kingdoms or any who crossed between. Seriously, it shook me that angels and vampires even fought whole wars in front of the humans, but the non-magicals never saw a thing.

Trust me, knowing the truth hurt, but living a life of ignorance would've been worse, despite the delicious cocktails, donuts, and coffee…

Holy hell, I needed a soy latte like *now*: a flat white, an espresso, I mean, I'd settle for a cappuccino…

Slowly, I cracked open one eye and then the other to find myself staring up into Amadeus' crimson gaze. It was as startling and sinfully beautiful as the first time that he'd danced for me at my wedding feast in Wild Hall. For a moment, however, he looked troubled, before he bent to kiss me again with such intensity and passion that I gasped. His hair swept across my cheek and I could taste the rich chocolate of his lips, but also his pain like just by being in his kingdom, he'd lost me.

He was still wearing his gloves, which were his only item of clothing (and boy, was that look a turn-on), and their soft touch made my skin tingle at each sweep down the hollow between my collarbones. I licked his lower lip, before curling my tongue gently into his mouth.

I'm right here...you didn't lose me... You can't please me, if you act like we're not pack...

Amadeus whined, tumbling back from me and scattering the cushions. Emperor caught him, holding him against his chest and throwing an accusing glare at me.

I shoved myself to my knees. I'd been dressed, whilst whatever drug in the air had kept my guys asleep enough to be *undressed,* in a red satin ball gown with black crescents and a billowing train that mimicked my shadows. It was gorgeous in the same way that this whole Lunar Shrine was, as if I was just another statue in it to be worshiped. Plus, since the whole shattering into itty pieces of my great-grandmother's statue, I wasn't so eager to go the whole sculpted route or do this venerated Wolf Witch thing either.

I wrinkled my nose against the damp earthy scent; the shrine was underground like the rest of the Kingdom of the Gods.

From my glimpses last night, it was a vast bunker or burrow. There were no windows and the pale light shone from crescent lanterns that swung over tinkling fountains. Water foamed down the corner of the room in a waterfall. In the central wall, a giant closed door that was shaped like the full moon, trapped us inside the shrine. There were no seats, only the luxurious cushions strewn over the floor like this was a sultan's tent, which reminded me uncomfortably of the *Only Pretty Betas* tent back in the Wilds, where Amadeus had reigned as king.

This was Amadeus' kingdom; I'd better not forget that my Charm was also a seducer and schemer who was the only one who knew how to survive here.

And I'd just pissed him off somehow.

I crossed my arms. "Hey, what did I do?"

"Excuse me, is this a new guessing game?" Mischief lounged against an arched alcove. The fact that he was safe and free from the witches, whilst his magic crackled in waves down his wings made my throat too tight to speak. Okay, that and how scorching hot he was when naked, *and the royal prick knew it.* "Oh, goodie, it is then...? I'll go first. The Charmer punished her incubus for displeasing her. Do I win the prize?"

I blinked at him. Jesus, incubi were vulnerable to control and abuse if they could be hurt even by their partner's fleeting displeasure. I'd only *thought* that Amadeus couldn't please me because he didn't feel like *mine* anymore or at least, now that he was back where he was prince, I knew that there was something he wasn't telling me.

And when had those words ever meant anything good?

My shadows wound out, stroking down Amadeus' chest and running over his nipples as light as feathers, until he arched; in every touch, I whispered just how much he *pleased* me.

When Amadeus turned to look at me again, his smile was soft. "I forgive you, see, as long as you want me still."

I curled with guilt. "I'll always want you, remember?"

Moon blinked sleepily, rubbing his eyes. "By my fur, enough angst, furless. There's cuddles for everybody."

When Moon stretched his long pale limbs, he looked angelically beautiful amongst the satin. The memory of the knife slicing into Moon's neck and matting his fur scarlet had me launching myself into his arms like he was a year's free supply of soy lattes.

Cuddle time…hmm, addictive.

To my surprise, Emperor also dived into Moon's hug, as quickly as Amadeus who snuggled down with a slinky wiggle of his hips. Yep, I wasn't checking out my brand on Amadeus' cute ass…*except, duh, of course I was.*

I wrapped my shadows around all of my Charms,

caressing across them, whilst they held onto me. Moon's curls were ticklish against my nose, and his chest was hard beneath me, but nobody could cuddle like him.

Mischief snickered. "Am I suddenly counted as *nobody*? What happened to me being your god?"

Ramiel rolled his eyes. "Will I do?"

He pushed up, stalking to Mischief, before caging him against the wall.

Mischief stiffened. "I believe you may have misunderstood the definition of a *cuddle*."

Ramiel's hair fell across his face, as he tipped Mischief's head back to kiss down his throat. "And perhaps you've forgotten our discussion about *not demanding worship*?"

When he rested his long fingers warningly on Mischief's hip, Mischief squirmed.

Maybe Mischief should be renamed the *Spanked God*...

This time I couldn't hold in the giggle.

Mischief sniffed as he eyed me. "I'm delighted that I'm providing entertainment for the witch. My mistake, I hadn't assumed that requesting I be held and loved equally was worship. I'll remember my place—"

Instantly, Mischief was smothered in a feathery embrace, as Ramiel kissed across his cheeks. "I'm sorry, please, I'm sorry. Forgive me?"

Mischief blinked at him. "It's no matter. I love

having my heart torn in two by my lover's see-saws of unpredictability."

When a tear trailed down Ramiel's cheek, Mischief bent forward and licked the tear, before it could fall.

Ramiel's soft gaze was anxious. "I worry about the fanatics of this kingdom and how they intend to worship you. Even this shrine feels…" He shivered. "…*dead*. You more than any of us know the hollowness of worship. But sometimes, I act too much like my strict Glory, and I never wish to be cruel."

Mischief snorted. "Don't fret. You couldn't be *cruel*, even if your pretty pink-hair, poetry books, or savior over there depended on it." Then he touched his hand to Ramiel's wing, which had been clawed by the mechanicals and swayed as he took the pain, healing it. Mischief's skin was clammy and ashen, as he rasped, "Do you perceive now? It is *I* who worship *you*."

"Zophia, you don't need to prove anything," Ramiel chided, although his voice was laced with affection.

Ramiel supported Mischief to the ground, cocooning him in his wings in what looked to be an epic cuddle. So, all it took was courage, sacrifice, and pain to get into the angel cuddle-zone.

Angels were demanding assholes, go figure.

"I said *everybody.*" Moon flailed around in the cushions. "Moth? Aquilo? Get your behinds into this cuddle fest."

I froze.

How on Hecate's tits hadn't I noticed that they weren't with us? Okay, I had just awoken from a drugged sleep in an entirely new wolf kingdom, after a battle in which I'd seen my aunt torn apart. So, hello *trauma alert* here. Except, it was more like I'd been so relieved that *any* of us were still alive that I hadn't paused to take a headcount. I mean, did I need to start taking a register now?

The Alphas had upheld their bargain about healing my Charms, but they'd only promised that Aquilo wouldn't die. My heart beat against my ribcage so fast that my chest ached. *Why had I been so trusting?* My uncle had always drilled into me to be precise in business and never to leave loopholes because there was a disturbing amount that could be done to a person that wouldn't end up with them dead.

And that was just another one of the fascinating things that I'd learned this week: from painting to degrees of pain.

They wouldn't truly hurt my fiancé, right? Yep, that didn't even sound convincing to me.

Merlin's balls...

Moon struggled out of the pile of cushions, hurling himself against the door. When there was no *bang* or *clank*, I realized that it must be padded, which made me feel like we'd been tossed in a cell for crazy people.

Maybe this whole kingdom was one big padded cell?

"Let me out, you rotten bastards!" Moon hollered. "Where's Moth? Moth, can you hear me? *Moth...?"*

At Moon's anguished yell, Okami woke up with a growl, burrowing his way out of the pile of clothes. He poked his silky snout over Emperor's waistcoat, snuffling against the dank of the cavern and joined his howls to Moon's.

Okami had never bonded with anyone but me. But Moon had been the first true wolf that Okami had ever met; I didn't doubt that he loved him.

"Silence that howling and calm yourself." Mischief's cool drawl cut across their distress.

Mischief pointed at the lights, whilst leaning his head against Ramiel.

I scrambled out of Emperor's hold to stare at the lights, which were tracking Moon. "What am I looking at here?"

Mischief's brow quirked. "Smile at the nice cameras."

Moon's rude finger gesture and raspberry definitely wasn't either a smile or princely.

Mischief gave a delighted laugh. "Close enough."

I strolled to Moon, tipping his chin back with my red. He bit his lip, hard enough to break the skin. I didn't blame him because it was his brother somewhere in this kingdom, which from what I could figure was far from cozy with his own, just like it hated my mage fiancé. But violent behavior triggered Big Brother, and the only way to be taken as not hostile…well, was to act *not hostile.*

In the Wilds, Moon had been sent to re-education, whilst I'd been thrown down a well. Here, my pack and I had been stripped and imprisoned in luxury with fountains, cushions, and cameras. I figured that the Gods were so far winning on the host front and I didn't want to test it by rebellion that didn't change anything.

Because that was something that I'd learned from my Charms: rebelling was how you acted, not what you said. But it was also about what you *changed.* We could have tried to free the other Omegas at the Re-education Center along with Moon, but it wouldn't have freed *all* the Omegas.

And Moon and I *would* free them all.

Right now, however, we had to convince the Kingdom of the Gods that we weren't a threat, then we could escape this room and find Moth and Aquilo. Huh, I was locked in with three naked wolf princes, how could I show the peeping toms that the wolves were under my control and hey, have a little fun at the same time?

Sexy decisions, sexy decisions…

I smiled. "What do you say, we give the voyeurs something to watch?"

Emperor stretched his arms above his head, which rippled the muscles along his chest. "Kinky." He snatched Amadeus' hand, pulling him up. Then he prowling towards us, towing Amadeus along with him. "*I'd* say: not without us you don't."

Moon rubbed his curls against my neck, clutching my shoulders like I might disappear the same as his brother. His nod was tentative, but the way that he licked up my throat wasn't.

Emperor's fingers played down my spine across the fabric of my dress, teasing so lightly that I bit my tongue at the barely there touches, as I almost begged him to rip my new dress and just *touch* me already.

But only *almost* because hey, it was a gorgeous dress.

I didn't expect the way that Amadeus wrenched Moon's head away from me and pressed his finger into the thin cut along his neck hard enough to make him wince. "Look you, did something happen last night, whilst the rest of our sexy behinds were gassed, that you'd like to confess?"

Moon blinked with pretend innocence. "No fair, what happens in a witch's house, stays in a witch's house."

Amadeus growled, nipping Moon's ear; Moon yipped, casting his best sad face at Amadeus, which had no effect. Unless the desired effect was to make him nip his *other* ear.

Moon yelped, before rubbing at both his ears.

Mischief raised his eyebrow. "I'm sorry, does that hurt? Let me assist you: your neck is cut because last night you had every intention of sacrificing yourself to save the rest of us. Oh, I wonder if the incubus prince will bite anything more interesting this time?"

"Thank you, oh helpful god," Moon huffed.

Mischief inclined his head. "You're welcome, most grateful subject."

Amadeus' ruby eyes glittered dangerously, although he stroked through Moon's hair gently. "You want to take a guess where I'm imagining biting you?"

"Aye, right," Moon grumbled, even though he leaned into Amadeus' caress, "like I'll choose the method of my own destruction."

Amadeus' stern face slipped, and he snickered. "You wouldn't have to, see, if you weren't always trying to sacrifice yourself."

Moon grinned. "Fur and fangs, it's what I'm here for."

When Amadeus growled, I tensed.

Wow, the Prince of the Wilds had the trick of pushing the other princes' buttons, and he knew it too.

"Bad, bad, wolf…" Amadeus dived on top of Moon, tumbling him to the floor, which was padded in soft ivory satin, the same as the door.

Moon whined as he fell, landing underneath Amadeus, but his claws and fangs didn't lengthen, only his hardening dick. I remembered from pinning him down in the stream, after hunting him to Wolf Bite, just how much it excited him to be caught.

"Get off, wee idiot." Moon bucked his hips but then hissed as that only rubbed his dick against Amadeus'.

Amadeus winked over his shoulder at the hidden camera in the closest light: sin wrapped up in alabaster perfection. "How about we both get off?"

He writhed like a snake along Moon, whose eyes were now glassy. When Moon whimpered, I was right there with him.

I watched a bead of sweat trace down the curve of Amadeus' spine between the silvery scars, which made me tense just a moment because it reminded me that someone in this kingdom had whipped Amadeus to mold him into this seductive creature: *my pretty Beta prince*. Then I kind of lost concentration on the thought because the bead slid teasingly between his pale ass cheeks, and I caught the way that Emperor had been watching the same thing, and his tongue darted out to swipe his lips…

I twisted to Emperor, catching his tongue with mine, before swiping his lip in imitation of him. He hummed with contentment, dragging me closer against his powerful chest, and my shadows turned their attentions to his butterfly tattoo, tracing across the patterns and playing with the dark magic woven inside.

When I drew back, my heart was thudding as hard as I could feel Emperor's was. He curled me against his side, whilst eying the two wolves who were still struggling against each other on the floor.

Moon appeared to have remembered that this was a fight, but although he was larger than Amadeus, you could tell that he didn't want to hurt him, which put him at a disadvantage. It also flooded me with warmth that even roughhousing, he was protective of the other prince, just like Emperor and he had been in the memory that I'd witnessed of them as kids. Plus, Amadeus had a dancer's agility, which made him as fast as a ninja; he coiled around Moon nipping him with as much relish as Okami would have.

Maybe he had a biting fetish too.

Two wolf princes fighting shouldn't have been this hot. Then again, since they were naked and both panting with desire, whilst pretending to ignore the way that they were rubbing against each other at the same time, *maybe it should.*

Which one of my Charms would break and come first? I had my money on Amadeus because Moon's pleasure was feeding his incubus side; Amadeus' eyes glowed dangerously with the fresh power.

"Should we help?" I asked.

Like Emperor couldn't tell that what I actually meant was: *shouldn't we be dragging off my dress and diving into this hot wolfie orgy?*

I was the bad, bad witch…

Emperor gave a lazy smile. "Which one?"

I circled my thumb across the softness of his hip. "Both of them?"

Emperor clenched his jaw, although he quivered. "Why would I give up watching this adorable show?" Then he raised his eyebrow cockily. "Hairpulling and biting only. No kneeing in the balls because you may want them later." When Amadeus and Moon both froze, glaring up at Emperor, he swallowed. "Remember what I said about no kneeing…?"

I *eeped,* as my legs were pulled from under me at the same time as Emperor's. Moon caught me, whilst Amadeus pulled Emperor's arms above his head. To my surprise, Emperor held them there without needing to be told and like he was simply choosing to sprawl on the floor.

Amadeus grinned down at Emperor with way too much smugness.

Just how much had Moon's power strengthened Amadeus?

Mischief chuckled, although his voice was commanding and dark. "I believe that the prince negotiated *hair pulling*. Pull his hair hard, incubus."

Amadeus' wound his fingers into Emperor's golden-locks. Emperor flinched, before Amadeus had even pulled, and then I couldn't help the snicker because I knew that it was because his style had been messed up. Moon soothed over Emperor's chest as he nuzzled at my neck. Then Amadeus pulled...*hard.*

Huh, Emperor's moan was seriously one of pleasure

and not pain. His lips parted, as his chest rose and fell rapidly; his pupils were blown.

Moon snatched my hand, pulling me over Emperor, before he smiled that radiant smile that made my skin tingle and my toes curl.

Ever-living witches, I needed him to smile at me like that every day.

Moon cocked his head. "Aye, next was *biting*, right?"

Emperor's eyes widened, and his breath sped up. When his gaze met mine, I rubbed my fingers across his. Amadeus was the virgin here because this week was the first time that he'd been allowed to have sexy times in his male form. Before he'd become my Charm, he'd been forced as a Beta to transform and *play* as a woman. Yet Emperor, who I suspected had more experience than any of us in this room...well, possibly than Mischief because who knew how kinky angels were...was acting like the blushing bride on his wedding day.

He hadn't been like this when we'd been trapped down the well. *What had changed?*

Curses and hexes, *of course* Emperor was freaked out. This was *Moon* smiling at him, being intimate, and *loving* him. How long had Emperor suffered being *hated* by his friend? And why?

Plus, how hard was it for Emperor to give up his Alpha authority and play the submissive role in this set up? To lie here, pretending to be the Omega because this wasn't simply me as Chief Alpha this time, it was an Omega and a Beta.

Sometimes sacrifices weren't so obvious, but they hurt just as much.

When I squeezed Emperor's hand, his gaze focused on mine, until his breathing steadied. Then I slipped my red around him, sliding over his skin, until he shuddered from my caresses. I eased him around, even though Amadeus never let go of his hair, tapping his shoulders with my shadows, until he lowered his arms and leaned against the wall. Now he was no longer under us but equal.

Emperor grabbed my shoulders, crashing his lips against mine more savagely than he ever had before, as if needing to reassert his hidden Alpha status.

Yep, there was no complaining from this witch.

"On my fangs, I haven't forgotten to bite." Moon slid down to Emperor's dick, blowing across its head. When Emperor jumped, he peeked up at him from underneath his eyelashes. "I might cock block you, but I'd never cock *bite* you."

Then he kissed down the skin joining Emperor's hip and thigh to his inner thigh, sucking hard enough to form hickeys.

I pulled back from the sweet vanilla taste of Emperor's mouth. When I glanced over Ramiel, I noticed with a curl of warmth that unfurled deep inside me that Ramiel had one arm around Mischief, holding him firmly in place, whilst his other was wanking him slowly and edging him in time with Emperor's own spiraling pleasure. Mischief purred in a way that was thrilling.

It was no wonder that Amadeus was glowing with flushed power; my own shadows were thrumming with it through the bond. I clenched my fists to control the waves of heat that were washing through me. At least, until Moon's fangs grew. Then my crimson seethed with possessive rage at the threat of somebody else biting my Bitten, even in play.

My crimson wrapped around Moon's chest, just as I yanked him back by his curls. "I'm the only one who bites my Charms."

Weirdly, that no longer sounded wrong. Maybe I truly was transforming into this *Wolf Witch*.

The said Charms cast soft glances at me like I'd just said some romantic schmaltz like: *no witch has ever loved a wolf with her last breath, but you'd be mine…*

Did wolves give greeting cards? The lines inside would be epic.

When I met Emperor's eye, his grin had returned to its usual cockiness level. "Bite my gorgeous self, and let's have the wild, dirty, mind blowing sex that I know you've been dreaming about."

I knocked the cocky right out of him when my teeth clamped into the delicate skin of his inner thigh right over the purple hickey left by Moon. He quivered, as

Amadeus pulled his hair, yanking his head forward this time so that he was forced to watch, whilst I bit down with deliberate slowness.

Okami howled, darting across the Lunar Shrine to nip at the Charms' necks excitedly, whilst his tail wagged.

When I peeked up, I almost let go of the bite because — *witches' tits* — Moon had lowered his lips over the tip of Emperor's dick and was sucking at it with a fierce concentration, whilst he tentatively stroked Emperor's balls.

This was Moon's first time…*doing any of this.* Obviously, he wanted to make an impression.

When I caught Emperor's eye — trapped as he was between Amadeus, Moon, and me — he looked stripped of his masks, Alpha dickishness, and constant need to protect everyone else. This morning, we were looking after…*loving*…him.

He trembled under our attentions. He was spellbound by the new sensations, gritting his teeth with the effort to not entirely let himself go and boy, how many decades had he needed to just let go?

I stroked my red up his spread thighs, towards the pink furl beneath his balls. Moon pulled off Emperor's dick, stroking it now in time with Ramiel's wanking of Mischief. Their desire in the bond around me, was as thrilling as the thrumming shadows and Amadeus' power fed by the pleasure.

When I tapped over the tight hole with my red, Emperor gasped. He came in a pearly arc across his stomach, at the same time as Mischief. Both wolf and angel wailed.

Hey, I'd never made a guy scream in bed before. That was what came of having a wolf tag team.

Then Emperor banged his head against the door, closing his eyes. "You're aware that you just killed me?" He groaned.

Amadeus let go of Emperor's hair, before smoothing it back into place. Then he kissed Emperor in gentle pecks across the corners of his mouth. "A chance at a shag with a fine behind like mine is worth dying for, see."

I pulled my red back inside, before giving the bite mark a final lick and sitting up. Moon cuddled against Emperor's side, resting his head on his shoulder.

Emperor blinked, sleepily. "That…just then…wasn't simply mind blowing; it was…mind sucked out…brain dead now. What a charming epitaph I shall have: *Here lies the Prince of the Alphas who was screwed to death.*"

Moon patted him on the stomach consolingly. "So, I wasn't bad for a virgin wolf?"

Woah, and there was a witch's cauldron worth of insecurity.

Emperor gave a gentle smile, although he waved his

hand airily. "Let's not forget that you did have a gorgeous cock to work with."

Mischief snorted. "Talking of cocks…or more precisely dicks…" Mischief slunk to his feet, sauntering to the fountain to wash off his own sticky stomach. Moon nudged Emperor, but he shook his head, drowsily. Hey, if he wanted to become tacky and itchy, that was his affair. "Now that we've appeased the voyeurs, I've had time to think, and maybe we should address the blindingly bright white elephant in the room: the gang of Alpha dicks who brought us to this kingdom. Shall we put it down to coincidence that they turned up on the night of the centennial at your aunt's house? Oh yes, and that they weren't caged, which within itself broke the treaty. Now, what was it that I've always believed…? One coincidence is simply chance but more than that is *infernal betrayal.*"

Shocked, I withered myself at the ferocity of Mischief's glare, as his wings spread behind him, sizzling with popcorn smelling magic.

I expected Amadeus to nuzzle further into Moon's arms for protection or deny the accusation with a sexy pout. At least, I *hoped* that was what he'd do.

Instead, he launched up, glowing with his own power, freshly fed on pleasure. His skin was translucent under the pale light of the lamps, and his eyes sparkled. Then he stalked towards Mischief like a challenge.

My pack were about to fight, and it'd be real, rather

than roughhousing or sexy play. My breath caught in my throat because I was desperate for neither of my guys to be hurt.

Yet no matter what happened in the fight, *I'd* already been hurt because Amadeus had betrayed me.

CHAPTER 18

I stood, hugging myself in the Lunar Shrine, whilst my guts churned in a way that was becoming weirdly familiar: Secrets and Betrayal Tummy Ache, I was calling it. Before I'd returned to England to discover my part in the wolf and witch wars, I'd been cocooned safely with my uncle in a world that turned on the petty gossip of secrets: who was cheating on their millionaire partner, who'd paid the most for their new mansion, and the best place to buy coffee (The Golden Pear)...*son of a bitch, I needed an espresso.*

Licking my lips at the ghost memory of coffee, at least sort of took away the sour taste that'd been there ever since I'd realized that Amadeus' betrayal and hidden secrets hadn't been the sort that I'd known in America.

Instead, they'd been the kind that plotters held —

the ones who brought down kingdoms and won wars through stealth. But then, I should've known that, ever since Amadeus seduced and defeated Rhona. He could've...okay, probably *would've*...killed her on the night that he'd rescued Emperor and me from the well.

I'd always known that Amadeus was deadly, it was just that it was hard to remember that when you were also under his spell.

I studied Amadeus in the light of the crescent moon lights; his skin looked eerily otherworldly. Moon and Amadeus had flanked him; their eyes glowed, whilst their nails gleamed.

Had that been the plan from the moment the Queen of the Gods had chosen and trained Amadeus to become my Charm? Mesmerize the Charmer with a half incubus who could spy on and control her, rather than be the one to be controlled?

Honestly, it was smart.

No wonder the queen had never looked at me throughout my Claiming. If I'd had to give up my adopted son to my enemy, I'd have wanted more of a backup plan than a cross my fingers and hope she wouldn't burn him with silver and stick him in a cage...*like my mom had the Ambassador*.

My breath hitched, and I gulped in air, as my lungs ached. Alarmed, Okami wound himself around my neck like he could stop my sudden shivers.

Jesus, how hadn't I thought of it before? The

Ambassador was this kingdom's prince. The queen had already sacrificed her true son to my mom; she'd been through this ordeal before, and that time her son *had* suffered.

Now, he'd *died*.

It didn't matter what Amadeus had done on behalf of his kingdom because my Wolf Charmer ass deserved it.

How were any of the shifters to know that the worst Amadeus would suffer at my witchy hands was to be stuffed in a wardrobe (and that'd been by Emperor)?

Mischief spun his magic out into a lasso. "We are both aware that you're not only the sweet and pretty wolf who you've been trained to be. Submission and sex are such useful weapons, are they not?"

Amadeus' eyes narrowed. "They're ones that have been used against me all my life. None of you know how it feels to be an incubus or trapped inside, knowing that you're nothing but *the moon's sacrifice* chosen for the Wolf Charmer."

Emperor blanched. He took a careful step forward. "I apologize if we've assumed—"

"I lied," Amadeus sighed. "I was under Moon Oath to hide...but you can see the scars? Look you, I just wanted you to think that I was a pampered prince because then I could forget that I'm only an adopted one."

"Goddess Moon! What has *adopted* to do with it?" Moon growled.

Amadeus gave a smile that was so sad it twisted my insides. "*Everything.*"

"Enough of this mawkishness." Mischief swung his magic above his head.

I hissed out a panicked breath. In the terror that my pack would fight for real I knew that despite Amadeus' betrayal, I'd never want him to be hurt. In fact, my red stung me in fury at even the thought that I wouldn't protect my Charm. Nothing that Amadeus had been forced to do — and I wasn't so much of a dick that the scars on his back didn't scream *forced* — could stop me protecting him.

Maybe Wolf Care was actually simpler than I'd thought.

My crimson burst out, wrapping around Mischief's silver in calming caresses, until he shuddered. He glanced at me questioningly, and I shook my head. Slowly, he slipped his magic back inside.

I strolled to Amadeus, tipping up his chin, as I caressed over his fluttering pulse with my thumb. "You're my Charm and my pack, but I only have the right to know what you want to share. I won't rush you. The problem we have is that you've been holding out on us about the plans of your asshole kingdom." When Amadeus tried to look away, I kissed him lightly, and his confused gaze shot to mine like he'd expected a slap, rather than tenderness. "I love you and I don't give a damn about anything you've done. We'll figure it out, but I just need to know."

"You mean that," Amadeus said like he was testing it out.

"I swear it on a mage's dick," I replied solemnly.

"I object to that," Mischief grumbled.

"Then why don't you bring that mage dick over here?" *Why did everything sound so much dirtier in Ramiel's soft voice?*

Ramiel beckoned Mischief, who swooped over the fountain, kicking the water in a sparkling spray over Amadeus' head and snickering when he spluttered. Then he landed with his best innocent expression next to Ramiel, who by the way that he crisply pulled Mischief to him by his wingtips, wasn't buying it, go figure.

Amadeus shook his damp hair, before pressing his gloved hand to my cheek, which always felt more intimate than when we were panting in pleasure. "Princess Vala's gang of Alphas — the Crescents — were to secretly remain uncaged and untransformed."

I rolled my eyes at the memory of the iPhone wielding Alpha assholes who'd invited us as *honored guests* to the Kingdom of the Gods. So, these were Amadeus' adopted sister's gang...? Honestly, I hadn't been crazy about meeting her before and now I had a feeling that she'd simply drive me crazy.

"Seriously, I get that, but how did they—"

"*My true prince.*" Amadeus' face suddenly lit up, as he twirled to Moon like the whole *betrayal thing* had just been neatly washed away. "If the Crescents came for our sexy behinds, then please tell me that they saved the Ambassador as well?"

His hope was painful, as he rocked on his heels.

My hands clenched; my tongue was heavy in my mouth. Okami licked my throat, cuddling closer around me.

I remembered how the Ambassador had tried to shelter Amadeus from the sweet-smelling gas, as well as curling around him when he was unconscious. The Ambassador had barely been more than a teenager, yet he'd shown compassion to the one who'd replaced him as prince. And he'd died to protect a mage, even though he was the son of those who'd helped torment him.

Why couldn't the witches see that wolves were more than beasts? That they could be heroes, as well as killers…?

Moon and Emperor exchanged a glance, before Emperor marched over to Amadeus and me, enfolding us both against his chest.

"The young Prince of the Gods died protecting the Charmer's fiancé." Emperor paused thoughtfully. "He was as brave as any Alpha."

When Amadeus' knees buckled, Emperor held him up. Amadeus was ashen, but it disturbed me that he didn't make a sound like he'd been coached to hold pain deep inside like just another dance move. Only when I rested my forehead against his, did his eyelids flutter, and a single tear spilled from the corner of his eye.

"He was good," Amadeus whispered like each word ripped another part of him to pieces. "Kind. Loyal. *Everything I'm not.*"

"On fear of silver, that's enough of that daft talk," Moon snarled. Moon's own eyes gleamed with tears, and Okami darted away from my neck to wind around Moon's. Moon stroked him with a shaky hand. "You're our friend and our pack. We love you, even if some rotten bastards have been pulling your strings. Let me guess, you've been spying on us for your bitch of a sister, and she's the one you told about last night…"

All of a sudden, the waterfall thundered, transforming to milk-white like it was feeding a god. The fountains shutoff dead.

Amadeus quivered in Emperor's arms, as if he knew what was coming next and (*hey, what a surprise*), it wasn't the part where us honored guests were offered a breakfast of waffles and chocolate sauce.

Come on, Crimson, if you just wish hard enough for those waffles maybe…

"That *bitch* of a sister prefers to be called *princess*." A woman's husky voice wound out of the walls and floor like dark coiling smoke. Amadeus winced. *So, there were speakers hidden around the room, as well as cameras…* My witchy tech fingers itched to tear up the padding and work out the mechanisms. But I didn't think that desecrating a shrine would make the best first impression to my mother-in-law. "But you're right, Omega." This time it was Moon's turn to wince. "Wow, not all Wilds are as dumb are they are pretty or is it just their princes who are cunning? What am I saying? No one's as pretty and cunning as *my* Beta prince, of course."

There was a growl — *woah, that was me.*

Emperor quirked his brow. "Inside, we're all growling in agreement."

I'd hoped that Amadeus' family would offer us a true home here. Hadn't the Crescents said that Mischief and I would be *worshiped*? But worship wasn't the same as love, and I wouldn't allow anyone to speak about my Charms like that anymore, even their own families. Toads and frogs, *especially* their families.

The moon doors creaked open at the same time as My Chemical Romance's "Welcome to the Black Parade" burst out of hidden speakers in an Emo anthem of marching drums, guitar riffs, and screaming epicness.

Well, that wasn't ominous at all.

Princess Vala sauntered through the doors like the music was her personal anthem. She wore a dress that was slit so high that when she swung her hips on each step it revealed her creamy thighs; she could've been Amadeus' incubus sister, rather than his adopted one. Yet there was an edge of darkness in her eyes that wasn't in Amadeus', as if she hadn't made up her mind whether she wanted to tear out your throat, kiss it, or do both at the same time.

Her hair was twisted on either side of her head in coils like twin moons, but apart from the gleam of her collar, she wasn't adorned with any jewelery. Maybe she didn't want to distract from her thick eyeliner and eyeshadow that made her look like an Emo who'd fallen into glitter.

When she clicked her fingers, the music shut off.

"Aw, that's a shame," I smirked, "we were just getting to the part where you decided to join the Black Parade."

Vala's claws grew, before she forced herself to smooth down her dress. "Beta told me that you enjoy music playing in your house. A good host helps you feel at home."

Yep, Amadeus was getting my death glare.

Amadeus wriggled down against Emperor's chest like if he couldn't see me or his sister, and Emperor just kept holding him, then the contest he'd set up between us would just *poof* like I'd cast a Vanishing Spell. In fact, I wished that I *knew* a Vanishing Spell, then Vala wouldn't look so smug.

Wouldn't it be nice if life was that simple?

"Honestly, I wouldn't call a crazy spook playing music to torment my ass, *enjoying* music." I snorted. "And I have a feeling that you don't care about me feeling at home. We're like sisters-in-law now, so it's a pleasure to meet you, but Amadeus is *mine* now, right?"

A blazing jealousy passed behind Vala's eyes that made me tremble.

Okay, I knew that as a witch and a Wolf Charmer I was Vala's enemy. Her brother had been sacrificed to my mom, and her adopted brother had also been given to me. I understood why I wouldn't be on her cuddle list. But at the same time, Amadeus must've reported to her that I hadn't hurt him, as well as the fact that I wasn't the same as the other Wolf Charmers.

Hadn't he?

But what if I *had* hurt him somehow, and he hadn't been allowed to tell me? My breath became ragged, as my red reached out, desperate to stroke through Amadeus' hair, but he snuggled down further into Emperor's arms.

Vala's smile was sweet but edged with cruelty. "*Amadeus*: is that what Beta told you to call him? Naughty, naughty. That name is banned within these walls. Someone's earned himself a spanking." Amadeus whined, and I growled — again. *Maybe there seriously was something in this Wolf Witch.* She strolled closer. "How about I tell you his true nickname?"

"Nay, how about you don't." Moon blocked her, tilting his chin up in the gesture that made my stomach squirm with its *adorable* rebelliousness. "He gets to choose his name; that's his right."

"He's a mongrel," Vala hissed, "he has no rights."

"Say that again," Mischief said silkily, although his eyes sparked, "I truly dare you."

Vala laughed, but I'd been to enough tense dinner parties in the Hamptons to know fake laughter when I heard it. "You don't look like innocents. How sweet. Why do you think a kingdom would adopt and train an incubus as their prince?"

When Amadeus flinched, I surged with the same rage as made Mischief break free of Ramiel's hold and soar towards Vala, whilst his magic wound around him in sizzling sprays.

Every godly inch of Mischief was terrifying, awe-inspiring...and hot.

Vala stumbled, as Mischief landed. Her eyes widened in shock.

"Do tell me why you think it advisable not to cease your senseless prattle?" Mischief stalked towards her, and Vala backed into the corner. "Oh, that's right, because you're a brutal, prejudiced bully. I've heard rather a lot about your sort within Wolf Kingdom, and I've fought against more oppressors than you can imagine. You talk about Amadeus' cunning, but *you're* the one who imagines yourself clever. Let me assure you that I *shall* find out what you're scheming if your intention is to hurt my pack."

Vala tossed her head with pretend indifference, even

as her heels touched the waterfall. "The *pretty* god thinks that he can—"

"*Whoops*, did I just say *Amadeus*?" Mischief leaned in closer to Vala, who stiffened. "Pray, will you spank me now? I double dare you."

Then Mischief's magic shoved Vala in the chest, sending her onto her ass beneath the milky waterfall. She shrieked, splashing and churning the foaming waters, before gasping and pulling herself out, whilst her dress stuck to her.

Her eyeliner hadn't run though, kudos.

Ramiel gave a delighted laugh, but it was Amadeus' snicker, which was muffled against Emperor's chest that made something inside me ache. How many times had *he* wanted to stand up to Vala and you know, push her under a waterfall or trap her in a room with nothing but My Chemical Romance playing on full volume for twenty-four hours? Instead, I remembered the webbing of scars on his back.

Had Vala put them there?

My expression hardened. "You wear milk well."

"*Flame*," she spat, "*that's* his nickname because it's his role to be beautiful, deadly, and attract all you silly witches, wolves, and…yeah, I hadn't thought that I was this good a trainer…but *gods* as well, like moths." When Amadeus sobbed, I hungered to slap the sneer from Vala's face. My red flooded out from me, surging around Mischief's silver, whilst I prowled to stand at his shoulder. "He was taught one thing: to betray you all into thinking that you had his love, so that he could bring me your secrets." She wiped her hand over her damp face, before fluttering her lashes at me. "I'd say that you were all burned."

"And I'd say," Mischief's icy fury sent shivers down even my spine, "this is what happens when you dare a *god*."

Mischief's silver shot out, slamming Vala against the wall.

I'd expected her to yelp, but instead she smiled.

Yep, that was officially creepy.

Her gaze darted to the crescent lights.

Well, burn me at the stake, I'd forgotten the cameras and who might be watching. With Kolby's murder and Stella's attempt to start a war with the wolves, I'd learned all about the use of a pretext.

It appeared that Vala was already the princess of diplomacy and had just set us up for the pretext because we'd stepped right in to making the first hostile move...*but what for?*

Mischief met my gaze sheepishly, immediately letting his magic slip away from Vala. My shadows prickled, sensing ancient magics in the air. Pulse pounding, I turned back to my pack, only for chains to whip from the padded floors and wrap around my Charms, as well as Ramiel, at the same time as tearing them away from each other. Only Amadeus was left free.

My fists clenched at their howls. At least the chains weren't silver, since my Charms were naked — you know, it helps to be an optimist.

I glared at Vala. "Let them go, or I swear that I'll kick your loser ass."

Vala cocked her head. "Yeah, I'm not feeling that right now."

Was she for real? How much of my Wolf Charmer powers did I have to let out to earn some respect in this new kingdom?

"Do you wish to know what your *god* is feeling right now?" Mischief held his hands smartly behind his back, but when I caught his eye I read an anxious uncertainty there.

Vala knew the script here, and her wolfie ass *was* cunning.

"I believe that now is not the time to be playing the *bow down and worship me card*," Ramiel called from across the shrine.

His voice was strained, as he struggled to breathe; the chains pressed against his chest.

"Too late." Vala grinned. "Just because you're a god, doesn't mean that you rule in my kingdom."

"Isn't it your *mom's* kingdom?" I scoffed.

Wisps of magic that were as beautiful as moon-beams whispered from the fountains. Before either Mischief and I had the time to turn away, they'd captured us in their smoky embrace, dragging us into the middle of the shrine and pulling our arms and legs apart until we were spread-eagled.

My heart thudded in my chest, whilst my back itched with sweat. But I was paralyzed. I couldn't even thrash and struggle, as I was pinned in place like an icon next to Mischief to be worshiped.

My little finger was touching Mischief's; all I could feel was that one point where his skin touched mine. I thanked Hecate that I could feel him, at least. I wouldn't have been able to take slow breaths to calm the panic, as my magic was once more forced deep inside me, until I couldn't even throw my crimson shadows out to protect myself. Next to me, I could feel the same happening to Mischief, as he too fought to steady his breathing between his desperate pants.

Witches had once taken Mischief's magic through a brand on his neck; now the wolves were doing the same thing.

Mischief was brave, loyal, and a true hero to his people...who were now hurting him.

So, that was what it was like to hate your in-laws.

Vala struggled to her feet, smoothing out her dress like it wasn't transparent and outlining her nipples. Then she pointed at Mischief and me, until the wisps spun around us. Dizzy, I watched as we became encased in mists like twin moons had swallowed us.

The deity gig sucked.

"Here," Vala clicked her fingers like Amadeus was a

dog. When he cringed back, hugging his arms across his nakedness, as if he could hide from her, she frowned. *"Come here."*

Amadeus' gaze became steely. Boy, he had some courage to look at his sister like that when the rest of his pack was hanging from the ceiling or in chains. "You can do anything, see, *anything* you like to me, but please don't hurt my pack."

Vala's mouth thinned. "I'm your pack. Now, *come here.*"

Amadeus scuffed his feet as he edged towards Vala. He ducked his head, and his hair hung across his face. I hated the darkly possessive way that Vala drew him to her, and the same hunger in her expression as she studied him that I saw in every wolf's face who came under his thrall. I knew that he was adopted, but I'd hoped that his sister had at least loved him like a sister.

Boy, was I wrong.

When she touched his cheek both Emperor and Moon growled.

"Skin to skin," Vala ordered.

Amadeus' eyes gleamed with tears, as he shook his head. "Please, I did what you asked..."

"You're displeasing me," she snarled.

Amadeus staggered, gasping with pain.

"You please me, Amadeus," I hollered because Vala telling her incubus brother that he'd displeased her was equivalent to kicking him in the balls. "You'll freaking *always* please me, remember?"

Amadeus straightened, breathing hard.

Vala repeated, never taking her intense gaze from Amadeus'. "Skin to skin."

Amadeus bit his lip as he pulled off his glove, and reluctantly brought his hand to touch his sister's cheek. When he screamed, she caught him, cradling him to her chest like she hadn't just turned him into a sobbing mess.

What in the witching heavens had he seen in her desires and thoughts?

I quivered, blinking away tears from the corners of my eyes, but unable to even wipe at them.

"Goddess Moon! He was never ordered to fall in love." Vala rubbed Amadeus' arm. "I can feel his disgusting love for a witch coursing through him...*infecting* him. Yuck, all that tingly, sappy *first love*. You know what he can feel?" She flashed a smile that was more fangs than teeth. "Every dark thing that I've ever desired to do to him. And now that he's been dirtied up by your Claiming, why should I hold back?"

"I will kill you," Mischief's voice was soft but deadly, "if you touch him even once."

When Vala winked at the camera, I groaned.

Yet all I cared about was that I was trapped in a magical moon shrine, whilst the leader of a bunch of fanatics threatened the guys that I loved.

I didn't know whether I truly was the Kingdom of the God's special Wolf Witch, but I did know that I no longer wished to simply kiss or kill a werewolf, I also longed to lead their pack.

Vala had played us, however, and now *we* looked like the bad guys. I was pretty sure that Mischief and I had committed treason. I shivered with the thought that we could have escaped from the witches only to be executed by wolves.

CHAPTER 19

At least execution was quick. As I hung paralyzed in the moonbeams that held me spread-eagled in the middle of the Lunar Shrine, I imagined the snap of Vala's fangs into my jugular or the slash of her nails into my guts. I didn't want to die, but every day that I'd survived the massacre that had killed my parents and their guests, I'd been expecting it.

But torture was slow, and boy, was I being tortured...*with 1970s rock music.*

Next to me, held within his own moon bubble, Mischief was whining. He'd started a couple of hours ago. I thought that it was to try and block out the music, or maybe he was coping even less well than me with the way that the wisps that spun around us dampened our magic, binding it.

Honestly, Vala was one mean princess with a mean sense of humor.

I didn't know if the rest of our pack was lucky or not that the Crescents had forced them to dress and then hauled them out of the shrine, before the music had started up.

Styx's "Witch Wolf" blasted on loop from the hidden speakers, whilst the waterfall throbbed and thundered in sympathy with its screamed solos, double-bass drumming, and wild electric guitar. If there was a hell, I thought that sinners would be trapped underground like this with only one song for eternity, played over and over and...

"Stop this infernal, diabolical din this instant!" Mischief howled.

Woah, if he'd been free, those speakers would've been toast.

Why did I have to think of *toast*...? My stomach grumbled.

Glazed donuts, marshmallows, waffles...

Hey, bad, bad brain: no fantasy feasts, when the rest of me couldn't join in.

"She thinks that she's so smart," I grumbled, "but I'm the *Wolf Witch*. If she's going to drive me crazy, the asshole should at least get the name right."

Mischief's breath was ragged, but I didn't miss the snort of laughter. I thrilled at the sound, after so many hours of nothing but his panicked whine. Faint tremors ran along his wings that were pulled out taut, just like his arms and legs.

"Well, I'm certain that was her top priority. Although, the princess will undoubtedly have convinced her mother that she's merely providing us with appropriate entertainment." His eyes fluttered closed. "I rather think that I have been the foolish one to fear the witches but not know to fear my own people."

My heart clenched at the melancholy in his voice because how much did it suck that he'd given up his land, family, and lover to save these wolves, only for them to turn on him? Except, his *pack* hadn't... Plus, I wasn't about to judge an entire kingdom on the actions of its princess. That was the kind of dickishness that had motivated my aunt to develop the Wolf Tamer.

"I've been living in fear from the moment that I arrived in Oxford with brief pauses for sexy times and cuddles." Despite myself, my mouth curved into a smile at the thought of Moon's cuddles, even though my guts churned with worry at what could be happening to him. "My Charms, Ramiel, and you have all taught me that it's how I act *despite* that fear, which makes me truly worthy of calling myself a rebel. Trust me, I'm learning that lesson."

Mischief arched his brow. "Perhaps you do know more than a *damn thing* now, witch. Also, *perhaps*..."

When his brow beaded with sweat, I gasped at the

silver strands that drifted out of his body as softly as gossamer.

How powerful was he to break the binding, when my red was still caged inside?

The silky strands suffused the moon around him, although they were still trapped by it. I trembled at the beauty, as the moon glowed. Mischief's little finger touched mine; his skin was soft, and my nerves were on fire. His magic was electric: it zinged through my finger, lighting my moon as well.

I laughed, as Mischief caressed me with his magic. Hey, what did music torture count for, when I had my very own god to light me up with his magical touch?

It kind of hadn't struck me fully until that moment: *this was Mischief's shrine.*

At least, it was a shrine to the moon, and the shifters believed that the Seraphim (like Mischief) who they were descended from, were their gods.

Although, their gods had seeded and then abandoned them to be vulnerable to silver and the witches.

They hadn't saved them.

Okay, I got why they had conflicted emotions about Mischief's return. I wouldn't have been bowing down before him either, even though he wasn't a god in the way that they wanted him to be and hadn't known anything about their existence until a week ago.

Maybe he'd better not lead with that fact either.

"My, what arrogance of these wolves to believe that

they can bind a god and a Wolf Charmer." Mischief stroked his magic down my neck, and I shivered. "I shall escape from here and then I shall make them rue the day." Mischief sighed. "Until such time... I spy with my little eye, something beginning with *M*."

I blinked. "Dude, seriously?"

Mischief sniffed. "If you're forfeiting already..."

"It's *moon*, right?" I said, flatly. "Seriously, tell me that it's not *moon*."

"It's not moon."

"Did you just say that because I told you to?"

Mischief snickered. "Excuse me if I was attempting obedience."

"Then attempt your game with anything but freaking *moon*," I snapped.

Mischief rolled his eyes. "I spy with my little eye, something beginning with *C*."

I clenched my jaw. "If it's *crescent*, I'll make you *rue* the witching day with my hand and your ass."

"You know, that doesn't sound much of a deterrent." Mischief curled his tongue behind his teeth. "Oh, and you win: it was *crescent*."

"Trust me, you're lucky that we're caught in this..." I glanced around the mists that surrounded us. "What on a witch's tit is this?"

"It's interesting that the wolves would've developed such a monstrous trick to turn us into idols, is it not?" Mischief was more subdued all of a sudden. "I can only imagine that it's a Seraphim Trap. One could almost call it hubris."

"Or pride comes before a fall," I muttered.

"Oh, I hope so… The princess has already discovered how it feels to fall on her bony behind." Mischief's eyes flashed.

"Hey, we took on the asshole Houses of Seasons and Blood. What can the Kingdom of Gods throw at us that we can't handle? Wait, I take that back. Fates, karma, universe who seems to hate me…I take that back, right? But we have each other and we'll save each other because we're equal in this pack."

Mischief drew in a sharp breath. "My mistake, you still don't know a *damn thing*." My eyes smarted with tears at his harshness and the way that his silver drew away from me, back inside his own moon. *What had I said?* "The question is no longer simply about your pack; it's about *you*. Now that the past, which haunted you, has been stripped back, along with the lies, who will you become?" My pulse thundered in my ears, loudly enough to drown out the rock music. I remembered the ruins of the House of Silver and mom's torn cape lying on top. I'd lost so much. But what remained? *Holy hell, Mischief was right.* "These shifters need an Alpha. Can you be both Wolf Charmer and leader, without abusing either role?"

"I'd never abuse my wolves." My throat was tight even at the thought.

"I assure you that abuse of position and power is far more tempting and insidious than abuse of a single wolf." Mischief's tongue darted out to lick over his lower lip. "How sweet that you imagine there's a simple answer here. Yet I'll still ask the question: Will you choose to be buried by your past or freed by the truth to lead your own future?"

"Honestly, I think I preferred I Spy," I grumbled.

Suddenly, the moon doors slammed open, and — *thank Hecate* — Styx's "Witch Wolf" at long freaking last shut off. Mischief and I both let out a gasp of relief.

A parade of naked Omegas, who were decorated in glittering silver and white like the transforming phases of the moon, sailed into the room. Their blond heads were respectfully bowed and hey, I'd never realized how much I loved...and *needed*...Moon to meet my eye. When I'd chosen him in the Omega Center, I'd hated how the other Omegas had trembled, whilst their gazes had remained cast down. Despite his terror at being chosen by a Wolf Charmer, Moon had always tilted his chin *up* in defiance. His rebelliousness had always been a combination of adorable and courageous. I'd thought that even before I'd understood just how much bravery it'd taken him to meet my eye without submitting. So, I didn't blame these Omegas for bowing their heads.

Yet there was something different about the way that they held themselves. They had a confidence in their beauty and a respect in their deference, rather than a fear.

Maybe they weren't treated the same way as the Omegas were in the Wilds?

The Omegas slipped into the alcoves, raising their arms into classical positions like living statues.

Wow, that was both weird and scorching hot; I forced myself not to look down their naked...*perfect*... bodies because you can ogle a statue but where was the line on *shifters* as statues...?

Then I remembered the way that Emperor had been chained to my bed for his Claiming to be used as an object just like these Omegas, and the warmth pooling through me became cold in the instant.

An Omega with wavy blond hair to his shoulders who looked like a moonbeam sprung to life, peeled away from an alcove. He was carrying a pot that smelled sweet. My stomach growled in protest again, and I flushed, but he only smiled at me shyly through his hair. Then he dipped his fingers in the pot and held them up to my lips.

I sniffed: *honey*.

Maybe they thought that gods lived on ambrosia and you know, all the other bullshit facts that they'd stolen from myths across the ages. Next to me, Mischief tutted. Did they expect me to lick the stuff from the Omega's fingers like an animal?

Hey, I'd put on cat ears and a tail, if they were into that kind of play, for a chance at something to eat.

I tentatively darted out my tongue.

"You witless witch, what are you doing?" Mischief hissed.

"Sucking some random dude's fingers?" I ventured.

"The first rule of being captured is: don't eat and drink the offered sustenance. At least, if you don't wish to be poisoned because I've learned through harsh experience that it's likely drugged." Mischief glared at the Omega who shrank back with an offended blink of his large eyes.

"Hey, fingers over here, honey wolfie, I'm not done with that sweetness." I wagged my tongue out more like a dog than a cat, tempting the Omega back.

Who needed dignity, when I could have treats?

Mischief groaned, as I finished sucking on the (now pulling a smug face at Mischief), Omega's fingers. Although, it could've been the way that I worked the fingers in my mouth, licking and then sucking, which even had the Omega flushed. But it was epic to see that he no longer avoided either of our eyes.

What wasn't epic, however, was the way that he shook and instantly returned to the ducked head and hunched shoulders look, as soon as the Queen of the Gods swished into the Lunar Shrine in a dress that had such a long train that it floated behind like moonlight over water.

Queen Banan was fairy beautiful but aristocratically cold. Her eyes made me feel like a spook because they looked straight through me, as if I wasn't there or she was seeing someone else entirely. Her crown of crescent moons was stark in contrast to her waterfall black hair that fell to her waist...*and she cradled Moth to her chest like he was her kid.*

I gaped at the way that the queen wrapped a small ivory blanket around his shoulders, whilst absentmindedly rubbing at its corner herself.

Wait, was that a security blanket...?

I didn't mean to be a jerk about it, but I might just have put my finger on why the Gods were the kingdom who hadn't mixed with the other wolves, or fought before they'd been conquered. If their own queen had a security blanket and needed to take Moth as a cub teddy bear, then no wonder the witches had triumphed.

What chance had the shifters had?

Except, Vala was more than smart enough to trick even Mischief. Maybe the queen simply had a thing for cuddling Princes of the Wilds? Honestly, I had a serious weakness for that myself.

The Omega with wavy hair pulled his fingers free from my mouth with a wet *pop* that was embarrassingly loud in the sudden silence. Then he backed away without looking up and stepped into his alcove, freezing as if he'd returned to statue form.

Here was a creepy assed thought: What if the

Omegas always lived in this shrine as their duty and they waited here like stone with no more choice over their lives than the Omegas in the Wilds? But maybe it was considered an honor…

Yep, as much an *honor* as hanging trapped like mosquitoes in amber was an honor for Mischief and me. The type of *honor* that I could seriously do without.

Queen Banan sauntered closer to me. For the first time, she appeared to truly *see* me. Yet I didn't think that it was an improvement because she assessed both Mischief and me like stringing up your daughter-in-law and god like baubles was an amusing hobby.

My uncle had peered at my collections of magic tech like that when I was a kid.

Mischief sniffed. "I think that our greeting can be reduced to five words: Let us go or die."

I sighed. *Where was Emperor and his diplomacy when you needed him?*

"You haven't met Mischief yet, but he's a royal prick. So, I'm sorry for his…" *Crappy attitude didn't quite cover it.* "…Threats to kill." I grinned with an attempt to be winning. *Hey, I could pull it off.* "Seriously, he wouldn't be in apocalypse mode, if we hadn't been told that we were guests, but then had been chained with our magic bound."

When Moth peeked at me from his place clasped to the queen, I shot him a reassuring smile. This time I was glad that Moon *wasn't* here, either to do his rebellious kicking of diplomacy's ass or to do that thing where he begged to take Moth's place for punishment.

Woah, bad bad brain: first food fantasies and now images of *my* Moon nestled up to the Queen of the Gods.

I'd have whacked my own forehead but I was still paralyzed, and the only person who could release me hadn't even shown a flicker of emotion throughout my admittedly unpolished speech. But you know, that's what comes of being tortured with rock music for hours. Banan was lucky that I hadn't simply screamed...or whined like Mischief had...in her face.

Yep, that was why we needed Emperor.

At last, Banan tipped up her aristocratic nose like concentrating on me was a painful effort. "May the moon shine on you. I welcome you into my kingdom below." Her whisper was as icy as the moon's rays on a winter night.

I shivered; I could feel each word prickling my skin into goosebumps.

Banan had a matching Welsh lilt to both Vala and Amadeus', but then, all the shifters of the Gods who'd survived had come from the same tiny Welsh island. I shivered again as I remember what Amadeus had told me about how they'd been ripped from their *closeness* to be dragged here, away from their homes and land.

That must've been terrifying.

"Now that the *un*pleasantries are over," Michael sniffed, "release us, wolf."

Banan's gaze swung to Mischief. "My daughter showed me footage, see, that I hardly dared believe... until now. But your violence and threats can't be allowed to endanger my people. They've suffered too much already. Fur and fangs, it's my duty to protect my kingdom, even from our god."

I sighed. Okay, so she had a point. In her place, I'd at least have allowed my honored guests a hearing before I found them guilty. Plus, I'd never violate anyone by binding their magic.

I hadn't lived through the Wolf War, however, or watched my people decimated before me. I'd witnessed only moments of my great-grandmother in action, but it'd been enough to sicken me.

How far would I go to make certain that outsiders weren't a danger to my wolves, if I'd lived through the Wolf War as one of the shifter royalty who'd been forced to kneel?

Guilt churned in my guts. I might be forging a new path as a Wolf Charmer but I was only just beginning to realize how much I was asking of these wolves.

"Oh, I'm aware that you have a duty to make certain that I'm safe because I'm the enemy," I replied.

Next to me, Mischief choked. "Wait, she didn't mean *enemy*—"

I ignored him, forcing myself to continue in a rush,

"And hey, you're right: *I'm not safe*. I'm a Wolf Charmer and I can control wolves. That's what I do, right? But if Amadeus has been spying on me (and honestly, that's okay too because I don't blame him or you for not trusting that he was safe with me), then you'll know that I'm not the same as any of the other asshole Wolf Charmers. I didn't keep him in a cage, control him with my shadows, or force him... *I love him*." I met Banan's gaze with a steely determination, and I could've been imagining it, but the corners of her mouth twitched into a smile. "I don't think that wolves are *beasts*, *savages*, or *killers*."

The Omegas who'd been frozen in place as statues broke position in shock.

The Omega with wavy hair raised his head for a moment, staring at me in awe. What did I bet that I'd broken another witchy law with that rant? But it was worth it for that look alone.

"A single skin like you truly believes that?" Banan stepped closer, clutching Moth to her side.

I smiled. "Dude, I love all my pack. Please, just let me see that they're okay..."

Banan's eyes became shuttered. "That's no longer your concern, Wolf Witch."

"And the cub?" Mischief asked cautiously, sweeping his gaze over Moth like he was scanning for injuries.

Banan's sombre face lit up, and she grinned. The

weird transformation from cold to warmth was night to day, and she instantly looked much younger.

She petted Moth's hair. "You mean *my adopted son*?"

My eyes widened. *Mage's balls…* "I freaking *don't*."

Banan's eyes flashed, and I quivered at their fire.

She tightened her hold around Moth, until he winced. "*Your* mother stole my true son away, Wolf Witch, are you not aware?" I swallowed, whilst my cheeks reddened with a shame that felt like it wanted to eat me from the inside. Holy hell, I was aware…and I wished that I wasn't. *Were those tears making her eyes bright now?* "My true s-son would only be slightly older now if h-he…I mean, he *will* be… Look you, if he h-hadn't been taken from me, they'd be similar…" Then she bared her teeth, and they snapped into fangs. "*Why shouldn't I have a new son?*"

When she broke off, her eyes were wet.

Banan didn't know that her son had been killed. Hocus pocus, she was this distressed simply thinking that her son was in the hands of witches.

How could I tell a mom that her son was dead?

Painting in my studio had never trained me for this.

When I glanced at Mischief, he shot me a warning look. My squirming guilt doubled to keep the secret, but I knew that Mischief had a point: we were both at our weakest, and Banan adored her *true son*. So, now wasn't the time to admit that he'd been killed by witches to save a mage because put like that...it kind of sounded bad.

When Moth cringed at Banan's vibrating fury, she soothed him, stroking his curls, just like I craved to. Then she pressed the security blanket into Moth's hand like he was a kid who'd need it to protect it from his fears. Only, the nightmares had already taken both him and the Ambassador...*and they'd been the witches.*

The way that Moth wrinkled his nose at having the security blanket forced on him would've been funny, since he always insisted that he wasn't a cub, only Banan's grief as a mom was raw and agonizing.

How had my mom tucked me in every night — loved *me* as her kid — whilst knowing that she'd denied the same to another mom who loved her kid just the same? How had she been able to keep one of us upstairs, whilst the other was in the cellar? Had she truly believed that bullshit about shifters being nothing but *beasts* or was hate and the drive for power enough to corrupt anyone to commit such acts?

None of that meant it was okay for Moth to be used as a son replacement; he was a Prince of the Wilds and not the Gods. But then, I'd created Okami to be my therapy, and Stella had built the mechanicals.

Who was I to talk about healthy?

"The true prince would want you to have his blankie; he was always such a kind boy," Banan cooed like Moth was a tiny cub. "It was his, before he was taken away to be trained in that terrible center to prepare him for the witches. They didn't allow him to take it with him, no matter how much he sobbed." She stroked down Moth's cheek. "Now I have you as my son, and I shan't allow anyone to take you. I promise."

"I apologize for the cruelties visited on you and your son," Mischief said with an intensity that shocked Banan into glancing up at him, "but repeating the cycle is, I assure you, never the answer."

My heart suddenly sped up, as Banan's eyes became sheeted ice, and she stalked to Mischief with a *swish* of her trailing dress.

Banan reached through the mists of the moon to snatch Mischief's chin in a bruising grip. "*Cruelty*? By the furless heavens, like a god who watched the death and destruction of his people and did nothing to save them?"

When her hand slid to Mischief's throat and tightened, Moth begged, "*Ma*, please don't…"

I could tell by the way that he trembled how much that *ma* had cost him. Banan, however, lightened her touch, until she was only stroking over Mischief's fluttering pulse.

"You arrive too late, but I still have a role for you in this shrine, see." Banan let go of Mischief's throat, taking a step back. Mischief's eyes sparked, as he broke her gaze. Ashen, it was *me* who whimpered because I saw through Banan's mask to her seething hatred and boy, was that not pretty. "You'll be kept here always with your magic bound. A worshiped idol and nothing more."

Then Mischief *did* whimper and pant in distress, and I was right there with him because the wisps of moonlight in the Seraphim Traps began to crystallize around us, pressing our magic even deeper inside.

Banan had over a decade of grief and loss, which she'd turned into an ice-cold rage that was more terrifying because it was both righteous and justified.

Whilst my pack and I had expected sanctuary in the Kingdom of the Gods, instead we'd been brought here for atonement.

CHAPTER 20

I didn't miss the irony that the greatest danger I'd faced since stumbling into the supernatural world in England was because of a mom's love for her son. Of course, I'd spent the last decade hating on wolves because of my *own* love for my mom, who'd been killed by wolves.

Just like this mom's son had been killed by witches.

Okay, now I understood Mischief's speech about cycles of violence, although I didn't think that the Queen of the Gods cared about more than having her chance to be the one to kick some ass for a change.

Banan's eyes were flinty, as she stroked both Moth's curls and her son's blankie and watched the twin moon's crystallizing around Mischief and me in the Lunar Shrine.

When the last whispers of Mischief's silver magic

were drawn back inside him, he groaned. I shivered, even though beads of sweat plastered my ball gown to my back, and I couldn't feel either my fingers or my shadows anymore. Maybe this Seraphim Trap was like magical frostbite.

I giggled. *Hold it together, Crimson; this is your hysteria alert.*

My giggle transformed into a sob; I reached for my red, and there was nothing but a sigh at the back of my mind. I retched at the horror.

"You're killing them," Moth gasped, "*please, please, please…*"

"I'm *saving* them from themselves," Banan snarled.

Her dickish words were the slap to the face that I needed.

Suddenly calm again, although still shaking from the agony of the quelling of my magic, I took a deep breath through my nostrils of the dank shrine air.

I could do this because I was more than my crimson shadows or Crimson Tide: I could also play a mean game of tennis, mix a blow your mind cocktail, and I'd been on the Debate Club, although only because my cousin had fancied the cruel but sweet assed Captain. And don't get me started on my music because I had a playlist that'd rock these shifters' non-existent pants off.

I mean, I knew that those weren't the kind of talents that helped when you were trapped by wolves but they were still *me*.

What I didn't need was anyone else to cage me like a beast to save me from myself.

"I won't say that I get your pain because I've never had a kid," I said, softly. Banan's gaze darted to mine. "Honestly, I'm only just married and before I came to Oxford, I could barely care for a houseplant. But you've every right to feel like you do. I know that. So, I'm not arguing about...*this*..." I waved at the spiked moon around me, "on my behalf because I've already promised that I'm different to my mom, and either you believe me and trust me or you don't. I can't do a damn thing about that." My expression hardened. "But seriously, you need to understand that Mischief isn't some all-seeing asshole god who chose to ignore you. He's a shifter who's sacrificed the same as you." My tongue swiped across my dry lips. Wow, there was a reason that my witchy ass didn't normally give scoldings: *I sucked at it.* "So, all I'm saying is," I took a deep breath, "don't be a dickhead about it."

Mischief snickered, and Moth attempted to mask his giggle in the blankie.

Banan's piercing stare focused on Mischief. Her words were whispered and wrung from her painfully, "You would've come to us in the Wolf Wars if you'd known...?"

Mischief's lips thinned. "In a heartbeat."

At last, Banan's expression softened, and the God Trap transformed to mist once more.

I gasped, as my red rushed back to the surface, even if it couldn't escape.

I could've kissed the cruel boy with sweet lips who'd been the only reason that my cousin had dragged me to Debate Club. What I truly wanted was to kiss Mischief who hung next to me with his little finger touching mine.

Yet I couldn't even turn to him or do more than feel the soft skin of his finger tingling against me.

Banan pointed regally at Mischief. "Look you, if you give me your Moon Oath to bring no violence—"

Mischief sighed. "Oh, what a splendid way to die, unable to even defend myself."

"Your Moon Oath to attack no one within the Kingdom of the Gods," Banan corrected through gritted teeth, "then I shall permit you both free. Although, as our god, you shall be moon leashed and on my queenly word, can be drawn back inside the shrine."

Yep, I hadn't missed the warning. Neither had Mischief who flinched.

"I give my Moon Oath," Mischief reluctantly agreed, "to allow you to leash your own god to wait upon your word, as if you believed me your *dog*."

Woah, now *that's* a masterclass in passive aggression.

"Unbind," Banan commanded, and the wisps of moonlight dispersed like whispers on the night.

Mischief and I fell flat on our faces.

Yey, for padding.

When I pushed myself to my knees, the Omega with wavy hair caught my elbow helping me up and fussing at my dress to straighten it, whilst Mischief stalked to his feet. Then the Omega froze as if just realizing that he'd sprung to life from his place in the alcove. The other Omegas were watching him with scared expressions, unable to believe his daring but also a touch of wistfulness, as if they wished that they'd been the ones to break free.

My red flowed around me in hissing waves at its mistreatment, even before I noticed the silver band around Mischief's ankle: *his leash*. The queen could kick Mischief's ass or mine but she wasn't punishing an Omega for rebelling and trying to help me.

I'd learned from Moon that royalty and leaders had responsibility and it meant protecting your subjects.

I rested my hand on the Omega's arm, and he leaned into the touch, just as Moon did. Maybe he received just as little gentle touch as Moon had before I'd Claimed him…?

"You forget yourself, your duty, and the purity of the light that resides within your Omega body," Banan scolded the Omega and holy hell, was she better at it than me. "You know what happens if you become sullied."

The Omega wrenched himself away from me so quickly that he swayed, almost falling on his ass.

Hello, *sullied*? I've been called a lot of things but my witchy hands *sullying* a wolf kind of stung.

"Are these your Acolytes?" Mischief demanded.

I didn't understand why his wings pulsed in violet fury.

Banan shook her head. "On my hide, they're Goddess Moon's priests and *my* precious Omegas. Come to me, my children." She held out her arms and the Omegas flocked from the alcoves to huddle around her and Moth, nuzzling against her joyfully. Huh, I hadn't seen that one coming. Except, she didn't mean her *true* children, right? She appeared to read the question in my eyes. "These are the children that I could save, see. The witches allow me to choose Omegas to keep as priests: chaste and chosen. That way, they don't have to be sent to the Omega Centers to be…" She rubbed her chin against an Omega's blond head, and he whined. "*I can keep them safe.*"

Mischief's expression was troubled, as his gaze met mine.

Hey, if I was an Omega then I'd be grateful to my queen too for choosing me as her *child,* even if it meant that I'd be shut up in a shrine and forced to never screw or love, if the alternative was to be sent to an Omega Training Center and Claimed by an enemy witch to be caged or end up as a pelt on a wall.

These were the Omegas that the queen saved because she hadn't been able to save her son, and witching heavens, she didn't even know yet just how much she hadn't been able to save him.

When the waterfall thundered, I startled. Then Vala slunk with a swing of her hips into the shrine with a smug smile.

What was it with her and dramatic entrances?

My nostrils flared, and I bit my tongue hard enough to taste the tangy blood, however, when I saw who she was dragging in by his sweep of white-blond hair. I was desperate to spring at her and wrap my shadows around her coiled black hair; *let her see how she liked it yanked on.*

On the other hand, that was just what she wanted, right?

Vala must've been watching from the cameras. Her mom had decided to free me, and now Vala wanted to prove that I couldn't be trusted with that freedom, so she was going to push my buttons.

Jesus, she knew just how to do that.

Aquilo's eyes burned with an ice-cold fury that could've put the queen's to frozen shame. But he still winced, as Vala tugged his hair harder, doubling him over to hurry behind her. Then she shoved him to his knees, before petting him *just like Aquilo's mom had petted the Ambassador.*

Aquilo quivered, but he didn't try to raise his head. He'd been too well trained by his own sister.

"Did you imagine," Mischief said with the quiet but

deadly precision of a sword being drawn, "that my warning of *touching* extended only to Amadeus?"

Vala bared her fangs. "Yeah, make more threats, silly god. You're under Moon Oath and wearing a leash. Look at this, I'm *touching*."

She extended the claw on her thumb, tracing it down Aquilo's cheek and tipping up his head. When I caught sight of his long…*gorgeous*…pale neck, I remembered that he was no longer forced to wear the blood pendant that bound his magic. Maybe he could've fought his way to escape, but where could he have gone without me, when his magical engagement contract would kill him within the month? And *maybe* he loved me (I blamed the honey for forcing out that word), just like I was certain that I loved him. In the House of Seasons when I'd thought that he was dead, I'd almost been unable to take another breath.

That was love, right?

I'd only asked Aquilo to marry me to save him from my family but now he was mine, like I was his. No scheming princess with an incubus complex was going to take him away from me.

"Tell your dick daughter to get her hands off my fiancé." I loved the way that Vala bristled at the same time as Aquilo's chest puffed out with pride at my Alpha posturing.

Okay, so hex my Charmer ass, it felt epic to mouth

off and claim Aquilo as mine, after hanging around for so many hours, helpless.

Plus, the squeal of the guitars had left me with a headache that pounded at my temples, and I didn't have the patience for diplomacy.

Banan cocked her head. "By the light of the moon, why so distressed? All mages who are thrown to the wolves are given to the princess and her Crescents for first choice. After them, the Alphas take their pick. Surely you of all witches know this?"

I pushed my nails into my palms to stop myself dragging Aquilo away from Vala, as she pulled him up by his throat, whilst never taking her gaze from mine.

Whatever Aquilo suffered it was because of me.

Yet this was what happened to men in witch families who discovered that they had magic. It would've happened to Kolby, Aquilo's friend, if he hadn't been murdered by the joint efforts of the Houses of Blood and Seasons.

Had Aquilo lived the last decade in terror that his mom would decide to send him into Wolf Kingdom if he didn't hide his magic, marry, and obey? How on earth had Aquilo not broken under that sort of pressure? I hadn't appreciated just how brave he'd been to help my Charms and me, until that moment.

Ancient traditions sucked.

I scowled. "Nope, I'm kind of new to all this witchy tradition crap or hadn't you noticed?" When Vala and

Banan exchanged a sly glance, I stiffened. *What were they hiding?* "Plus, Aquilo wasn't thrown to the wolves, he came here as an *honored guest* with me."

"On fear of silver, silence!" Banan shrieked.

When the Omegas cowered, Mischief soothed the Omegas' bowed heads with gossamer silver that swept across them as soft as kisses. They nuzzled into his caress, relaxing.

Banan's eyes narrowed in outrage. "Your intended is of the House of Blood. By the moon, they're our most vicious enemy who've bathed in the blood of my precious Omegas for a hundred years." Vala scraped her claw down Aquilo's cheek, beading scarlet against his blanched skin. "If my daughter hadn't found the mage's fair hair as pretty as any Omega's, I'd have taken great delight in burning him by the river as an offering to Goddess Moon."

Mischief sniffed. "I'd have rejected the offering, just so that we're clear."

Vala nosed along Aquilo's neck, scenting his cool skin in a way that made me shudder with the memory of his tantalizing smell of sunshine and fresh linen that was all wrong trapped here in the stench of the earthy underground.

My chest ached at the thought of the other mages for over a hundred years who'd been held here...who were *still* being held here.

When Vala clicked her fingers at the Omega who

was clutching the honey, he lowered his head, padding closer and holding it out to her. He was back to staring at the ground. Not that I'd want to look into Vala's *Emo does glitter* face.

Vala dipped her thumb into the honey, before raising it to Aquilo's mouth like a sweet pacifier or something else that would've been hot if it'd been anyone but Vala and Aquilo had been willing.

Aquilo merely turned up his pretty nose at her offering. Holy hell, I craved to feather kisses along it. Who knew that him being a snooty asshole could be a turn on for me?

"Didn't I give up enough dignity already?" Aquilo drawled coolly, even though he shot me an agonized glance. A blush bloomed all the way down his neck. "Am I to be a pet or your cub surrogate as well?"

He arched his brow at Moth who was still clutching his blankie.

Aquilo had a point, but crappy timing.

Startled at his disobedience, the Omega raised his gaze to Aquilo warningly. Then he nodded at the honey in encouragement.

Vala let go of Aquilo's throat and backhanded the Omega. Aquilo let out a hiss of protest.

"One look at a sexy mage and you forget your place, Omega," Vala snarled. "I think that this one's skill sets are more suited for the Omega Training Center, mother."

The Omega whined as he cradled his scarlet cheek.

"Don't you freaking dare," I growled.

To my surprise, Banan tutted at her daughter, ushering the Omega into her arms. I held my breath, but she pressed a kiss to his injured cheek, before rocking him.

Yep, that wasn't disturbing at all.

My pack and I were at the mercy of a queen (I had a feeling it was an entire kingdom), who were searching for surrogates for their missing cubs.

Or someone to punish for the fact that they'd lost them.

"Our god will be angry with us if we hurt his priests," Banan singsonged.

Mischief's wings sprung out in dark splendor. He was a cuffed god, but he was still a god. "Your god is already angry with you. Release the mage."

Banan's face drained of warmth. "The House of Blood oppress us. After the Wolf Wars, we thought that it'd stop. That we'd be allowed this corner of Wolf Kingdom to be ours and that us survivors would be free. *That was a lie.* Why would you speak for them?"

I knew that Mischief shouldn't have played the god card.

"I'm shockingly intimate with pain and loss," Mischief murmured, "but not with yours. Yet may I request that *you get over it*?" My eyes widened. *Hell, he didn't just go there, did he?* "This mage and witch have as little to do with the war as your cub. Tell me again, pray, why innocents should suffer for the actions of their ancestors?"

"On the moon, you're not yet ready to be free," Banan growled. Mischief yelped, as the silver circling his ankle yanked him backwards, pinning him to the wall. "Whilst the Blood boy and you," Banan pointed a shaky finger from Aquilo to me, "must see and understand your true legacies."

Vala's grin was creepy assed and way too pleased with herself to mean anything good. She snatched Aquilo by the hair, which must be her favorite way of dragging mages, then stalked to me. I dodged out of the way because I had a sensitive scalp and I didn't want her tugging on my curls and frizzing them either. Instead, however, she caught me by the scruff of the neck.

I'd promised to be on my best behavior and I meant it. At least, until I could find my pack and free Moon.

I realized that we truly had to take back the kingdoms for the princes and that the Omegas needed to be saved from more than the centers. Yet now that we'd defeated Stella and the witches, I was starting to understand that the wolves would be as hard to rebel against — *screw that, harder* — because I had to prove myself better than the previous Wolf Charmers.

I had to control the Crimson Tide.

I battled with my billowing waves of red and the

instinct to struggle, as Vala squeezed my neck and pulled me towards the door. "What am I *seeing*?" I gasped. "Is it a romcom because then Aquilo and I can snuggle with popcorn."

Aquilo shot me a disgusted glance that I was certain had more to do with the choice of romcom than the snuggling or popcorn: maybe he was more of a fantasy fanatic? He'd had Harry Potter stashed in his attic, after all. Okay, that sounded like a euphemism, and now I couldn't stop the hot images...

Vala's claws bit into my neck, and I grimaced.

"*Death*," Vala hissed, "that's what you'll see. Because haven't you worked it out yet? We're all dead here."

CHAPTER 21

I hunched in the pitch black, smothered in the sensation of being buried alive. If Mischief had been allowed off his leash to come with us, he'd have cocooned me with his warm popcorn scented wings against the rank dusty smell and dark.

Instead, Princess Vala had dragged me along with Aquilo down a rabbit warren of corridors, before shoving me through a tiny door and slamming it behind her. Then she'd pushed me into the corner — alone — like a kid who needed time to think about what they'd done.

The crescent-shaped sign outside had read, **MUSEUM OF DEATH**.

Trust me, after that sign I didn't expect the princess showering Aquilo and me in chocolate sauce, whilst the

Crescents swung each other around in a cheerful dance to Imagine Dragon's "On Top of the World."

Hey, I'm an optimist but I hadn't cast a Self-Delusion spell.

Yet I also hadn't been prepared for the crushing despair that quivered through my shadows, which trembled and clung close to me. I'd never felt their fear before, only rage, joy, desire, and even distress. But not fear, even whilst they'd been bound.

When I shifted from foot to foot on the uneven floor, something cracked.

Crunch — crack — crunch.

What on Hecate's breath was I standing on?

"What a truly terrible host I am." Vala's husky voice filled the museum. "Poor little witches and mages need *light.*"

On her bellowed *light*, the entire circular ceiling lit ghostly pale, but still bright enough after the dark to make me squint. I blinked, as my eyes watered, peering at the circular room, which appeared to be…a catacomb. Unless, you know, there was another name for somewhere with walls stuck with skulls.

Wait, there was: *The Museum of freaking Death.*

What kind of screwed-up *grave* had Vala brought me to, where the skulls weren't the most disturbing thing? That honor went to the stuffed Omegas who were posed all around and watched me with glass eyes.

My crimson burst out in an instinctive effort to protect me, pooling the room in blood. My hands shook.

Son of a bitch, the asshole wolves seriously believed in the power of the hands-on learning experience.

I glanced at Aquilo, wishing that I could hold him, even though he wouldn't lean into my touch like Moon would. It didn't matter though; I knew that he'd need the reassurance as much as I did.

Yep, I'd say he needed a big ass hug of reassurance.

Aquilo was ashen, and his eyes looked haunted. I hadn't noticed the shadows underneath them before, but I did now. He looked exhausted, and as if he understood more about this museum than I did with a weary sadness. How hard had it been for him to survive his family's torments and find a way to escape to seek the vampire's help? He'd been holding himself together for so long, would he shatter now?

Not if I could witching help it.

The way that Vala stroked the back of Aquilo's neck was surprisingly gentle, even though her words were sharp as a blade, "Are you enjoying your family's work? One thing you can say for Bloods, they take great pride in their murders."

Aquilo fell to his knees with a *crack*, before bending over and puking. *Screw staying in my corner like a good witch.* My fiancé needed me and he wasn't unwanted and thrown to the wolves: *he was loved by me.* The magical contract of the blood bracelet screamed my claim on him in throbbing scarlet, even if I hated the dickish ownership part of that.

Vala could play with Aquilo like a doll, but it didn't change that he was *my* pack. And my pack was spitting up on the floor, whilst shaking and pale, because of Vala's cruelty.

I crouched next to Aquilo, stroking his sweaty hair back from his fevered forehead; his blue eyes welled with tears like the rising tides in the Arctic ocean. Then I sneezed on the bone-dust.

Yuck, yuck, and *yuck.*

My foot crunched again beneath me, and I glanced down, before recoiling. The floor was a sea of bones and skulls like the walls. I'd been standing and walking on the dead.

Was this the dead that the queen had meant? Why had Aquilo and me been brought to this grave?

Vala cocked her head as she scrutinized Aquilo's anguish. "Interesting. It's almost like you're *not* proud, single skin of the House of Blood."

Aquilo wiped his shaky hand across his mouth. "Please believe me, I'm not."

Vala brushed her hand down her hip in a move that would've been seductive, except...*hello, bones.* "Why should I believe anything that a *mage* says?"

I dug my nails into my dress to stop myself shooting

out my red and pinning her in a web amongst the lights. Why couldn't ball gowns have pockets? I needed to stuff my hands into them to resist the temptation.

Oblivious to my struggle, Vala slunk between the stuffed wolves, stroking each one in turn — on their snout, down their back, or behind their ear — in a ritual that appeared familiar as if they were childhood friends and this was both a greeting and a blessing. It was kind of like they were still alive and her own family.

I hugged my arms around myself because her love for these stuffed wolves was too close to Emperor's own tender blessing of the stone wolves who'd been trapped in the courtyard of the House of Blood.

It was easy to forget that both were royalty. But then, that was because Princess Vala was a dick.

"Dude, your daytrip is going to receive a seriously low score." I pushed myself to my feet. "I saw your kingdom on a map at my aunt's, and it was next to the river and everything. But all you can come up with to show me is bones?"

For a moment, Vala's fangs extended so far in her fury that I thought she'd partially shift. My shadows whipped around me in case I had to defend myself (hey, if Mischief could have that clause in his Moon Oath, I was certain that it could extend to me as well). Then she shook her shoulders as if to calm herself, although she still spoke through a mouthful of fangs.

"Witches paint murals and paintings of their victories. These aren't bones: they're the legacy of your great-grandmother — the Crimson Terror of the Wolf War." I gaped at her. Zetta had called my great-grandmother the *Crimson Hero of the Wolf War*. I guessed it all depended which side of her shadows you stood, and since I'd watched the hell that she'd unleashed on the shifters, dashing them into the Thames, *Terror* sounded about right from their side. "Surely you want to revel in her greatest achievement?"

I cringed, understanding my shadows fear now: here were the accusing dead killed by my ancestors, and boy, did I feel the weight of my family's crimes.

"Nope, I truly don't want to *revel*, charcoal a quick sketch in commemoration, or throw a "Witches Won" party," I replied. "I hate that my ancestors did this to yours, and I'll fight to stop another such atrocity. I *have* fought to save you from a second war. I can't promise that this will never happen again because duh, just look at the world, it *always* does. But I'll battle to make certain that it's not whilst I'm here because my shadows do more than control, they can protect as well. So, are you done dicking around with the scare tactics now?"

When Vala prowled closer, I stiffened, but she only leaned closer. Her breath was hot against my ear, as her fingers played up and down my arm.

"Yeah, I'm not feeling your heartfelt speech, Wolf

Witch," she whispered, before continuing like a mantra or prayer, "By the light of the moon, I am the dead, we are the dead, and shall remain now and always *dead*." When I flinched away, her fingers suddenly tightened around my elbow. "We Gods honor our fallen by becoming them and never forgetting. Let me help with our Forever Memory Cave."

Aquilo leapt up, blocking Vala. "Don't do this. The Charmer has risked everything she has to save *your* prince and her other Charms. That's what I've witnessed, lowly mage as I may be."

Vala growled, sinking her claws into Aquilo's shoulder and dragging him aside. By her standards, that was being gentle.

When a miniature whirlwind surged on Aquilo's palm, I shook my head at him, even if it bathed me in warmth that he desired to protect me.

I wasn't in this kingdom to fight with the wolves but to try and find a new home with them as weird as that idea was. I didn't know if they'd ever accept me, and it was looking even less likely every second. But until my pack were safe, I'd play along, which didn't mean that I wouldn't remember every time that Vala had made the guys that I loved hurt.

I'd never been in the revenge business before, but the pain of my pack burned me like nothing else.

Vala shoved me in front of a low arch; the cave

beyond lay in gloom. Then gleaming letters burst above my head:

REMEMBER ALWAYS.

Yep, this was going to suck.

When Vala pressed her body against mine; I could feel the rapid thudding of her heart. Her narrowed gaze burned me.

"If there's a light side of the moon, then there's also a dark," she murmured, tucking one of my curls behind my ear. "*You're that dark.*"

Then she hurled me through into the Forever Memory Cave on my knees. A stone slab slammed across the entranceway, trapping me inside with a *bang*.

I was alone in the earthy damp of the cave, and my stomach took that moment to growl.

Son of a leaky cauldron, could this day get any worse?

My eyes slowly adjusted to the gloom, and I crawled forwards, feeling around the edges of the cave. The sides were gouged with deep claw marks like someone...*or a lot of someones*...had been tunneling to get out. Except, it wasn't a neat tunnel, more like one dug in chaotic panic. Plus, whoever these wolves had been who'd been shut in here like me, they hadn't succeeded in their escape because the shallow tunnels stopped.

I felt all around the cave, before glancing upward. Then I gasped in shock: the claw marks continued all the way almost to the cave's ceiling.

Yep, this day could get worse.

I swallowed bile. How was this my great-grand-mother's legacy? What had happened in here to make the wolves so desperate that they'd clawed the walls?

My eyes pricked with tears at the thought of the shifters' fear. As a kid, I'd hidden in the dark of the wardrobe and panted with terror of the monsters prowling outside, during my parents' murder, and I'd dreamed of that night ever since. Then I remembered how my Charms and Moth had been raised knowing that they'd be sacrificed to me as Tribute, yet that they'd also been taught I was a *monster*.

I fell back on my ass, allowing the tears to fall down my cheeks because hey, there was no one to see me.

Moon had tried to tell me when I'd first chosen him, but I hadn't understood then.

But I did now.

My princes had known that theirs was a noble sacrifice to save their kingdoms, whilst I was the dragon.

I'd been sketchy on even the basics when I'd become the Wolf Charmer, stumbling into centuries of hatred and war between the supernaturals. Each of my Charms, on the other hand, had lived for decades with the aftermath of the war and the knowledge of their kingdoms' expectation: that they'd be Claimed by the great-granddaughter of the Crimson Terror.

I shuddered because it freaked even *me* out.

Yet if they'd had decades knowing that they'd be

sacrificed, then did that also mean they'd had the same length of time to plan and scheme?

I'd caught glances between my Charms that I didn't understand. I knew they wished to free the Omegas, but what else did they want? Both Stella and Zetta had warned that my Charms were controlling me and attempting to change me to become theirs.

Yet I *was* theirs, and if they had any schemes or plots, then I simply wanted in on them. There were monsters in both the witch and wolf worlds but they weren't me. I longed to help my pack free their kingdoms.

Suddenly, a hologram flooded the chamber with light. I blinked, but then yelped, pressing my back to the wall. The hologram wolves were all around me...*hundreds of them* packed into the cave. Their howls shook me; I pressed my hands over my ears.

The wolves were naked, and boy, were they thin; their ribs showed through, whilst I thought that their legs would snap if I even looked at them the wrong way. They scrambled on top of each other, scratching at the walls with their filthy claws — okay, so that explained the marks — in futile attempts to tunnel out. They clambered on top of their fallen friends to scratch at the higher earth.

I shrieked, as a hologram Omega swiped its claw through me at the wall behind.

How long had they been shut in here?

My stomach clenched, as dizziness rushed through me. Lightheaded, I wrenched at my hair like pulling out the curly strands would stop the truth whirling through my head.

She wouldn't...even my great-grandmother couldn't...the asshole, dickhead, son of a bitch...

When an Omega started to howl, the other wolves joined in. It was eerie, beautiful, and freaking *wrecked* me...because it was the howling of the dead.

Zetta had shown me back in the House of Silver how the Omegas had been made to kneel by the river Thames. Then how my great-grandmother had chosen her harem in the first Claiming from the kneeling and frightened Omegas.

Yet I hadn't thought about what had happened to the Omegas and Betas who she *hadn't* Chosen.

A small number must've been allowed to return to their kingdoms. But the rest...

I clenched my teeth to stop their chattering as I forced myself to watch the wolves who'd died down here in the dark, frantically clawing to escape and starving without moonlight, just like Moon had in his **REJECT** cell.

My great-grandmother had done that, and mom had known about it. No wonder my uncle had hated seeing my powers and had raised me as non-magical. Yet my shadows wept within me as equally distressed by the wolves' pain as me; they were mine and as innocent of these killings, as I was.

I knew now why Aquilo had puked when he'd been faced with the bones and stuffed wolves in the Museum of Death, which were a memorial to those who'd died inside this cave.

My crimson shadows wouldn't be The Terror. It wasn't like I'd be a hero in any war either, since I sucked at even my martial arts. But I would make this cycle of *death* stop.

I'd already exorcised the ghosts that haunted my own past, now I had to find a way to help the Gods exorcise their own. By living on the ground where their families had died, they'd become the dead themselves. And that wasn't healthy, right? It wasn't like I thought that they should forget, but the problem was that they couldn't forgive, whilst they were still suffering and dying. It had to be their own choice. But until they were free of the collars, Tributes, and centers — the whole Treaty that had followed the Wolf War and oppressed them — how could they forgive or build a fresh future?

Honestly, Vala and Banan's grief and rage combined was more dangerous than I'd even realized because it wasn't based on the loss of a single son but on hundreds. Jesus, maybe *thousands*.

Who could say it wasn't righteous?

I was the Wolf Witch, however, and it was time that everybody stopped living in the past.

Righteous didn't make something *right*.

I forced myself to my feet, billowing out my shadows. The wolves' howled louder, before falling on top of me to scrabble at the walls. I screamed as I was buried beneath the dead.

CHAPTER 22

I scratched my nails until they bled against the stone slab of the Forever Memory Cave, desperate to escape the howling holograms, like I'd rubbed my wrists raw in the Beta Apprentice's tent in the Wilds. Except, when I'd first been thrown to the wolves, my Beta guards had been a sinfully hot harem with Amadeus as their wicked but pampered prince.

They'd danced, screwed, and laughed...*wildly alive*...whereas the wolves all around me reeked with death.

Only Pretty Betas, the painted sign had promised.

I shivered because what if the sign was both simply the truth but also a warning that only the pretty Betas had survived...and *would* survive...?

What sort of messed-up world had my great-grand-mother created in this Wolf Kingdom, where the lesson that she'd taught had been that *Only Perfect Omegas* and *Only Pretty Betas* would be tolerated?

I'd already had a taste of the Omega and Re-education Centers that trained (which is asshole speak for brainwashed), Omegas into being *perfect*.

When I'd first chosen Moon and brought him back to the House of Silver, he'd been resigned to me starving him, simply because I hadn't known that he fed on moonlight.

And now I knew why.

Amadeus had been chosen by Queen Banan to be Claimed by me because he was the *prettiest* Beta in his kingdom. But I already knew that his image of pampered prince was a lie: I'd traced the silvered scars webbing his back.

What would happen if he revealed that he was far more than simply *pretty*?

Around me, the Omegas and Betas from a hundred years before died. Yet my pulse pounded too loudly in my ears because I was certain that Vala hadn't shown me these visions merely to punish me.

I'd learned the lesson well with the Oxford covens that everything was a pretext, and I had the serious suspicion that this was Vala's justification for a second war, which would slaughter both witches and the new generation of perfect, pretty, innocent, and *beautifully alive* wolves.

I slammed my fist against the door again; my throat

ached from screaming. My shadows flooded out in crashing waves, drowning the caves and its ghost wolves in crimson.

Suddenly, the slab slid open, and Amadeus slipped inside along with a low hum of music. I stumbled backwards, as he hushed me, clasping his gloved hand in mine and glancing anxiously through the gap back into the Museum of Death outside.

He held me back like he was watching for something.

I clung onto his hand, as if his touch would save me or could freaking absolve me. When my tremors shook through him, he raised his surprised gaze to mine. Then his expression became soft with concern, and he squeezed my fingers.

Holy hell, these were the times that Okami would've wound around me, but he was with Moon, and I didn't even know where either of them were. I needed his touch and to feel something blossoming inside me, instead of the numbing guilt.

"Kiss me," I commanded.

Amadeus' eyes lit up, hungrily. Then he caged me against the slab, slamming my hands above my head.

Woah, he was more powerful than he looked.

When Amadeus pushed his thigh between mine, his dick hardened against my leg. My red twitched, before it wove around him, caressing his sides. Then his lips were on mine, insistent and savage, as if he could sense my need and was responding to it. Yet the way that his hard-on tented in his tights, he needed it in just the same way. When his tongue darted to swipe at mine, it tasted of sweet chocolate.

I lost myself then: in Amadeus' kiss. His body, touch, and taste banished the *death, death, death* all around us. I kissed him hard enough to bring myself to life again because I felt like I'd spent a decade shrouded in death, just like the ghostly wolves that scrabbled at the walls all around us and the entire Kingdom of the Gods had spent a hundred years…*and something had to free us all.*

It hit me like a hex: my Charms were my life now, and I'd do anything to save the wolves. Maybe being a Wolf Witch meant sacrificing for the shifters just as Mischief had.

I'd die for them, and wasn't *that* the ultimate rebellion against witch tradition…?

Amadeus moaned, as I bit at his lower lip. Who knew that the stroke of Amadeus' tongue, which I caught between my own and sucked, would be what brought me fully to life?

Amadeus would be a smug…but sinfully hot… asshole now. And I couldn't help the way that I imagined Moon kissing me just like this.

Please…please…let Moon kiss me soon…

When I panted, Amadeus whined. His gasps were swallowed by our kiss. My shadows coiled around him, driving his pleasure higher. I bunched my hands in his top, reveling in his captivating beauty and the desire that glittered in his ruby eyes.

When his incubus side was fed, he looked deadly.

Finally, I reluctantly pulled back, and he cupped my cheek. I was surprised to see the wetness on the tip of his gloved thumb, when he wiped underneath my eye.

Wait, I was crying...?

I pressed a quick kiss to his thumb in thanks, because sexy times was one thing, but tenderness he hadn't been trained for: *that was all him.*

My heart clenched at the love in his gaze, which I knew was reflected in my own. This wasn't all about seduction and simply pleasing me because of his nature and role, right?

Hadn't Vala been furious that he'd broken his mission with me by falling in love?

I examined the open fragility and wonder in his look. "How don't you hate me?" I murmured. "I'm the freaking Wolf Charmer."

"I have **WCH** branded on my sexy behind, see. As your property, it's a not like I can forget who you are."

I caught Amadeus' hand, before he could pull down his pants to show off the brand.

Why had those words hurt so much since they were true? After all, I imagined that it'd hurt way more when I'd scorched my name onto his ass.

"If you could stop feeling yourself up for one

second…" When Amadeus caught a snicker in his palm, I stroked through his hair, "…I meant—"

"I'm not daft because I'm pretty; I know what you meant." Amadeus' eyes were as sharp in the dark, as his voice was steely. "You're not some ancient Wolf Charmer. You're *Crimson*. I'm yours, and you're mine. That's all that matters."

Amadeus might not have the head tilt mastered yet like Moon but he was just as much a rebel. As a half incubus and under the possessive eye of his adopted sister, how dangerous would that be for him?

His sister…

My eyes widened, and I blanched. What had the princess been doing to Aquilo, whilst I'd been trapped in the cave? My crimson drew back inside, seething at the threat to my fiancé.

"Dude, we need to get Aquilo away from your asshole sister," I demanded.

Amadeus wouldn't meet my gaze. "He's safe."

I swallowed and nodded.

Amadeus pulled me back to the gap in the slab, peering out. Then he dropped to all-fours, nodding at me to do the same.

I rolled my eyes because I'd already been tied up and trapped and crawling didn't do it for me, unless in kinky play and on floors that didn't graze my knees.

Amadeus gave a slinky wriggle of his hips (yep, I was checking out his ass and he knew it), before crawling silently out of the Forever Memory Cave. I took a steadying breath, before I followed him.

I winced, as the bones in the museum dug into my palms and knees, flinching at each *crunch*. Yet the sound was muffled by the mesmerizing sultriness of Lana del Rey's "Gods and Monsters", which sang from speakers in the ghostly lit ceiling.

So, still with the irony.

Yet I hesitated because boy, was the filthy mouthed eroticism of the song not appropriate in a room built out of skulls, especially after I'd just been forced to relive the nightmares in the cave beyond.

What frog kissing freakiness was going on?

When Amadeus sensed that I wasn't still crawling after him towards the door, he peered over his shoulder, and I caught the flash of guilt in his eyes.

Aquilo was safe, my witchy ass.

I edged closer to a stuffed wolf, peering through its legs.

Don't let its fur touch me...not after knowing that it'd once died here.

I could only catch a glimpse of Aquilo's black jeans and Vala's shimmering dress. Frustrated, I forced myself to crawl on my elbows underneath the wolf, shuddering as its belly rubbed against my head. Amadeus' huffed breath was hot against my ear, as he wriggled in next to me.

Then I clasped the bones beneath me in order to bite them into my palms and hold back the gasp.

Son of a thrice hexed witch…

Vala pinned Aquilo to the wall with her thigh hitched up in full femme fatale mode. Trust me, if there'd been a pole in the museum, she'd have been dancing around it. There was nothing petals-on-silk sheets about the way that she seduced Aquilo through the music. Instead, she swayed aggressively with her arms linked around his neck, bumping her hips against his. Except, I'd have bet anything that his dick wasn't hard, unlike the way Amadeus' had been. He looked more terrified than turned-on.

I still couldn't help the cold churning my guts and the furious raging of my shadows at seeing him dirty dance with someone else. As a kid, I'd have washed my own mouth out for even suggesting that I'd have cared what my elitist bully did. But now, I shook with the thought of the princess' hands touching his smooth skin, when all I wanted was to be the one who wrapped my arms around him and…okay, so dancing sexily to this music without standing on his toes was pushing it, but in my fantasy, he wouldn't even care because it was *me* holding him.

I glared at Amadeus. "Son of a bitch… *Safe*…?"

Amadeus' lips thinned. "By my hide, don't you trust him? How do you think I could sneak in to you? I've never been naughty…except in play…before *you*,

Charmer. You should trust the mage more because he's bright, see. He's the one who chose to distract my sister…like that."

When I glanced back at Vala, she'd guided Aquilo's hands to her waist and was kissing up his jaw, whilst slow dancing to the song's beat like she was screwing him right there against the wall…just taking his *every-thing*…through the power of the music and the graze of her fangs against his throat.

It was dark, erotic, and messed-up.

"I don't think so," I fiercely whispered.

When I tried to wriggle out from underneath the wolf, however, Amadeus snatched my sleeve. His expression was troubled. "I'm sorry if I didn't please you, but it was Aquilo's idea. My sister's treating him like a favored Omega, and there's nowhere *safer* in this kingdom than in my sister's favor. Doesn't Aquilo get the choice to protect you, or are we truly your slaves?"

Woah, Amadeus knew how to snap a witch's broomstick.

If I respected Aquilo as an equal, then I had to let him choose, even if he was being dumb. I'd never allow him to die for me, but Amadeus knew this kingdom better than I did; I had to trust him as well.

Amadeus nodded towards the door, and grudgingly I nodded.

Yet I froze when Vala unbuttoned Aquilo's black velvet shirt. She teasingly revealed his sculptured chest, the sweet dips of his collarbones, and his pink nipples; I craved to lick and kiss between them, until he melted into my touch. I was desperate to show him that he should be quivering in pleasure, rather than holding himself with the same stiffness and terror as a kitten dangled by the scruff of its neck about to be drowned.

Aquilo was no incubus seducer…

In the House of Blood, I'd overheard Aquilo's mom warn him that as the male he was only the *breeding stock* and had to make sure I was happy in bed because then maybe I wouldn't *hurt him too badly.*

Yep, that hadn't made me want to hurl at all.

I'd promised Aquilo that we wouldn't be following the typical witch model, but what were my words and a couple of tender hugs when compared to a lifetime of lectures, whippings, and fearing your arranged marriage?

Then Vala slipped out her iPhone and wrenched Aquilo's shirt away to reveal one snowy shoulder. He yelped, cringing back. My shadows whipped out, and I battled to restrain them.

Vala held up her phone with a grin. "Say *silver.*"

Woah, Aquilo's glare could've frozen her into an ice statue, but she still snapped the photo.

"I didn't imagine that the desire to see me in such a state of undress would be high amongst the Crescents." Aquilo tried for casual, but hey, he didn't pull it off.

Vala licked up his neck, and he shuddered. "Guess

again, Blood boy. By the face of the moon, do you even know how many families have lost children to your House? You're a celebrity." When Aquilo ducked his head, Vala tilted up his chin. "Why don't you drop your pants? Let's see if it's true or not that Bloods steal our Omegas because their own males have no dicks."

Okay, screw all that noble stuff about trust and choices. There was no way on earth that Aquilo's pants were coming off.

Aquilo and I were going to have a serious chat about acceptable diplomacy tactics because Aquilo wasn't Amadeus or Emperor who'd both been taught to wield seduction as a weapon. Maybe that was why Amadeus didn't understand the danger.

Ivy had once asked me to be careful with her son because he was an *innocent*. It wasn't like *I* had a lot of experience before I came to England because hiding my magic from non-magical boyfriends had made anything more than a couple of coffee dates like a Bond movie. But Aquilo was a virgin, and I wouldn't let Vala steal his first sexual experiences because Aquilo had some warped view of his role as my fiancé.

Like a weirdly overdressed worm, I squirmed out from underneath the stuffed wolf to face off with the real one. Behind me, I heard Amadeus sigh and heave himself to stand next to me.

"Hands off my fiancé, bitch," I growled.

Vala dropped her phone, which clattered amongst the bones.

Aquilo's neck and chest blushed a pretty pink, as he bit his lip. I shivered with the desire to take his lip between my own teeth, and then to suck away the hurt. Except, even more than that, I had the itching urge to bite a certain wolf princess and not in a sexy way, who'd smugly swung her arm around Aquilo's shoulder.

It wasn't like I could miss that message.

"*Flame*, I thought that I'd taught you better than that." Vala's claws tapped Aquilo's nose. "If you'd meant to disobey me, at least you could've done it well. What's with the unstealthy?"

Amadeus whimpered, hunching his shoulders at her disapproval. Wait...so, she was most pissed off that his ninja assassin skills hadn't been perfect?

What on earth had they taught Amadeus?

"You're still handsy," I snarled.

My shadows burst out, casting the skulls and bones in a red like they were seeped in blood.

Vala's mouth tightened. "See, that's because he's *my* mage."

I clenched my jaw. "Would it turn you on if he cried?"

Vala's eyes glowed golden. "*I'm not a witch.* That's what turns on Wolf Charmers. Didn't you spend long enough in the cave to learn that?"

I flushed. What did I say that came close to how I'd

felt in the Forever Memory Cave, unless you know, it started with *I'm sorry my family murdered your family*? Wait, maybe that was okay. "I'm sorry—"

"Please, *apologize* for your family's genocide of mine." Vala's teeth elongated, until she was partially shifted.

My breathing became ragged, as I snapped shut my mouth. Huh, in dumb ideas of the week that ranked highly.

Only then did I notice that Vala was herself shaking, whilst she stroked Aquilo's hair back from his forehead more to soothe herself than him.

Why in the witching heavens hadn't I realized it before? The Alphas of Vala's generation were as messed-up as the Omegas and Betas, simply in a different way. They'd also lived through the Wolf War as kids, witnessing their parents' humiliating defeat, their relocation into the Wolf Kingdom, and their oppression ever since by the witches.

Yet the danger was that the Alphas were in a position of power to do something about it. They'd had a hundred years to plan how to damage the witches back, and by the blazing glare that Vala directed at me, I was certain that she planned to.

I had to free my princes and my people from this wounded generation, or they'd prove the witches right about them being nothing but *beasts*, *savages*, and *killers*.

Jesus, I couldn't even think about the deaths of my hot, sinful, and glorious wolves if they lost a second war.

Amadeus slunk to Aquilo, doing up his shirt because Aquilo's hands weren't steady enough. Aquilo flinched even at his gentle touch.

Then Amadeus peeked up at his sister through his eyelashes, before touching her cheek. "If it pleases you, sister, the Charmer's not what we always thought. She's as much a wolf as a witch, and she could help—"

Vala shoved Aquilo into the wall, before snatching Amadeus by the front of his top. She was taller than him, and his toes scrabbled in the bones, throwing up a mist of dust. "Don't try and manipulate me, brother. *Ever.*" Amadeus was breathing in harsh pants; his eyes were blown wide with fear, as he nodded. "*You are not pleasing me.*"

Amadeus whined, high and pained.

Vala was hurting him, simply through her displeasure. I gritted my teeth, rocking back on my heels to stop my crimson from ripping Amadeus from her grasp.

Control, control, control…

My shadows throbbed through me like a red tidal sea, but I couldn't act like just another dickhead Wolf Charmer, no matter how much I craved to show this jerk of a princess how I protected my pack because that'd be repeating my great-grandmother's mistakes.

Plus, once I unleashed the crimson tide, I didn't

know if I could stop them washing away every wolf in its wake.

"Remember what's stamped on your wolfie ass," I ordered because commands helped Amadeus, and anything that'd win in the verbal war with Vala was an incubus approved weapon. "You're mine, and you please me, right?"

Amadeus's whine transformed into a moan of pleasure.

Boom — that was how to explode the pleasure bomb.

I wrinkled my nose. I even made my own brain shudder with that image.

Vala clutched her brother's bicep, shaking him. "Since you've returned, you've done nothing but displease me."

Amadeus panted like she'd punched him in the gut.

My nostrils flared. "Honestly, you *always* please me."

Amadeus' eyelids fluttered; his fingers opened and closed compulsively, caught between the twin sensations of pleasure and pain.

"*You bring me no pleasure,*" Vala whispered, hot and cruel against his ear.

Amadeus' knees buckled, and she let go of him, allowing him to tumble to her feet with a howl. I bit my tongue, whilst my own shoulders quivered.

A curse on a mage's dick, how could she hurt her own brother like this?

"Look at me," I commanded. When Amadeus raised his gaze to mine, peering through his black hair that was stark against the translucent white of his skin, I remembered the way that he'd looked at me with such love in the cave. I hoped that he remembered the love that'd been in *my* eyes as well. "Pleasure...your tongue...my mind blown."

Aquilo pulled at the frayed bottom of his shirt as he muttered, "You don't need to crow about it. How mind blowing can a kiss be?"

Amadeus snickered. "She didn't say where the kiss was, see?"

I hadn't thought that Aquilo could blush any deeper, and boy, did that make me wonder what he'd be like caught in the tangle of an angel, wolf, and witch snuggle fest, which made me flush almost as pink as him with desire.

"Mind...blowing." I arched my brow like it was a fencing sword at Vala.

"Yeah, I'm not playing the Does He, Doesn't He Please Me Game," Vala growled. I swallowed because the way she'd announced that made it sound like a kid's game that was popular with incubi stuck in the middle. She hauled Amadeus to the door. "On fear of silver, don't speak and go to the Isolation Room. You don't deserve to feed tonight."

Like the Kingdom of the Gods hadn't been starved enough...but then, the witches had taught them that trick.

Amadeus' voice was thick with tears but also a blazing fearlessness, "Goddess Moon! Why don't you see that I'm not yours anymore to punish? I don't have to please you, only my Charmer."

Vala froze; her cheek twitched, even as her claws sank into Amadeus' arms. Jesus, his words must've hurt her after decades of raising Amadeus (and don't think that I'd missed how she loved him possessively), to be rejected for the *monster* who the entire kingdom feared.

Yep, karma was a witch.

Vala tossed her brother out of the museum without meeting his eye. "Now do you see why you displease me?"

When she swept back towards me, I stumbled because you know, I'd never understood how someone could have a murderous glint in their eye but I did now. Her sharp claws extended even further, whilst her fangs gleamed.

I was trapped in this underground kingdom, whilst Mischief was leashed, and the rest of my pack was hidden somewhere apart and alone from me. I shivered, chilled at the rage and hatred that swirled in the princess' eyes: I'd known that we were enemies.

In my arrogance, I'd grown too used to wolves either loving or fearing me, rather than hungering to tear out my throat. I'd spent so much of the last week battling to stop the witches murdering the wolves, that I'd never thought the wolves would fight back.

Yet Vala prowled past me, snatching Aquilo by his hair instead and pulling him after her. My throat burned, as she straddled the back of a wolf like she was riding the Omega.

Aquilo's desperate gaze met mine. He thrashed in an attempt to stop himself being dragged onto the wolf as well and being trapped in front of Vala.

Vala pulled Aquilo up, however, holding him in place like they were lovers on a motorbike.

I understood Aquilo's panic because his House had killed almost as many Omegas as mine, and it was one thing to know that and another to literally ride the dead.

He was going to hurl again...

"What a *clever* Wolf Witch stealing my Beta," Vala hissed. "Only, if he's no longer *mine*, then your mage won't ever be *yours*."

I clasped my hands behind my back to control the red. It'd been easier when I'd been bound in Cosmos Tower by Ivy, before she'd thrown me to the wolves, because all my power had been taken from me. But now I had to control myself and do the *adult* thing that would save all sides in these supernatural wars.

Huh, this was what it felt like to have true responsibility: it was kind of like a panic attack combined with heartburn.

"I take it your loser ass isn't aware that I can say a couple of words and our magical engagement is broken?" I cocked my head, ignoring the way that Aquilo flinched. *Please let him realize that I didn't mean a damn word of my bluff.* "Check out the markings around his wrist. If I break the bond, it'll kill him. It looks like you better release him, huh? After all, he can't give you any kinky fun if he's cold and stiff."

Vala's eyes blazed, as she raised Aquilo's wrist to study the blood bracelet that was now throbbing violently; Aquilo whimpered. Then she traced over it sensually with her tongue, never lowering her intent stare from mine.

"By my fangs, every time that I believe witches can't invent a worse cruelty, they find a way to impress me with their heartlessness." To my surprise, Vala slipped off the back of the wolf, handling Aquilo as gently as glass as she helped him down. "How could you murder such beauty? You don't deserve him or *any* of them."

I blinked. "I never asked for a wolf as a birthday present or the Tributes. Plus, the angels were just sort of in my basement and attic. Okay, I did propose to Aquilo but..." I trailed off. "When did I say that I deserved them?"

"Yet you'd kill them." Vala shoved Aquilo stumbling across the museum, and I caught him in my arms.

When he peered at me through his mop of hair, I smiled at him. "Whereas I wish to bring my pack to life."

"Just to be clear, you're not breaking the bond...?" There was a resigned acceptance in Aquilo's question, even though it was threaded with hope.

I hated that.

I dragged Aquilo into a cuddle worthy of Moon, despite his muffled protest. Yet his head relaxed onto my shoulder, and he let himself be held like this was what he'd needed but would never have asked for.

He'd never need to ask me for gentleness.

"I've already watched too many people who I love die. I'll never break the bond. You're kind of stuck with my Charmer ass." I rested my forehead against Aquilo's.

Vala's eyes narrowed. "That would truly get me right in the feels, except for the number of wolves who I've loved and had to watch die or be sacrificed. Yeah, way more than the witches that you saw massacred. So, you mum and dad died, what do you think it felt like to have my brother ripped from my arms?" She stroked her hands across the back of a stuffed wolf. "My mum thinks that you're a god, but I know that you're a devil in disguise. And unlike my mum, I bite. *Gods arise!*"

Suddenly, a rumbling growl echoed through the museum.

That didn't sound good.

Then the stuffed wolf's fur bristled and the wolf turned its head to glare at me with flaming glass eyes.

I *eeped*, stumbling backward and dragging Aquilo with me.

Yep, zombie werewolves not good at all and worse even than the nightmares that had haunted me for the last decade.

All around us, the stuffed wolves were shaking their heads and arching their backs like they were becoming familiar with their bodies after a long time asleep.

And for asleep, read *being dead.*

As if with a hive mind, the wolves turned and howled, launching themselves at me. I screamed, falling on my ass, but my crimson shadows webbed out to cocoon a shield, whilst Aquilo blasted wind at the wolves.

I tensed, waiting for the howl, clash, or snap of jaws…*something.* I stared around the gloom in shock: the zombie werewolves had vanished like they'd been no more than ghosts.

My shadows coiled around me in comfort, stroking down my sides to distract me from the unease.

Vala gave a hollow laugh. "So, the mighty Wolf Charmer jumps at shadows. Fool witch, why fear the dead, when the living will soon be at your throat?"

And there it was: the dark threat crossing behind Vala's eyes that promised pain, war, death…*and a plot that I had to uncover.*

I forced myself to my feet, staggering across the bones to her. "Would you, the living, and the dead go for it, if I said let's chill out, have a glass of wine together, and be friends now?"

I grinned winningly. Unless you were an Alpha who hated me, in which case I might as well have waved a wolf flaying knife in front of her to piss her off.

Vala grabbed me by the curls, slamming me against the wall, whilst her fangs descended to my neck. I yelped, as her teeth nicked my skin, and my blood trailed down like warm tears.

My eyes widened in terror. *The dickhead didn't plan to Wolf Bite me...?* I wasn't anyone's Omega, and I'd never be the princess'.

Then Vala murmured, as her breath huffed against my ear, "By the light of the moon, my mum is buried in her grief and so sits on a throne of bones in the dark amongst the dead, forever remembering. *I* will lead our kingdom into one of light and life. Then *you* will wish that the Wilds had torn you to pieces as they should've done because a crimson tide is coming." I jumped: *Crimson Tide...?* I became ashen, as a wave of dizziness hit me. What if my family's motto had been about more than my shadows because the Wolf Charmer line was connected to the royal line of wolves in a way that was more complex than I yet understood? "*A tide of blood.*"

When Vala's fangs pressed harder against my neck, I

shuddered. I'd thought that having been thrown to the wolves, I'd become leader of the pack.

Instead, I was nothing but an icon like Mischief to be used to rally a kingdom to war.

I'd escaped the Wilds, saved Moon from Re-education, and triumphed against the witches. But my own great-grandmother had been the Terror of the Wolf War. I might have my shadows, but I couldn't taint them by using them against these wolf survivors.

Yet in the name of Hecate, how could I survive the coming Crimson Tide without them? My shadows curled around me because I knew that I wouldn't.

Instead, the wolves would bring themselves to life with my death.

Trapped in the Kingdom of the Gods, just like my parents, I'd die on a werewolf's fangs.

TO BE CONTINUED...

CONTINUE CRIMSON'S ADVENTURES IN
ONLY PROTECTOR ALPHAS, BOOK
THREE IN THE REBEL WEREWOLVES
SERIES.

Continue Crimson's adventures in ONLY PROTECTOR ALPHAS, Book Three in the Rebel Werewolves series.

https://rosemaryajohns.com

Thanks for reading Only Pretty Betas. If you enjoyed reading this book, **please consider leaving a review on Amazon.** Your support is really important to us authors. Plus, I love hearing from my readers!
Thanks, you're awesome!

AUTHOR NOTE

Only Protector Alphas — Book Three in the Rebel Werewolves series — is already written, so you can continue Crimson and her pack's adventures! The trilogy is COMPLETE and available to order NOW! I wanted to put a twist on both witch and shifter myths, as well as explore the wicked seductiveness of incubi. I live in Oxford, and I've spent years imagining these worlds. I can't wait for you to discover in the next book the deadly secrets and crisis of the crimson tide, Alphas, and the final wolf kingdom in the sinful climax of the trilogy!

You're total stars for your recommendations, word of mouth, and reviews because it's how my books reach new readers. I'm truly grateful to you. Even a single line review raises the series' visibility.

I love Crimson and her Charms. I hope you do too!

Thanks, you're awesome - my Rebel family :)

Rebel here, yeah?

Rosemary A Johns

REBEL ANGELS
READ THE COMPLETE SERIES NOW!

YOU MAY ALSO ENJOY...

REBEL ANGELS – ENEMIES-TO-LOVERS
FANTASY ROMANCE

The beautiful...*naked*...vampire gazed up at me. I stared in shock at the soft cat ears that poked out of his hair.

"How flexible are you on collars?" Ash smirked.

"He's adorable. Can we keep him?" Mischief's gaze darted to mine.

I grinned at my angel and vampire lovers, before sitting cross-legged in front of the Cat Vampire. He shied away, curling his tail around himself to shield his modesty.

"I'm not adorable," the Cat Vampire hissed, "I'm Tiger." He nuzzled his chin against the studs in Rebel's jacket, scenting them. Then he peeked at Mischief. "And I'm not the one with glittery hair, angel."

Mischief arched a brow. "Meow, the cat has claws. I hope he knows that I scratch back?"

This box set includes over 1,500 pages of thrilling magic, dark romance, and adventure with twists that you'll never see coming.

Vampires and angels are locked in a deadly war. But first, they want their daughter back.

Grab Rebel Angels and fall in love with the dark angels and vampires. **Discover MISCHIEF'S story and where the Rebel worlds began...**

APPENDIX ONE: OXFORD'S WITCH COVENS

House of Silver

Crimson Tide, the Wolf Charmer

Zetta and Daniel, Crimson's parents

Crimson's legendary great-grandmother

House of Seasons

Stella, Crimson's aunt and leader of Oxford's covens

House of Blood

Ivy, the Blood Witch, mother to the twins

Lux, twins with Aquilo

Aquilo, a mage

APPENDIX TWO: CHARACTERS

WOLF SHIFTERS

Ambassador, Stella's wolf and true prince of the Kingdom of the Gods

Okami, magical wolf created by Crimson

Crescents, Vala's Alphas in the Kingdom of the Gods

SUPERNATURALS

Mischief, (god, mage, angel name 'Zophia', from the Realm of the Seraphim)

Ramiel, Addict angel

'Zetta', magical essence of past Wolf Charmers, ward in House of Silver

Dual, Duke of Oxford's vampire court and Fallen angel

ACADEMIES

Rebel Academy, where 'bad' supernaturals are sent

Alpha Academy, where Alphas are schooled

Omega Training Center, where Omegas are trained

Re-education Center, where rebellious Omegas are 'corrected'

Kingdom of the Wilds

Omega Prince Moon (Moon Child) – First Charm

Omega Moth, Moon's brother

Queen Rhona

Princess Morag

Countess Lyall

Kingdom of the Gods

Beta Prince Amadeus (half incubus) - Second Charm

Queen Banan

Princess Vala

Kingdom of the Alphas

Alpha Prince Emperor ('Cursed Alpha') – Third Charm

Queen Aurora

Princess Hope

ABOUT THE AUTHOR

ROSEMARY A JOHNS is a USA Today bestselling and award-winning fantasy author, music fanatic, and paranormal anti-hero addict. She writes sexy angels and werewolves, savage vampires, and epic battles.

Winner of the Silver Award in the National Wishing Shelf Book Awards. Finalist in the IAN Book of the Year Awards. Runner-up in the Best Fantasy Book of the Year, Reality Bites Book Awards. Honorable Mention in the Readers' Favorite Book Awards.

Shortlisted in the International Rubery Book Awards.

Rosemary is also a traditionally published short story writer. She studied history at Oxford University and ran her own theater company. She's always been a rebel…

Want to read more and stay up to date on Rosemary's newest releases? Sign up for her *VIP* Rebel Newsletter and grab two FREE novellas!

Have you read all the series in the Rebel Verse by Rosemary A Johns?

Rebel Angels
Rebel Legends
Rebel Vampires
Rebel Werewolves
Rebel Academy

Read More from Rosemary A Johns
Website: https://rosemaryajohns.com
BookBub: https://www.bookbub.com/authors/rosemary-a-johns
Facebook: https://www.facebook.com/RosemaryAnnJohns
Twitter: @RosemaryAJohns
JOIN ROSEMARY'S REBELS FACEBOOK GROUP TODAY FOR NEWS AND EXCLUSIVES

Printed in Great Britain
by Amazon

81534355R00222